THE GOOD DOCTOR OF WARSAW

ELISABETH GIFFORD

CORVUS

First published in Great Britain in 2018 by Corvus, an imprint
of Atlantic Books Ltd.

Copyright © Elisabeth Gifford, 2018

The moral right of Elisabeth Gifford to be identified as the author of this work
has been asserted by her in accordance with the Copyright, Designs and Patents
Act of 1988.

Quotation credits: permission gratefully received from Sandra Joseph, editor
of *A Voice for the Child: The inspirational words of Janusz Korczak*, published
in 1999 by Thorsons.

Picture research and credits: many thanks to Yad Vashem, Israel; Ghetto
Fighters' House Museum, Israel; The Emanuel Ringelblum Jewish
Historical Institute, Poland; The Korczakianum Centre for Documentation
and Research, Poland; Roman Wroblewski Wasserman; and the State
Archives of Warsaw, Poland.

10 9 8 7 6 5 4 3 2 1

A CIP catalogue record for this book is available from the British Library.

Hardback ISBN: 978 178 649 3415
E-book ISBN: 978 178 649 2470
Trade paperback ISBN: 978 178 649 2463

PRINTED AND BOUND BY MBM PRINT SCS LTD, GLASGOW.

Corvus
An imprint of Atlantic Books Ltd
Ormond House
26–27 Boswell Street
London
WC1N 3JZ

www.corvus-books.co.uk

MIX
Paper from
responsible sources
FSC
www.fsc.org
FSC® C117931

You do not leave a sick child alone to face the dark,
and you do not leave children at a time like this.
Janusz Korczak

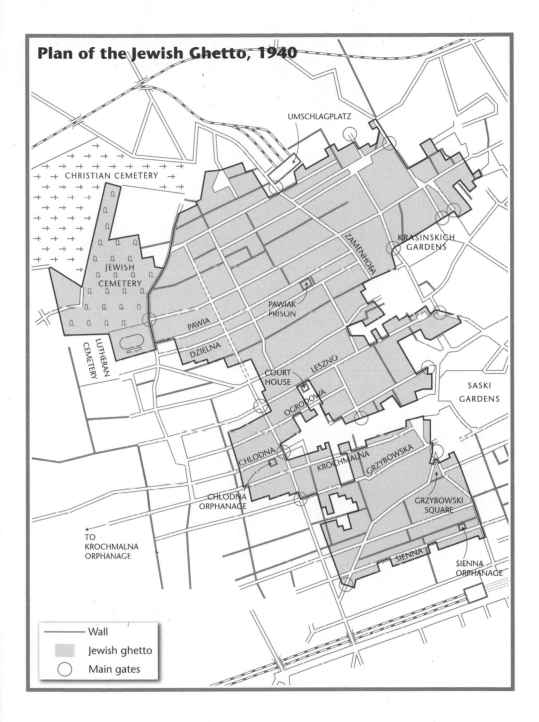

Plan of the Jewish Ghetto, 1940

CHRISTIAN CEMETERY

UMSCHLAGPLATZ

JEWISH CEMETERY

KRASINSKICH GARDENS

ZAMENHOFA

PAWIAK PRISON

LUTHERAN CEMETERY

PAWIA

DZIELNA

LESZNO

COURT HOUSE

OGRODOWA

SASKI GARDENS

CHLODNA

CHLODNA ORPHANAGE

KROCHMALNA

GRZYBOWSKA

GRZYBOWSKI SQUARE

TO KROCHMALNA ORPHANAGE

SIENNA

SIENNA ORPHANAGE

Wall
Jewish ghetto
Main gates

CHAPTER ONE

WARSAW, 17 JANUARY 1945

Two hours before dawn, Misha stood on the bank of the Vistula, looking out across the frozen river towards Warsaw. In his hand was a photograph of Sophia, no bigger than his palm. He had cut around her outline to make her seem more real over the years. Two small holes in her shoulders where he'd tacked her up above his bed in various training barracks, a holy icon for a believer. In the dim light her pale eyes looked out at him, serious and afraid. He knew the rest of the picture by heart, her fair hair drawn back, her beautiful face too thin. Two years since he last held Sophia's warm face in his hands and kissed her lips, or breathed in the faint smell of almonds that her skin carried. The wind chilled him with a relentless blast, an ache in his body from her absence. He pulled up his collar and slipped her back inside his canvas wallet, beat his hands against his arms to get the feeling back.

'Here, Misha, have some of this.'

A few yards along the bank he could see the outlines of Russian guards in thick winter coats, eating from metal tins, the steam rising in the frozen air as they talked and laughed loudly. One of them held out a bottle. Misha walked over and took a swig. The guns had fallen silent now, but you could still smell the smoke drifting from across the river. The Russians were in a good mood, relaxed and laughing about who was going to dance with big Irina that night.

Irina, a broad-faced woman filling her uniform with a massive body and a large bosom, grinned down at them in the gloom, spooning up her bean stew.

'Don't even bother asking,' she snorted, pushing her cloak back over one shoulder. 'I'd eat you lot for breakfast. But if anyone was asking, I might say yes to Misha.'

She looked at him with a greedy glint. Misha was used to women behaving strangely around him. His dark amber eyes with their green flecks were as beautiful as any girl's – at least that's what Sophia had once told him. He was tall and fine-boned, and the Polish uniform of high boots and jodhpurs gave him an old-fashioned, almost aristocratic air, but then with his easy-going humour Misha had a way of being friends with most people. Even though he was a Pole – and a Jew at that – the Russians included him readily as one of them.

Misha dipped his head as Irina bellowed with laughter. Having Irina for a girlfriend would be a dangerous business. There was a rumour going round that her last lover had died, not from a German bullet, but from Irina's pistol after a jealous argument.

'If you find any of Hitler's friends still over there, give them my best wishes with one of these.' Irina patted her gun in its holster.

They all clapped him on the back, magnanimous and hearty, Warsaw's liberators.

As part of the reconnaissance group for the Polish First Army under Russian command Misha was always first into the enemy territory ahead, scouting out safe passages for the tanks, tensely looking out for German stragglers. Today, his small unit would be the first to enter Warsaw. Three years since he had last set foot in the city.

The line of four Willys jeeps was waiting at the edge of the snow-covered river. Between the breaking clouds, scraps of black and a sliver of metallic moon. Franek, Misha's driver and self-appointed guide and counsellor, was at the wheel of the first jeep, the flaps of his sheepskin hat pulled down over his ears.

'Hurry up, man, before we freeze to death,' he yelled. 'We want to get across before there's any light.' Warsaw was still held by night but at their backs, dawn was already a pale red line. Their brief was to send back a wireless message on the situation before the Polish infantry began to cross on foot as dawn broke.

Misha hauled up alongside Franek and pulled the door shut, but the cold wind still managed to whistle in through the gaps, the jeep rocking with its blows. He took his pistol from its holster. In front of them, the river shone white, a long and meandering plain of snow, far brighter than the wadding of clouds above.

His breath fogging and rising in front of his face, Franek leaned forward as the wheels bumped down onto the snow-covered surface of the river. Misha felt his muscles tense but the ice held, half a winter in thickness. Sliding and jolting, they began to track across the rutted surface, four black shapes, no headlights, driving slowly, the engines' noise low. Snow had softened the shapes of burned-out army trucks and the frozen bodies of dead horses and other debris, casting long shadows in the ghostly light. To their right, the broken girders of the Poniatowski Bridge rose up out of the ice at drunken angles.

'Hard to believe,' said Misha. 'Here we are, the first to liberate Warsaw. Going home.'

'Do you mean liberate in the Russian sense? Sit on the opposite bank saying you're waiting for supplies for six months until the Wehrmacht has crushed the Polish resistance into the dust, wait until the Germans have pulled out, and then roll in? A nice clean slate for Russian occupation.'

'Have you heard any more from your brothers?'

Franek shook his head.

'I'm sorry, Franek,' said Misha.

Franek had heard through intelligence that one of his brothers had died during the Warsaw uprising. Another had died in the unauthorized breakout of the Polish army in an attempt to cross the river and come to the aid of besieged Warsaw a few weeks after they arrived. They had been beaten back with terrible losses. Beneath the frozen ice were hundreds of corpses from the Polish First Army. The Russians were furious. They had dismissed their Polish general and replaced him with someone more obedient.

The jeep banged down into a deep rut in the ice and Misha's free hand flew out to grip onto the dashboard. The dark shapes behind braked. Franek spun the wheel, gained purchase again and drove carefully around the rutted area. Misha looked back. The others were following. He unpeeled his hand from the cold metal and rubbed his frozen cheeks. His skin prickled with the naked feeling, waiting to hear a shot ring out from the opposite bank.

They were now more than halfway across the ice. For years, Misha had crossed the Vistula back home into Warsaw, taking for granted the town's long silhouette floating between the sky and the wide river, its elegant steeples and church towers, the bulk of the palace fortress.

All that was gone. As he trained his binoculars on the approaching bank and the bridgehead up on their right, he scanned nothing but empty spaces and eroded stumps in the toneless light. Rising smoke drifted against a dirty sky. He swung the binoculars round to the head of the broken bridge.

'Stop, Franek. Stop. Up there, I can see a sentry.'

Franek braked sharply. Misha heard the jeep behind squeal to a halt.

Misha passed him the glasses, and pointed to a red-and-white box just visible on the bank. 'No cover out here if he fires.'

'He's not moving. Can't have seen us.' Opening the window flap, Franek clicked the gun catch, sighted and fired. The noise of the shot ricocheted across the plain.

'Shit. Missed.' Franek reloaded hurriedly, waiting for the sentry to return fire. He quickly took a second shot. The guard shuddered, a spray of matter from a direct hit, but the man remained leaning rigidly against the wooden box.

Misha took the glasses back.

'There's snow on his shoulders.'

'My God, frozen at his post.'

Approaching the bank cautiously, Franek pulled up alongside the sentry box. Light was beginning to gather in the sky, and the snow cast an eerie light up on the dead man's grey face. A rime of frost dusted his helmet and the wool of his coat. A second sentry was leaning inside the box like a toppled skittle, a rifle slung across his front.

'Warsaw's being guarded by corpses,' said Franek.

The small convoy of jeeps carried on up the slipway alongside the smashed bridge piers. At the top, Franek stopped the engine.

In front of them lay a sight that defied words in the cold half-light, nothing but long vistas open to the livid sky, miles of ruins and rubble blanketed with snow. Not a single building intact, chimney stacks left like broken trees. Here and there ragged remains of walls stuck up with gaps for windows, black against the luminous snow. They listened tensely for the click of a gun, a lone sniper watching them, but there was nothing. A deep silence, even the air frozen and dead.

'Which way?' said Franek.

Misha shook his head. 'If we go ahead that was Jerozolimskie Avenue.'

They began moving slowly along a narrow track between the slopes of bricks and scree, one wheel jolting over rubble. The substantial shops and offices of the commercial district were gone, replaced by ruins and avalanches of bricks and dust. Drifts of snow had whitened the debris, the blackened ruins of the walls rising like tombstones in a winter cemetery. Not a single living person anywhere. A thousand years might have passed since elegant shoppers and businessmen had thronged the avenue with its red trams and polished cars.

At the corner of Jerozolimskie they stopped and looked along the main thoroughfare. Marszalkowska Avenue was another endless vista of buildings crumbled into mounds of rubble, the remaining masonry black and fire-damaged. Franek cut the jeep's engine again. Misha tensed but no shot rang out. No snipers waiting. The uncanny quiet made the skin along Misha's back contract. An atavistic fear thickened the air. Something wicked brooded over the city in the twilight of the winter morning. Only the dead should linger in the underworld.

'But there's got to be someone here,' Misha said. It sounded like a plea. The blankets and medical supplies that they had brought with them in the back of the jeep for civilians were beginning to feel like a sick joke.

A strained moment when the jeep failed to start again in the cold. Franek pulled the choke two or three times and the engine made a whining screech.

'Not too much, it'll flood,' Misha said, his voice more anxious than he expected. Finally, the engine caught and they jolted forwards over rubble along Marszalkowska Avenue.

They came to a section where the rubble had been cleared, apartments with less damage. In the distance, they could see buildings that were more or less intact. The unmistakable sound of a lorry engine moving away.

'The Germans must be using the buildings ahead as barracks,' said Franek.

'Sounds like they're pulling out. Better continue on foot.'

Misha opened the jeep door carefully and unfolded his long frame into the deep cold, signalling for Franek and three of the men behind to follow. They skirted along the side of an apartment block, crouching down, running across the next junction in turn. As the last man crossed there was the whish and snap of a bullet and he doubled over. He limped across, holding his thigh, a dark stain spreading. Misha scanned along the building opposite. A sniper on the roofline. More cracks as they exchanged fire and the sniper fell. Yelling in German from the street ahead, the roar of a lorry pulling away. The sound of the engine faded and a thick silence fell again.

'They're only interested in getting out,' said Franek.

Misha radioed back to headquarters while the men drank from flasks and the wound was bandaged.

'The infantry will be across the river in two hours,' Misha told the waiting men. 'We carry on scouting out the full situation but don't engage unless we have to. We'll split into two groups.'

There was no way to check if the streets ahead had been mined by the retreating army as Misha, Franek and one of the radio boys headed north. A reddish dawn was spreading at the edge of a white sky like a wound behind a seeping bandage, showing with increasing clarity details of the broken landscape: a field of wooden crosses standing inside the ruins of a roofless church, an iron bedstead rising from the snow, an upturned child's pram.

They carried on along Senatorska Street towards Theatre Square, hoping to see something of the Warsaw they had known. Nothing but more rubble. The Opera was gone, the town hall eradicated. Along Midowa to Castle Square to another demolition site. The column of King Sigismund lay in pieces, the defender of Warsaw face down in the mud and snow. Market Square was charred ruins, stumps of buildings like gravestones in the toneless light.

They headed west down Dluga Street, past the wastes of Krasinskich Park. Every tree had been felled. Nearing the area that had been walled off as a ghetto, Misha felt his heartbeat rising. Abruptly, the bomb-damaged buildings ended. The ghetto wall was entirely gone as were the thousands of buildings inside it. Speechless, Misha got out of the jeep. He was standing in front of miles of empty land, a levelled field sown with snow and frost. Every brick and plank had been taken away, the ground razed flat. Nothing remained of the ghetto except for a church half a mile away, marooned in a white and frozen sea. Three years ago, he and half a million other Jewish people had lived here, crowded together in a constant hubbub of so many voices. Now, there was only the sound of the wind blowing unimpeded across this scraped-clean demolition site. He walked out a little way. He was standing alone in the blank luminosity, the cold penetrating his boots and his gloves. There were no other tracks except for his.

Misha made his way back to the jeep, feeling frozen to the bone.

'Do you think we've time to go past Krochmalna Street?' Misha asked as he got back in. 'If you don't want to risk it . . .'

Franek nodded his assent and the jeep started along what had once been Leszno Street, now a ghostly track through a desert.

Mounds of broken masonry blocked Krochmalna Street. Misha got out of the jeep, scrambling over rubble towards the place where he had lived and worked as a teacher only three years ago. By some miracle, several buildings in Krochmalna Street were still standing. And there it was. The children's home was still there. The dormitory windows had been blown out, the roof was gone, the front pitted with shrapnel, but it was still there. His heart contracted in the silence. No voices of children shouting and laughing as they played in the yard in front of the house.

There was the noise of someone following him over the rubble. Franek appeared beside him, looking up at the building's remains.

'I heard a rumour that Dr Korczak and the children escaped. That they're alive in the east somewhere.'

'Yes,' said Misha. 'I heard that rumour.'

He looked up at the empty window frames. With a pain in his chest, he thought back to the last time he had seen the doctor and the children, the Sienna Street home inside the ghetto walls. He had been out of the ghetto all day as part of a work detail for the Germans, clearing broken glass in the Praga barracks, the bored guard holding his rifle loosely as he watched over them.

When he'd got back to the orphanage late that afternoon, the children were gone. Half-drunk cups of milk and bread lay cold on the tables, chairs pushed back and tipped over. Looters had already been through the building, splitting open pillows, and spilling the contents of the children's keepsake cupboards across the small ballroom of the businessmen's club that for the past year and a half had served as a crowded dormitory, schoolroom and dining room for two hundred children.

Before the war, he had walked with Sophia through Warsaw towards Grzybowski Square, making her laugh with stories about the children, children who were naughty and wise and so full of life.

Tears streaming down his face now because they had been taken, because he hadn't been there to save them. He stood in the cold wind that blew across the broken bricks of Krochmalna Street, his face stripped bare as driftwood, scoured down to the bone by pain.

CHAPTER TWO

WARSAW, MAY 1937

Korczak is still mourning the loss of his wireless broadcast. Millions tuned in across Poland each week to hear his message of understanding and respect for children. But now it seems a Jew may not speak on Polish air. Contract terminated. What is he if he isn't Polish? He thinks and he dreams in Polish, knows the streets of Warsaw as well as he knows his own palm. Truly, the poison of the Nazi insanity is spreading across Europe.

At least he still has the lectures, the chance to influence a new generation of teachers who will one day care for Poland's children. He's wearing his tweed suit with a fob watch in the waistcoat, a bow-tie.

Korczak slows his steps so that the small boy at his side can keep up as they climb the stairs. Around them the smooth surfaces of the hospital echo and re-echo with footfalls and with distant doors closing.

'Good afternoon, Dr Korczak,' a nurse calls out as she hurries by, glancing at the skinny urchin holding his hand. She evidently wants to ask what the doctor's doing here today, years since he resigned to take care of a house full of orphans. A bachelor father, caring for a hundred children.

Outside the radiography door, Korczak kneels down to talk to little Szymonek.

'We'll go inside, there will be lots of people there, and then I'm going to ask you to stand behind the special machine. Are you ready?'

Szymonek nods. Large serious eyes. 'Because it will help the grown-ups understand children.'

'You have great courage, my little man.'

Korczak stands up and opens the door. He's still angry and shaken by the discovery yesterday that one of his own teachers in the orphanage on Krochmalna Street had dragged a boy down to the cellar and left him there in the dark.

'What else could I do, Pan Doctor?' the teacher had asked, expecting sympathy perhaps. 'Jakubek wouldn't listen to me. I was so exasperated I even raised my hand, but he just yelled back, "Hit me and Pan Doctor will have you thrown out." I'm not proud of it, but I saw red then and pulled him down to the cellar. He went quiet after that.'

'You left a child alone in the dark?' Korczak had closed his eyes, speaking almost in a whisper. 'But how do you know he wasn't acting badly because he was suffering? You're the adult. You had the chance to find out what was wrong, to teach him that he doesn't need to lash out when he's upset. But no, what do you do? It's into the dark, into the cellar.'

Korczak had had to rush away at that point, the tears close.

A few days later, they learned why Jakubek had been so difficult. He had been out on a Saturday to visit his beloved grandmother only to find that she had passed away.

The room is filled with chattering students. They are all puzzled as to why they've been asked to vacate their usual lecture room in the Institute of Pedagogy and walk over to this laboratory in the hospital. They fall silent as Dr Korczak enters, expectant. No one falls asleep in Korczak's lectures.

But his attention is only on the child, speaking in a low voice to him as he leads Szymonek to stand behind a square glass screen. The blinds are down, the boy's skinny chest luminous in the gloom. His eyes follow the doctor as the lecture begins.

'So you've been with the children all day. I understand. It's not easy sometimes. Some days you're worn out. You can't take any more. You feel like yelling at them, feel perhaps the impulse to raise your hand.'

Dr Korczak switches on the fluorescent lamp behind the child. The glass screen lights up with an ethereal glow showing a portrait in dark pencil, a small child's ribs. Inside is the shadow of a heart, beating fast, jumping like a panicked bird.

'Look carefully. This is how a child's heart behaves if you shout at them, if you raise your hand. This is what a child's heart does when they are afraid. Look carefully, and remember.'

Korczak turns off the lamp, puts his jacket around the boy and picks him up. 'That will be all.'

Korczak leaves with the child and the stunned room breaks into a buzz of chatter.

A boy taller than anyone else in the room, a long athletic frame, a slightly receding hairline above a broad forehead that gives the impression of good sense, is packing away his notebooks hurriedly. Misha is thinking about how he's going to write a letter to his father that night, explaining why he isn't going to get an engineering job now he's finished his degree. Instead, he's going to begin a teaching degree at night school and carry on working at Korczak's orphanage as a barely paid student helper. His father will be furious. He knows from his own job as a teacher that there's no money in education, no jobs. He'll blame Korczak for this catastrophe, which will be correct.

If you want to change the world, change education.

As he crosses the room, a pen falls from Misha's canvas bag. He kneels to retrieve it and looking up sees a girl still sitting on a chair, lost in her own thoughts, reflecting on the talk. He sees fair hair drawn back from an oval face, clear blue eyes, generous lips, a white blouse with a Peter Pan collar. Just a girl.

But he can't move, he can't look away; deep in his chest there's the unmistakable hum of a tuning fork, the inevitable true note around which all the other notes will harmonize. This girl. He badly wants to speak to her, to sit by her and take her hand.

But what's he thinking of? He'll be on duty at the home soon. And let's face it: he's going to be too poor to fall in love for a long time. He should be strong. He has that letter to write.

He shoulders his bag and leaves.

*

But the girl won't leave him. Over the next few days Misha finds himself back in that moment again, gazing up at a pale, open face, impelled to speak to her.

So at the next lecture, he decides, he's going to do it. He's really going to find a way to talk to her.

But a crowd of friends surrounds her. A boy in a chalk-striped suit, oiled hair, calls out, 'Sophia.'

Her name. Misha picks it up like a treasure.

He watches the eager-faced boy, notes how he laughs self-consciously at something she says. Is she smiling back because she likes him too? Is she just being polite? Misha finds he dislikes him intensely.

Next time. He'll go up and speak to her next time. Sophia.

But there is no next time. Korczak's lectures are cancelled. No reason given, though everyone knows why. Only true Poles can be trusted with the education of Polish minds.

Now Misha has no business going to the university any more. Misha's studying for a teaching certificate at the night school. He was only there at the Institute lecture because Korczak invited him.

It's for the best, he tells himself. He's being ridiculous, falling in love with a stranger. And no, he certainly isn't going to let himself go back to the Institute and hang around the gates in case she comes out.

He waits for his crush to fade, like a graze on a child's knee that will heal itself in time. But she ambushes him as he's crossing Saxon Park in the cool of the evening. She ambushes him when he's standing by a window looking over the yard where one of the boys is playing a harmonica, 'My Shtetl Beltz'. Her face comes back to him like a longing for home.

He finds himself hoping he will bump into her somewhere. It feels as though it's something that is meant to happen, will happen. But the months go by, summer comes and goes. The air begins to have an unpredictable tang of cold.

Autumn is almost here, and he still hasn't seen her again.

CHAPTER THREE

WARSAW, SEPTEMBER 1937

Sophia takes her identification card back from the university registrar. There's a rectangular stamp inked above her photo. 'What's this?'

The registrar shrugs. 'If you're Jewish you sit on the allocated benches this term. There's a notice down in the hall.'

Students are crowded around the board, reading the announcement. Rosa's there, her nose screwed up in disgust. She turns as Sophia joins her.

'Of course they'll say it's for our own protection, to stop incidents like that poor medic who had his face slashed last term.'

Rosa sighs and takes Sophia's arm as they head for their lecture. 'I don't recognize Poland any more. It was hard enough getting a place here, and now this. Sometimes I think your friend Tosia has the right idea. We should join one of the youth movements and quietly prepare to leave for Palestine.'

Sophia looks at her in horror. 'How can you say that? Never. We're Poles. Poland is our home. The harder they make it, then the more determined we just have to be. It's nonsense, this talk of segregation in lectures. There's never been a ghetto mentality in Poland, and as far as I'm concerned there never will be.'

A hot anger stays with Sophia but she still feels a flutter of apprehension as they enter the hall. Several of the tiered benches on the left are empty, nothing more than a piece of paper on them. The girls join the students standing at the back, talking in buzzes of indignation.

As Professor Kotarbinski enters, everyone hushes. He walks down through the benches and takes his place on the podium. Almost six feet tall, a military moustache waxed to two points, Kotarbinski commands the room as he surveys the empty benches in silence. A bang of wood on wood resounds as he picks up his chair and places it decisively to one side.

'Until the university can devise more satisfactory seating arrangements, I will be renouncing my right to sit.'

With a rattling of benches several more non-Jewish students rise to join him. Sophia feels a tight lump in her throat. They're not without friends.

She can still feel the sting of heat in her cheeks as she makes her way down to the podium at the end of the lecture to thank Kotarbinski. Really, the whole thing is simply embarrassing.

'It's a bad business, but you mustn't let them bully you out of here, Sophia. Promise me you'll finish your degree.'

'Nothing's going to stop me, sir.'

Across the main gates students in white caps with green ribbons in their lapels have rigged up a banner. Black ink is bleeding through the sheeting, the message clear even from the back: 'Ban Jews from university'.

The girls look at each other. No choice but to walk beneath the insulting slogan. Rosa adjusts the tiny Tyrolean hat perched on her newly waved black hair and they lock arms again.

'Here goes,' says Sophia.

'Honestly, Father could buy most of this lot out any day,' Rosa mutters as they walk under the banner.

Sophia feels exhausted as they wait for the tram. Mostly it's the basic hurt of being disliked, the unpopular girl shunned in class. Infantile and deeply wounding.

'Let's forget about all this,' says Rosa as they board the red tram. 'Come to my place this evening. A little party. We'll put some records on. Dance. And how about a smile? When you're as pretty as you are, Sophia, you've no reason to ever look down in the mouth.'

The tram takes them to Grzybowski Square where they embrace and part. Sophia has lived in this area all her life and she can feel herself relaxing once again as she makes her way through the familiar bustle of the Friday market. On Twarda Street she turns into the courtyard of her apartment block. Women are taking down the washing from the wooden clothes dryers, gossiping together. A busker is playing 'My Shtetl Beltz' on an accordion, looking up at the windows in the hope that someone will throw down some coins. Children are playing hopscotch – just as they have always done, just as they always will.

She opens the door to the apartment and breathes in the comforting smell of Father's books, Mother's flowers out on the balcony. But something's going on. In the kitchen, Mother is already in her apron, stirring a pot on the stove. The wooden board that covers the enamel bath in the corner is piled with serving dishes and bowls of vegetables. Krystyna is shelling peas into a colander and looking mischievous.

'So what is it? What's happened?'

'She wants to know what's happened,' Mother says. 'What makes you think something's happened?'

'It's Sabina,' Krystyna blurts out. At fourteen, Krystyna isn't much good at keeping secrets.

'Really? Has Lutek said something?'

'That's for Sabina to tell us,' says Mother. 'Anyway, they're both here for supper so you'll know soon enough. And look at the time. It'll be dusk before we know it. Krystyna, I want you to lay the table, the best cloth mind, and Sophia, I want you to go down and get a nice bottle of wine from Judel's and some other things. I've written you a list.'

Sophia takes the list and goes down to the market. Six peaches and a bunch of parsley. Women in long skirts and headscarves stand behind baskets of bagels and barrels of herring. A young woman in a smart rayon dress sits by a board heaped with rolls of cloth. Sophia could close her eyes and know exactly where she was just from the mix of fried onions and lemons, of baked bread and cabbages, of tarry pine boards baking in the sunshine.

She walks on past the teenage boys in their short gabardine coats and girlish side locks streaming out of the Yeshiva school, past the people hurrying up the steps of the church with its two square towers for their evening communion. Then on to Sosnowicz's delicatessen, run by the mother of a school friend, where diners sit at tables eating her famous sausage with cabbage. Seeing Sophia, Mrs Sosnowicz calls her to the front of the queue and pops an extra parcel of red sausage in her basket as a gift.

'I hear there's good news for Sabina,' she whispers and slips back to her customers.

At Horowicz wine shop Judel comes to meet her at the door holding out her arms.

'A wedding in the family – may he whose name may not be mentioned be praised. And people always want something special for a special day, and at a special price.' She shows Sophia the bottle she's already picked out and takes the coins in exchange.

'May I live to see so much happiness for my own daughters,' she adds with a sigh.

At the baker's, Sophia buys a plait of sweet challah bread. Looking around now at the crowded shop, women in shawls bringing in pots of cholent stew to cook overnight in the baker's oven, she wonders what her fellow students would see. As a child, growing up speaking Polish, and going to a Polish school, Jewishness always seemed to be little more than a family quirk, like red hair or having a peculiar aunt. But now, with work so hard to find, with the Far Right gaining power, she's often hurt and angered by certain newspaper articles, by offhand comments from people she thinks of as friends. Do they really think almost half of Warsaw should pack their bags and leave for Madagascar or some place? Warsaw is and always will be her home.

By the time Sophia gets back, the best dinner service is set out on the table, the candles ready to light for the Sabbath meal. Krystyna has changed into her best dress.

'Mrs Sosnowicz in the delicatessen tells me Sabina is engaged.' Sophia unloads the fruit carefully onto a plate. 'Mother, how come she knows before I do?'

'So she knows. People like to know. And did Judel give you a good price on the wine? Ah, yes. She's found something nice for Sabina here.'

'I can't believe it. Sabina's getting married.'

'Well, twenty-three isn't too young to be thinking of getting engaged, Sophia. Or twenty even.' Her mother pauses expectantly.

'No, Mother, there's no one I'm hiding. Anyway, I'm sure Judel or someone would know about it before me. And Mother, I'm not getting married. I've no time for all that.'

Her mother nods knowingly.

The door opens and Sabina and Lutek come in followed by Father in his long coat with its astrakhan collar. 'See who I found in the street outside, Mother,' he calls out. 'Looked like they could do with a good meal so I brought them with me. You wouldn't happen to have cooked anything, would you?'

She laughs, indicating the sideboard laden with cold meats, flaked cod and pickles. Sabina kisses everyone, a glossy fox fur over the shoulder of her hourglass suit. She unpins the little beret from her immaculately lacquered hair.

Krystyna takes the fox stole and strokes it with a little sigh. 'Sabina, you're so lucky getting to buy such lovely things, and at a discount.'

'When you work as a model at a top couturier's house, you have to look as if you've just stepped off the train from Paris,' says Mother proudly. Sabina is the acknowledged beauty of the family, with her ethereal, pale skin, enormous dark eyes and silky black hair. Krystyna and Sophia are blonde like their mother's side of the family and grew up like two sturdy little puppies, tumbling over each other noisily, while Sabina looked on with wide eyes, her dress clean, the large ribbon in her hair still in place.

Mother takes the fur from Krystyna and stows it carefully in the hallway.

'You can borrow it one day if you like,' says Sabina, seeing Krystyna's face fall.

'Really? You're such a darling. But isn't it expensive?'

Sabina shrugs. 'I don't mind.'

'Now all my girls are here, we can light the candles,' says Mother, her voice mellow with happiness.

They gather around her at the tableside as she strikes a match and carefully sets a little flame to each wick. She circles her hands above the candles, drawing in the scent of wax and flame, then covers her eyes to pray. When she removes her hands, she's been crying a little. 'My girls,' she says. 'Growing up.'

As the dusk falls, lights begin to glow in the windows around the courtyard for the Friday supper. A skein of song from somewhere outside, a deep male face joined by the voices of children, *Shalom aleichem*, peace be with you. Sophia too begins to hum and the rest of the family join in around the table and sing a couple of the old verses.

They're not a strictly religious family, but for Mother the Friday meal is sacrosanct and her face is radiant and a little proud with all her girls around her. The peppery scent of so many books along one wall, the lemony musk of Mother's flowers through the balcony windows, mix with the challah yeast and dusky wine.

Does it change you to be so loved, to love? Sophia wonders. She studies her sister's face in the candlelight for clues, and finds unhappiness in her eyes. It's true that Sabina is often shy and a little anxious, but this is something more. She's about to lean across and whisper to Sabina, and ask her what's wrong, but Krystyna has an urgent question.

'So what will your dress be like, Sabina? It's going to be so wonderful with Madame Fournier helping you at the salon. Imagine.'

'Oh. Well, you see . . .' Sabina stops. She drops her head. Two pink spots flush her cheeks.

Lutek puts his arm around her. 'We didn't want to talk about it today, but . . .' he says in a low voice.

Sabina's shy eyes look up, startled and ashamed. 'Madame Fournier's fired me.'

'She's fired you, Sabina? Why would she fire you? She's always sung your praises. Her best model.'

'Turns out I don't have the right looks to be a model at Maison Française after all. They said I looked French and now I'm too Jewish, it seems.'

'Well, that's ridiculous,' says Mother hotly. 'Whatever are they talking about?'

'Sabina was going to resign soon anyway,' says Lutek. 'Father will be more than glad if she can start with us in the office at the printing firm.'

Sabina smiles at him gratefully, but a quiet sadness lingers on in her face through the rest of the evening.

After supper, as the family get out the cards to begin a long game of Bezique, Sophia slips away to Rosa's apartment across the street.

'So you're here at last,' says Rosa, rescuing her from her mother who comes out to greet everyone in the hallway, prospecting for family news and cheerfully flashing the many diamond rings that never leave her fingers even as she weighs out meat in their butcher's shop.

'Come on. There's someone here you'll want to meet. He actually works with your favourite lecturer, Dr Korczak.'

Sophia groans. Now that Rosa is engaged, she has taken on the mission of finding Sophia the perfect match.

'Please stop doing this, Rosa. That last boy you made me talk to for hours.'

The large parlour is filled with ornate furniture in the style of a Polish hunting lodge, any spaces between crowded with friends. The balcony windows stand open onto the mild night air. On the gramophone a tango is playing, the hit from the summer, 'In a Year's Time'.

'There he is,' says Rosa.

Over by the window, taller than anyone else in the room, there's a young man with a remarkably nice smile. Sophia sees a head that is neat in the way of a cat, eyes that slant in a slightly eastern fashion. And so tall. Really, he is Mr Giraffe, she thinks and yet there's a strange feeling of things being just as they ought to be.

Misha's about to leave when he sees Rosa threading her way across the room towards him; a girl in a summer dress is following behind her.

He pushes away from the window frame with a jolt. Blonde hair pulled back from an open brow, the same full lips, her skin tanned against the white of her dress. It's her.

And she must wonder why he's grinning like an idiot as she offers her hand.

'Rosa tells me you work with Korczak,' she says.

'That's right. Yes. I'm a student helper at the orphanage. I do.'

He's not making much sense, distracted by the impression of a soft hand in his. But her eyes are on him, enquiring, direct. She deserves a sensible conversation.

'And so you're training to teach too?' he tries.

'Oh, dear. Did Rosa tell you that or can you guess by looking at me?'

'No, no. I saw you before, at a lecture that Korczak gave, in the X-ray room.'

'The little boy and his beating heart! Wasn't it remarkable? Not so much a lecture as a complete change of perspective. But I would have remembered you if you were there, surely.'

He likes that. 'There's no reason you should. We didn't speak. And the lectures were cancelled so suddenly.'

She frowns. 'Wasn't that terrible? He must be so upset.'

'Yes, but the thing that has really depressed him is losing the Polish children's home he opened. The board of governors sacked him. No longer allowed to see the children he'd taken care of for years. Half his family.'

'That's shocking.'

Her eyes blaze. She barely reaches his shoulder but he feels she equals him, vital, a force to be reckoned with. And yet there's something of the dancer in the way she holds herself, at ease, gracefully aware of her body. And those eyes. Is there a name for that shade of blue, translucent and limpid? They size him up.

'I really envy you, working alongside Korczak, learning his methods with the children first-hand. It must be wonderful to work with him.'

'To be honest it can be very confusing to begin with.'

'How do you mean, confusing?'

'He doesn't teach a set method, you know. He believes that you should get to know each child individually. Work out what they need from there.'

'But don't all children need clear rules? And how can the teacher know if they are doing the right thing? Why are you smiling?'

'I like how enthusiastic you are. Really.'

She bristles slightly. 'You were saying, about Korczak. So he doesn't give any instruction?'

'He does in his own way. We meet up each evening with either him or with Stefa, the house mother, and we talk about the children. And he gives a sort of talk to all the teachers once a week, though if you're not used to him, he seems to ramble on, make jokes.'

'Jokes?'

'When Korczak's playing the fool he's often making his most serious points. He likes to make you think. His philosophy is that you can't learn about a child from reading a book or listening to some professor. You have to find your own way when it comes to caring for children by getting to know each child. It's not always easy at Korczak's home to begin with, but the children at his home are some of the happiest I know, even the little hard cases who come off the street.'

'So you're telling me Korczak's a famous writer who doesn't tell his students to read books? But what do you think about Piaget's new book?'

'I haven't read it yet.'

'He hasn't read it. But you must. Why don't I lend you my copy? I'm nearby. I can run up and fetch it for you later.'

'I'd like that.'

At some point the music stops playing. They look up to realize that the room has emptied around them, although they still stand as close together.

'Shall I get that book?'

They walk side by side under the lamplight, quietly, like two people who have settled on some understanding. He waits under the archway leading to her courtyard while she runs upstairs, the night air buzzing in her absence. A glimpse of her white dress in the dark stairwell and she's back, a little out of breath. She places the book in his hands. It's new, smelling of ink. He takes the weight of it and holds it against his chest. But no, she has to take it back and point out the passages he must absolutely read.

She doesn't seem in a hurry to go. He looks down at the tiny path of pale skin in the parting of her hair, so vulnerable and exposed, and wants to protect her from the chill in the air, from the world as it is. The lamplight illuminates a fine down on her cheek. Would it feel like the down of a peach if he placed his lips there, the skin cool to the touch?

But she'd be offended, hardly knows him.

'I was wondering,' he offers. 'Perhaps you might like to meet again?' Holding his breath.

'I'd like that.'

He can feel himself grinning broadly, never so happy before this. 'Tuesday perhaps? Say nine-thirty?'

'Yes. I can be free on Tuesday.' She's smiling too.

They will meet in Castle Square, by King Sigismund's column at nine-thirty on Tuesday. The place where lovers meet.

CHAPTER FOUR

WARSAW, SEPTEMBER 1937

Misha is sitting at the desk in the little office between the boys' and the girls' dormitories, a window and a door opening out onto each so he can keep watch. He likes sitting in this lamplit cockpit, piloting the children through a safe night's sleep. Usually, he spends the small hours studying, but tonight the words keep dancing out of his head.

Tomorrow morning, in Castle Square.

Korczak comes in, still wearing his coat and broad-brimmed hat, smelling of cold air and smoke from the train and of his beloved cigarettes.

'Thought I'd see if they're all settled.' The rustle of paper. He's stopped at the Turkish bakery to buy his favourite raisin cakes. He offers one to Misha. Two of the boys are sitting up, watching through the glass with interest. He waves them in and lets them share the bounty before sending them back to their dormitory, important and blessed with cake.

'You've been giving a talk to one of the youth groups?' Misha asks.

'At a Jewish community centre in a little town called Oswiecim. So many young people who want to make the journey to Palestine soon, but it's a thorny issue.'

He sits down and takes off his wide-brimmed hat, slips off his bow-tie and loosens his collar.

He eyes Misha with a wry scrutiny for a moment. 'And you, my friend? I take it she's beautiful.'

'Someone told you about Sophia?'

Korczak chuckles. 'Your face, dear Misha, it's as good as newspaper headlines. "Man falls dangerously in love."'

'She's a great fan of yours in fact, Pan Doctor. She wants to be a teacher.'

'And very pretty.'

Misha colours.

'Yes, I see. I diagnose a hopeless case.'

'Well advanced, I'm afraid. Do you have any advice for me?'

'From me? An old bachelor? I never give advice. All I can tell you is that a beautiful life is always a difficult life. We must all find our own way. And I wouldn't advise following mine. That was just for me.'

Korczak rises and pats Misha heavily on the shoulder like a commiseration.

Misha watches the door close. Pan Doctor will go up to his little room in the attic next to the fragrant apple store. A narrow bed with an army blanket, his father's old desk with Pan Doctor's notes for his next book. An oriel window overlooking the yard where the sparrows will greet him in the morning as he scatters crumbs for them. Misha has begun to think he will follow Korczak, a life dedicated to children.

Misha watches the dawn grow. Finally, finally, it's time to turn off the nightlights.

He's early. Misha sits on the steps beneath King Sigismund's column and leans back on his elbows. Warsaw has never looked more beautiful, the royal castle with its red bricks and verdigris spire, a pure blue sky, the vast dome of St Anna's guarding the road to the bridge. He's sitting facing the broad reach of Krakowskie Avenue. He thinks that's the way she'll come. Trams and sleek Austin cars sweep round the square while horses and droshky cabs thread in and out like a parade.

He takes out his pocket watch. She's a little late, but no matter. His father handed it on to him the day he left Pinsk to travel three hundred miles from Polish Belarus to the excitement of studying in Warsaw. Running the chain through his fingers, Misha can almost smell the water of the Pinsk marshes again. He'll take Sophia there one day and he'll row her across the endless lakes that mirror the sky, black-and-white storks taking off from their nests in the reed banks, the church spires of Pinsk rising up like a ship on the sea.

He flips open the cover again. She's certainly late. She'll have a good reason, she'll come running up the steps. You'll never guess what happened.

Every twenty minutes he checks his watch, trying to spot Sophia among the crowds along the boulevard, mistakes her several times. An hour goes by, then an hour and a half, and still he waits. This is a moment that will change his life, when Sophia walks towards him across the square.

When the bells begin to sound eleven across Warsaw, he rises in a daze, his legs stiff from sitting on the stone steps so long, blinking to adjust to this unexpected reality. She's not here. She's really not coming.

There'll be a message back at the home to say why. He hurries back to Krochmalna Street.

There's no message.

He almost calls her several times over the next few days, but a gentleman should allow a quiet refusal. He won't pester her.

All the same, he checks each day at the gatehouse in case there's a note or message until Zalewski finally says, 'Listen, Pan Misha, if I hear I'll let you know. And please, I see all the girls making calves' eyes at you. Put one of them out of their misery and ask them out.'

But there's only Sophia. The weeks confirm his diagnosis. It's Sophia or it's no one.

One foggy afternoon in early autumn, Misha returns to the home with a group of children he's taken for a trip to the cinema.

In the orphanage hallway, Pani Stefa leans over the banisters, arms full of clean nightshirts, good-natured, middle-aged face mischievous. 'Phone for you in the office. A girl. And she sounds cross.'

'It's about my book,' Sophia's voice says coldly. 'I'd appreciate it if you'd let me have it back.'

He's so astonished he can't reply.

'I have to say,' she blurts out. 'I was surprised that we made an arrangement and then you didn't turn up. I waited there until it was quite dark, and rather cold.'

'You were waiting in the dark?'

'What do you think? Half past nine, of course it was dark.'

'But I was there in the morning. Half past nine. I waited for you for hours.'

'Oh.' A silence on her part now. 'You were waiting for me? But who makes a date at nine-thirty in the morning?' She's still cross, but her voice has a note of hope in it now.

'Sophia, I'm so very sorry. I thought I'd explained. I always work in the evenings. I'm only free in the morning.'

He puts down the phone, his face lit up by a huge smile. It was all a misunderstanding. He's going to see her again.

They meet by the fountain in Saxon Gardens, at midday. No mistaking midday. The autumn sun is cold but there's a small rainbow arcing in the mist above the great bowl of the fountain. The palace windows glint yellow and gold through the colonnades of Saxon Square. She's wearing a coat with a small fur collar, her cheeks pink with cold.

After a moment's hesitation they carry on almost where they left off the night of Rosa's party, all those long weeks ago, both talking at once – no, you go first, no, you, please. They walk through the avenue of winter trees, the white statues each side gesturing mysterious messages. Before they realize it they've walked across Theatre Square and on into Old Town.

He reaches out and finds her small hand in his, its shape there behind every thought as they wander on down the stone steps of Old Town that lead to the riverbank.

He says her eyes are the same colour as the sky. Poetry, she says. She must think of something poetic to describe his. She stops on the steps down to the river and examines his. They're piwne, she says, beer-coloured, with tiny flecks of green glass.

The sun is lighting the wide expanse of river with gold and lilac bands. Behind them the medieval outline of old Warsaw, in front of them the chimneystacks of industrial Praga beyond the trees. The wind comes in from the east, undeniably cold, taking the last leaves from the willows on the opposite bank. He puts his arm around her, opening his jacket to shelter her inside as best he can.

In the space of a moment she's stood on tiptoes and brushed her lips against his cheek, her softness against his rougher skin. A magnet drawn across his body.

He answers with a kiss and then another. Everything that passed before a hint, a shadow. He will always want these kisses.

CHAPTER FIVE

WARSAW, SPRING 1938

The light stings his blue eyes as eight-year-old Erwin leaves the factory. All night he's been watching the metal press, the hiss of hot air as the plate came down with a thump, big enough to squash him flat. And each time, it was he who did it, who pushed the black button to set it all in motion.

It was Erwin's idea to get a job in the factory. Now, he can feel the weight of coins in his pocket as he walks down the cobbled street. Shopkeepers in their long gabardine coats and side locks creak back their wooden shutters to let the light into small caves of cloth, or metal pans, or rye bread. Above them are hand-painted signs for all the things people need – and for all the things people don't have money to buy these days.

Mother will be awake by now and will realize he's missing – but when she sees what he's going to bring her…. He buys a loaf of dark rye bread and a large smoked fish. His stomach begs him to break into the bread now but he wants to give the loaf to her whole and beautiful.

He saunters into the dim coal shed. It's as dim and dusty as the bottom of a mine. Gritty anthracite particles hang in the cold slices of light coming in between the planks. His sisters, wild-haired and grimy, are still sleeping on sacks by the black stove. His big brother Isaac is sitting and looking about.

A thin sad mother, coal dust in the lines of her face, is feeding small lumps into the red heat of the stove. A couple of feet away from the stove the shed stays as frosty as the street outside.

When Father was alive Mother was pretty and soft. Father made them all laugh with his tales of the people he met as a porter on Nalewki Street, the things he had to carry on his back. They had food every day and they had beds.

Mother doesn't shout when she sees him come in. She looks at him sadly. He takes out the loaf and the fish and puts them on her lap.

Such a noise from his big brother and sisters. They cook the fish and tear it up with the bread. Such smiles. And he did it. His big brother Isaac wouldn't know how to find food for them, with his soft brown hair and his love of books. All Isaac wants is to go back to the Yeshiva and study. It's sturdy little blond Erwin with his ready fists and quick wits who has to take care of everyone. At eight, he's already a little hustler.

Tonight he'll go back to the factory in Wola and ask if they want him to work again. Right now though, he's sleepy, his arms and eyes heavy. He pulls some empty sacks behind the stove and lies down.

Korczak has two visits today, two prospective new children. Misha is coming with him. In time Korczak hopes Misha will be able to take over the visits to new children, and many other things in the home. After all, he and Stefa are not getting any younger. It's time to start thinking about how a new generation will carry the home into the future. He and Misha got on from the beginning, perhaps because they both lost a parent early, had to tutor as teenagers to help support the family. Misha is athletic and happy to take the children ice skating or kayaking, play football in the yard, but he has an instinctive understanding that children have an inner life, and that some of them carry a deep sadness.

It's only a few hundred yards along Krochmalna Street but they've left the small factories, green lots and new apartment blocks of the street's Polish end where the orphanage stands, and are walking through the clamour of Jewish Krochmalna, famous for its poverty, its streetwalkers and its small-time crooks. It's teeming with ragged children playing between the low, tar-roofed houses. Two girls are singing, a clapping game in Yiddish.

They turn into a courtyard, a babble of voices from the rows of open windows. Yiddish curses from a knife-grinder mix with prayers from a front room Yeshiva. On its doorstep, a rabbi's wife in her wig nods at Korczak. A baker in a ripped shirt, red-faced from the heat of his basement oven, stands at the top of his cellar steps and waves to him. They all know Pan Doctor.

Misha follows Korczak down one of the sets of worn steps to a tiny barrel-roofed cellar ripe with old damp. The only light comes from a grimy window slit, legs walking past on the pavement. There's a single bed, a tiny iron stove that smells of frying, bowls and pans hang on nails along the wall for washing or cooking. A woman is sitting on the bed, thin, with a tubercular cough. A girl of about eight, equally wasted and pallid, sits on the bed as if she sees no one. Long, uncombed red hair in matted curls. The saddest eyes Misha has ever seen.

'What can I do?' the woman says. 'I'm too sick to look after a child. And what should she eat? I have nothing.'

'And the parents have passed away?'

The woman gives Korczak a vinegary look, yellow and sharp. 'Only ever a mother. She's passed away to Paris where she thinks business will be better. Child doesn't understand what her mother is. Doesn't understand much at all, it seems to me.'

Korczak crouches down in front of the child. Halinka looks out at him, then returns to her sadness. But he's seen a flicker there. She's intelligent, alive. If they can find her.

The matted red hair will have to come off, crawling as it is.

'Bring her on Friday, before the Sabbath meal. The children bathe then.'

Then on to the next address. A coal shed behind a factory.

It's late afternoon when Erwin wakes behind the stove. There's a man in the gloom, a bald head, white beard, talking with Mother. Next to him is a tall young man with a canvas bag and a notebook, writing things down as Mother talks.

'They don't go to school any more, Pan Doctor. They help me bag the coal, or they wander the streets. Three months now since their father died and we lost the rooms on Piwna Street. We only got this because a friend took pity on us.'

Erwin goes over and listens in. The old man wears a pale dustcoat, has white hair. Mother has written him a letter. The man looks at Erwin, bright eyes behind wire-rimmed spectacles.

'So this is the little worker who does a night shift in a factory. A man already.'

Erwin swells into the space he stands in.

'So?' he says.

'Erwin, Pan Doctor has a bed for you. He can take you and Isaac.' Mother is agitated, animated. This is important.

'Take us where? To a hospital?'

'To his home.'

'So come and visit us next Saturday. If you like us, you can stay.'

'We'll come, Pan Doctor. Thank you.'

But Erwin knows he won't like this home, this hospital. He holds his mother's hand. When the two men have gone he notices that his stomach is empty again, but the day has lots of hours left, and all of them cold and long and hungry.

Mother makes the boys wash in a basin, the water black with coal dust. They walk along Krochmalna Street and stop at the gates outside a rich man's house, white and tall with big windows and a balcony, children playing beneath a large chestnut tree. Inside, Erwin is dazzled by the rows of clean, white beds, by the smell of freshly baked bread, of meatballs in broth.

The doctor is kind. His blue eyes look right into Erwin's soul, even when he's standing above him as he shaves off all Erwin's hair and then weighs and measures him. Next, Isaac has his head shaved. Lastly a little girl called Halinka with thick red curls who won't look at anyone.

He eats five times that day. He can't believe it. He is shocked to find that the beautiful white bed he is shown to in the dormitory is only for him. This house is where Erwin wants to live for ever. The next day he goes to school and no one beats him up for killing Jesus when he has to wait in the corridor while the priest teaches the Polish children.

No one beats up a Korczak boy. Everyone knows who Korczak is with his famous children's books and his radio broadcasts.

And no one beats you up, or yells at you, or steals your stuff in the big white house. And best of all, Pan Doctor sits in the sun and listens to him, lets Erwin sit as close as a son next to a father while Pan Doctor nods and listens to whatever Erwin has to say.

He's not waiting any more. His life has begun. Every Saturday he goes to see Mother in her room in the big house on Sienna Street where she's a maid now – only the two sisters are allowed to live with her there – and he tells her wonderful stories about his past week. He's good at school. Clever, they say. Who knew?

He has friends, lots of friends. But as he plays under the great chestnut tree, he sees the new girl, Halinka, playing with no one. She walks around the courtyard like a little shorn lamb, eyes far away, singing to herself, trying to look as if she likes being alone best of all.

Erwin knows all about looking as if you don't care, when you're hungry, when you're lonely. He tries to talk to her, but the boys laugh at him for playing with the girls. Is he in love?

Two months, three months, the other children get tired of asking Halinka to play. They forget about her. She wanders around the edge of the yard like a small ghost while Erwin's heart breaks a little more for her each day.

Then a great commotion. Pan Doctor has done something terrible. He's put Halinka on top of the big cupboard in the library and walked off. She can't get down. How is she going to get down?

A whole crowd of little girls stands in front of the cupboard, discussing what to do, shouting up encouraging messages. Erwin runs for Pan Misha. He's tall enough to lift her down in one movement and Halinka is safe on the earth again. She goes off surrounded by a gaggle of clucking nurses and friends.

Pan Doctor comes in from the hallway where, Erwin realizes, he's been watching everything. Pan Doctor's puzzles always have a purpose.

Erwin sees what Pan Doctor has done and his heart swells with thanks. After that day, Halinka is never forgotten again, never lonely again. Her hair grows out in two thick, frizzy red-gold plaits, a sprinkle of freckles across her nose and forehead, and each day Erwin is a little more in love with gentle and kind Halinka.

Of course, Pan Doctor has to go in front of the children's court for putting a child on top of the cupboard. Eight-year-old Erwin stands up in Pan Doctor's defence, and he speaks well, his round blue eyes indignant. The children are almost persuaded. But Pan Doctor is having none of it.

'Same rules for everyone,' he says. 'You must give me the same punishment that you would give to any child if they did such a thing. Only fair.'

Erwin and his friend Sammy Gogol are standing at the window, scrubbed and combed and looking out for Pani Sophia to come through the gate. As soon as they see her they yell to Pan Misha and dash out into the courtyard to meet her.

'So we're going to the music store on Marshall Avenue?' says Sophia as the boys crowd around her, each giving their version of the story. She glances up at Misha. He smiles as if to say, I guess I'm going to have to share you today.

Sammy's parents were both gifted musicians. He can wander up to the hall piano and pick out any tune. Day after day Misha has found the new boy standing at the top window of the stairwell looking out over the courtyard of the Polish apartments next door, listening to a boy playing his harmonica.

'If I could,' he'd whispered to Pan Misha at the supper table, 'I'd buy a harmonica just like that. If I had some money.'

'But you do have money,' Erwin had pointed out. 'Haven't you lost two teeth since you arrived? Don't you know that when you hand your teeth in to Pan Doctor he writes it down in his book and banks a zloty for you?'

Sammy's eyes had lit up. His own money. He swung round to check with Pan Misha, hope across his small face with its long nose and big ears.

'Is that enough to buy a harmonica?'

'I should think it is.'

So now they set off to choose Sammy's harmonica. The boys walk in front as they cross Saxon Park, Erwin blond and compact, beady blue eyes assessing everything. Sammy taller, a long aquiline nose and sticking-out ears, his dark hair in compact curls. Erwin has come to advise on how to get a good deal, waving his hands as Sammy listens carefully, nodding at tips on driving a hard bargain.

On Marshall Boulevard with its grand offices and shops, they enter a music shop and buy a gleaming harmonica with a mellow, resonant tone. Sammy holds it like a holy relic. A trill of three recognizable notes emerges among some wheezing first tries as the boys march down the street. Sophia claps as she and Misha follow behind. But up ahead, a crowd of people are gathered around the news-seller, almost snatching the afternoon paper from his hand.

Headlines are scrawled across the poster in front of the stand. Hitler has annexed Austria.

'Perhaps he'll be satisfied now,' says Sophia as they walk back to the home in more sombre mood.

A few weeks later, Hitler marches into Czechoslovakia and claims the Sudetenland as part of the Reich.

'Why is no one in the civilized world doing anything to stop this madman? Whatever will he do next?' says Mrs Rozental as she mends a stocking in the kitchen.

Mr Rozental switches off the wireless. Slight and greying, he points at the room with his pipe. 'These claims that part of Poland is German territory are going nowhere. He'd never dare cross over into Poland.'

Sabina looks down shyly from the white droshky decorated with white roses and carnations. Her veil fits closely around her head like a princess in a medieval painting, a silk flower fastened to one side. Lutek waves his top hat and the white horse sets off. Sophia and Krystyna wave madly, Mrs Rozental dabbing her eyes. She takes her husband's arm as they watch the carriage set off along Twarda Street to Grzybowski Square.

Next to Sophia, Misha wears his new suit, his father's watch in the waistcoat pocket. Both his sisters, Niura with her blonde curls and Ryfka with her plaits, are studying in Warsaw now and Mrs Rozental has decided to take them under her wing. They crowd along the pavement next to Rosa and her new husband, along with the neighbours and friends who've known Sabina since she was a little girl, everyone waving and cheering as the carriage sets off around the square. A band has come out of the courtyard to play, a clarinet and accordion. The carriage takes two more turns around the square to eke out the splendour of the moment, then drives along Twarda Street and turns into a side passage. Hidden away in a little square, the tiny white Nozyk Synagogue waits, pretty as a wedding cake.

The wedding party follows in groups, arms linked, chattering and smiling. Inside the synagogue, they fall quiet, enveloped by the solemn smell of polished wood, of hot candle wax and the air of anticipation.

The cantor is highly regarded, known for his ability to make everyone cry, the sign of a good wedding. Sabina and Lutek are married beneath the carved marble canopy. They each tread on a glass folded in a napkin, a reminder of the destruction of Jerusalem, and then they are back outside in the April sun, stopping for a photograph before Mother says they should move into the hall where the food and the band are waiting.

Later, as the dancing begins, Sophia recalls her lace gloves, a present from Sabina. She must have left them inside the synagogue. She slips out to get them.

The building is empty. She breathes in the peaceful air, looking around at the pretty fretwork screens and the delicate white and gold of the building. One day. In this very place. Misha will be waiting under the canopy as she walks towards him.

She leaves the building and runs across the courtyard, unable to be away from him for a moment longer, running towards the music and singing from inside the Nozyk hall.

A few months later, the world is shaken by a violent pogrom against Jews in Nazi Austria. There have been restrictions on Jewish life in the Reich, but this brutality is a new departure. How can people be arrested, robbed and beaten up, on the streets of civilized Vienna?

In her new flat, Sabina has no interest in newspapers. White as a sheet, her face thin, she is throwing up constantly.

'What's wrong?' asks Krystyna, holding back Sabina's long, black hair from the bowl on her knee.

Mother wipes Sabina's forehead tenderly. 'Nothing's wrong,' says Mother calmly. 'This is good news.'

Sabina goes shakily to the mirror, tries to tidy her hair.

'So long as the poor baby has your blonde hair, Mother. I look like a complete witch.'

'My beautiful girl. Such a thing to say. A little nap this afternoon will help you feel less down.'

They hide the evening newspaper from Sabina with its pictures of shops in Vienna with broken windows and paint daubed across doors: 'Jews get out'.

CHAPTER SIX

LITTLE ROSE SUMMER CAMP, JULY 1939

For weeks Sophia's been looking forward to spending a month at the Little Rose summer camp: a whole month to be with Dr Korczak and the children and a chance to learn from the great man himself.

And a whole month spent with Misha. They've been a couple for two years now, but since he lives at the orphanage as a teacher and she with her parents, both of them studying, it feels as though they are constantly saying goodbye, always waiting for the next time they can meet.

But since they arrived, three days ago, it honestly feels as though Misha's been avoiding her, distant and jumpy.

The wooden table is warm from the afternoon sun, piled with little stacks of paper and sticks from her kite-making club. Halinka is helping Sara colour in the bows for the string of her kite. The rest of the children have gone to play in the field nearby, the grass rippled with light, the clear trebles of their voices coming and going on the breeze.

Across the field she can see Misha towering above the boys in their vests and shorts as he supervises a football game. Her heart clenches. She's barely spoken with him all day. She loves him so much she's never considered for a moment that he might not always feel the same. She can't imagine a future without Misha at its centre.

'Are you sad, Pani Sophia?' Halinka asks. Really, you can't hide much from a child like Halinka with her gentle ability to pick up on other's feelings.

'Am I frowning? On such a lovely day.' Sophia takes the finished kite that Sara hands to her. Beneath Sara's straight fringe, the scar on her forehead shows silver against her summer tan.

'We'll fly them as soon as it's windy enough.'

She watches the girls run down the sloping field, calling out to the others.

At least people have stopped doing that sort of thing now, gangs of boys throwing stones at the children as they walk home from school.

There's a new feeling in the air at Warsaw. They all need to stand together. Hitler has swallowed Austria and the Sudetenland and now he's making rumbling threats about taking a slice of Poland's northern sea coast.

A horrible new thought. A cold shadow passes across the day.

Perhaps Misha's moody because he's going to tell her that he wants to enlist. Sabina's husband has already joined up.

But she couldn't bear that either, if Misha had to go away and fight.

Misha's sister Niura joins Sophia at the picnic table.

'How was chemistry club?' asks Sophia.

'My budding scientists are all still alive, I'm happy to say.'

Niura has the same high cheekbones and slanted eyes as Misha, the same lilting eastern inflection to her Polish. She's become a good friend over the past two years.

Niura waves to Misha across the field but he looks away as if he doesn't want to acknowledge the girls.

A boy falls over in his eagerness to get the ball. Misha helps him up, examines the knee and soon the boy's laughing.

'You know,' Niura says, 'Father tried to do his best when Mother died, but he's a military man. It was Misha who carried on Mother's warmth in the house, who used to read to Ryfka and me when we were little. He was the one who listened to us when we were upset. He hasn't got an unkind bone in his body.'

'But don't you think he seems worried about something? Something's wrong.'

Niura gives her a funny look. 'Not at all. He's never been happier.'

They watch as Misha leads the boys away towards the long wooden dachas behind the garden of hollyhocks and lettuces. They pass Korczak in his wide-brimmed straw hat, sitting on the grass nearby with a group of children.

Korczak gets up, exchanges a few words with Misha and pats him on the shoulder.

*

Pan Doctor sits back down on the bank alongside the children, sleepily listening as they discuss their project. Szymonek and some of the younger children are building a city of sand and twigs for the ants. Behind them long bleached grasses shiver in the breeze. Yellow butterflies tumble above like blown petals. He breathes out. It's a relief to be away from Warsaw and the ominous headlines shouted out by the news sellers each day. Here, all that matters is a quarrel by the swing, a lost sandal or a bruised knee. And there are twenty new children this week, twenty little books to get to know and decipher – his favourite thing.

Pan Doctor takes out his notebook and writes something down. He likes to mull over how to solve the small problems that come up each day. The mystery of why Sara suddenly refuses to eat bread, for example.

And then there's the problem of boys. This year he arrived at Little Rose to find something of a mutiny on his hands, a roomful of little boys indignant with life's injustices. Erwin was chosen to voice their complaint. Why was it that Pani Stefa always favoured the girls, praised them more, gave them the best jobs to do, while the boys it seemed were constantly in trouble?

Dear Stefa, it's such a relief to see her back from her visit to Ein Harod. His depression lifted the moment she arrived home, handing out oranges and good wishes from their past pupils in the kibbutz.

And hasn't it always been Stefa who ran everything really, who kept a steady hand on the tiller, right from the very first day he'd met her? A very plain twenty-six-year-old, determined to make the neglected orphanage she'd taken on into a real home for a hundred underfed children.

Now they've worked together for what, over a quarter of a century? People talk about how homely Stefa is to look at, but there's nothing plain about Stefa; her face shines when she's with the children.

And what a joy it is once more to walk with his dearest friend through the gardens around the dachas each evening, discussing the children, she in her inevitable brown dress, he smoking a cigarette; a middle-aged spinster and a confirmed bachelor with a family of a hundred children to care for.

Of course it was two hundred children, before the board at his Polish children's home sacked him. A Jew can't take care of Polish children any more, it seems. So many years to build bridges of understanding between two cultures. Moments to tear it down.

It still hurts like a bereavement to think of those children. He hasn't seen them for over two years now. His children. They've always spent the summer camp together, but not this year.

Yes, he's scolded Stefa for coming home and cancelling her plans to retire and live in the sun in Palestine. But what happiness to see her again. Not changed one bit. You rarely see Stefa with her hands still. Stefa who endlessly mends, folds, sorts, puts a cool hand on the forehead of a child with a fever.

Is it any wonder that she sometimes finds it easier to be pleased with the girls, has always been tempted to love them slightly more with their clean pinafores, their brushed hair and their willingness to be neat and tidy?

So many years in a boy's childhood when you might ask what purpose boys serve exactly, with so many things broken and trampled and their repulsion for water and soap. Why is it always the boys who make all the mending, and largely the girls who do it? Perhaps he should introduce a day when the girls must rip their frocks and the boys mend them. He makes a note of that in his pocket book. Why not? It could go in the calendar, a fixture along with first snow day when everyone must miss school and the day when everyone gets up as late as they want.

At least he's solved the mystery of the ripped trousers. Stefa had said she'd never had to mend so many pairs.

He had the feeling it was something to do with the new mania the boys had for sliding down the wooden handrail on the veranda steps. He'd tested the theory, ripped his own trousers on a nail snagged away in the wood: *quod erat demonstradum*. Strictly illegal, of course, to slide down the banisters in the home, so he'd had to go before the children's court again.

Only fair, he'd told little Sara, only fair. We all have to abide by the same rules, from the youngest to the oldest. The law is a beautiful thing.

But that still leaves the problem of the boys sulking. How to make them feel proud of being boys? A child like Erwin, messy and noisy, but bold enough to find himself a job in a factory at only eight.

In time all their energy and boldness will serve them well, as men. Yes, life will demand all of that and more, but how to make them proud now of the little men they are today?

The bell in the onion-domed steeple of the convent nearby rings out midnight. Misha goes through the boys' hut shaking them awake. He signals for them to be silent as they pull on their shorts and jumpers. In front of the hut, Korczak assembles them in the darkness, a band of expectant and now wide-awake eight- to fourteen-year-old boys.

Stocky little Erwin and thoughtful Sammy with his long features and dark, almond eyes – among the older boys now at almost twelve – have been sent to break into the kitchen and fetch a sack of potatoes. Korczak's written a note for them to leave on the kitchen table promising that he'll replace them tomorrow.

Abrasha's missing. It's not like him to be difficult. Then Korczak sees the child's slender form, running from the wooden huts, his delicate features lit up with a broad smile. He's been back to fetch his violin.

The dark air is cool with scents of earth and grass. A full moon casts sharp, monochrome shadows. With muffled whispers, the boys set off towards the forest, torch beams arcing across the obscure grass, the thick stars crowding along the Milky Way above. The pine trees of the forest rise up like a dark wall.

They plunge inside. Glow worms blink on and off. The boys keep their voices low, awed by the sleeping giant of the forest at night; the rusty cries of a fox somewhere, an owl calls out.

They come to a clearing and under Jakubek's orders – the oldest boy in the home now – some gather firewood in the dark while others dig a pit to bury the potatoes in the sandy earth. They gather in a circle and watch the tepee of sticks catch. The flames grow and send up showers of red sparks.

Abrasha goes to one side in the shadows of the trees and begins to play 'Night in a Forest', eyes closed and face blissful. He's always wanted to stand among the trees with the stars above him and play these wild notes. The boys stare into the flames and listen, eyes wide. Then they sing songs, threading one after another, in Yiddish and in Polish. As the fire settles to embers that quiver with a layer of white ash, Pan Doctor tells a story from a book he wrote for the children when Poland became free, Little King Matt, about a child who tries to run a country and learns that it's not so easy to do the right thing – especially not to begin with. And an old tale of a boy lost in the forest with nothing but his wits and his good heart to save him, who stumbles across a flying ship caught in the branches of the trees.

Soot and ash on their faces, Sammy and Erwin help Jakubek rake back the embers and dig the potatoes from the sandy pit. The boys pull them apart with their fingers, blow on the fragrant insides as Korczak passes around a paper bag of salt. The best potatoes ever eaten.

Light begins to dawn as the band of boys walk back to the dachas, Sammy at the front playing his harmonica. The girls crowd at the windows of their hut, amazed to see the boys coming home at this hour. And each boy walks past waving, grubby and dishevelled and proud to be so – to be themselves.

Sophia is at the window with the girls, a long cardigan around her pyjamas, wondering why Misha did not tell her about the midnight picnic.

He barely speaks to her all day. Late in the afternoon, when the children are watching a film reel of Mickey Mouse cartoons, Misha suggests a walk, just the two of them. She almost refuses to go, she feels so cross and neglected.

He's wearing his best white shirt, his plus-four trousers, damp hair ploughed with fresh comb marks as if he had somewhere more important to go than a countryside ramble. Would he rather be somewhere else?

The warm air from the miles of open fields buffs her bare arms. The willows along the stream change to pale green and silver and back again in the wind, but she won't let it distract her from how unhappy she feels. She doesn't take his hand when he reaches across for hers. She falls behind him a pace or two, looking at his long back and wide shoulders with a feeling of loss, of homesickness for all her hopes.

The wall of dark pine trees casts a sharp shade across the grass as they approach the forest. Suddenly Misha stops and turns towards her. She closes her eyes. He's going to say something. Her heart lurches.

She feels a slight movement in the air and she opens her eyes to see him kneeling on the grass. She watches, amazed, as he reaches out to take her hand, feels the strange heat of his fingers and palm against her cool skin.

'I won't earn much, and I know you've still two more years of study but no one can ever love you more, dear Sophia. Would you? Would you be my wife one day? Please say yes.'

She can't speak. There's a minute tremor in his hand, thrumming like a message in a wire. He buries his lips in her palm. Everything in her melts.

'Yes, yes, of course, darling Misha.'

All the tense anxiety is swept from his face. He leaps up and holds her so tightly. They kiss deeply, then walk on, stopping to kiss again as they travel in a dream through the woods, bursts of sunlight illuminating the path when the treetops part above them. In a clearing they find a fallen tree covered in thick moss. They sit down, tight in each other's arms. Birds sing with the cadence of wine filling a glass. Tall pines enclose them, the sky their roof.

He looks down at her hand. 'I'm sorry I don't have a ring yet.'

She shrugs. 'It's not important. But two years. You don't mind waiting so long? Another two years until we both graduate.'

'It won't be so long. It's the right thing to do.'

She looks down at her hands, thinking of Sabina, white-faced and exhausted, holding her beloved baby Marianek nine months after the wedding. They both know that a pregnancy would mean the end of Sophia's degree. So they'll wait. She's glad he understands how important it is to her that she graduates.

But it won't be easy.

They kiss and embrace, tracing each other's warmth and contours. The singing of the birds fills Sophia's ears. She closes her eyes, not sure at times where her skin ends and Misha's begins.

Can they really wait another two years? She thinks of Rosa, who gave up her degree to marry Lolek.

No, she won't do that.

Misha goes still, whispers, 'Look.' Behind them, there's the shape of a deer through the trees. It's wandered so close in their quietness that they can catch the smell of its leathery goatiness. It shudders, bucks and flees away into the forest.

They walk out of the trees, dazed by the afternoon sun and by their immeasurable happiness, fingers laced together, the whole world surely a gift just to them. Across the fields, in front of the dachas, lines of white tea towels over the vegetable frames are fluttering like flags for a celebration. Niura sees them coming. She's been waiting for them, Sophia realizes. Niura runs towards them and seeing their beaming faces she too begins to cry.

'I thought I'd burst all day. I'm so happy, so, so happy.' She pauses. 'But you did say yes?'

Sophia laughs. 'I said yes.'

Niura hugs her and by now the children have caught on. They run out and jump up and down. Pan Misha and Pani Sophia are getting married.

'I should really give up education and go full-time into the matchmaking business,' laughs Korczak. 'Another pair of you tying the knot.' With the Newerlys and the Sztokmans, they'll be the third wedding from among the staff of student helpers.

'If it's with your blessing,' says Misha. Korczak has become a second father to him, or the mother he lost.

Korczak kisses them both on the forehead. 'When I see you dear children, such hopes for the future. With every blessing I can give you. But what blessing can I give you except for the longing for a better world, for love and forgiveness, for truth and for justice, for a world that may not exist today but may exist tomorrow perhaps?' He hugs them both to him, a little roughly, coughing away a thickness in his voice that sounds like a man close to tears. 'My children,' he says and then is all action and gaiety, clapping his hands. They must have dancing after supper, songs.

He sends Abrasha to run for the orphanage camera and Sophia and Misha stand on the dacha steps to have their picture taken. She is one step up to be more on his level, white ankle socks and strong tanned legs, a summer dress and her bright hair gleaming with the sun. He is in plus fours and a white open-necked shirt, and both of them with such smiles.

For the rest of the week, the little girls have a passion for dressing up and playing weddings, kidnapping various boys to act as grooms. Few of them stay long before they run off to play football again, throwing down their silk shawls. Apart from Erwin, who, bashful and shy, offers to be the groom for his adored Halinka, his face pink with pride.

He's always loved Halinka, from the moment she arrived at the home on Krochmalna Street as a shorn and skinny little lamb who refused to speak to anyone else.

So when she pushes the net curtain out of her eyes and promises to love him for ever, Erwin too promises. He will love her always, take care of her always.

Sara won't eat the bread she takes at supper. Sitting at the same table, Erwin is scandalized to see Sara push away her bread each meal. Wasting food. Erwin loves the beautiful meals that appear each day. The rule is, you can take as much food as you want, so long as you eat it. Even Pani Sophia, sitting at their table, can't coax Sara to eat it.

Pan Doctor is collecting up the soup bowls. He sees the bread, Sara's lips clamped shut. He crouches down next to her and whispers, 'Sara, the witches have gone away to the mountains and won't be back.'

She looks at him with hope in her eyes. Tentatively, she takes a bite, then eats all the bread. She runs off to play, holding Halinka's hand.

'How did you know that trick to make her eat it?' asks Sophia.

'No trick. I listened. I found out from Sara that her grandmother told her a story about witches living in bread crusts and since then Sara's been terrified of bread. Sometimes, you have to make up a new story to drive away the old one.'

Humming, he carries on along the tables with his stack of bowls.

The last day of summer camp. Sophia stands at the edge of the fields. The morning light renders the blades of grass translucent and mists through the air. She wants to hold this moment. It's hard to think of returning to Warsaw with its blackout and its oppressive atmosphere.

Sara and Halinka call to her. The kites are ready and everyone is setting out to the open fields to make them fly. A few sticks and pieces of paper have become birds that rise high on the wind.

'Pani Sophia,' says Abrasha as he tenses the string with his violinist's fingers each time the kite dips. 'One day, I'm going to fly all over the world and play music that sounds like kites on the wind. Will you come with me?'

'Yes,' says Sophia. 'In a silver aeroplane.'

On the way back to Warsaw, the train slows as it passes through fields filled with Polish cavalry on manoeuvres. The children crowd excitedly at the windows. The soldiers' uniforms and the flanks of the horses glow chestnut brown in the sun. Slender white pennants flutter above the soldiers' square caps with their poppy-red bands.

The train picks up speed again, and Misha turns his head to catch a last sight of them. Sophia holds his hand tightly. She knows what he will do as soon they get back to Warsaw.

CHAPTER SEVEN

WARSAW, 31 AUGUST 1939

Misha lopes down the steps of the recruiting office, his face set and angry. All morning he's been going from office to office, trying to enlist. They all want to take him, tall and capable and eager to serve for his country, but Misha's been to university which means he's been exempted from training, so where should they put him. Then there's the problem that university also puts him in the officers' rank, and since a Jew can't be in charge of Poles they're not sure if they are allowed to enlist him. No one knows if they are permitted to ignore the old rule – why hasn't it been abolished? Ridiculous. But in the end it's always a very regretful no.

Hitler has been demanding that Poland hand over control of Danzig and a slice of northern Poland for months and yesterday, he issued a final ultimatum. The Polish army, however, seems to have been taken completely by surprise, hopelessly disorganized and with no clear plan.

The cafés around Saxon Square are as full as ever, everyone trying to ignore the gritty walls of sandbags piled up in front of the palace. Baskets of petunias hang from the lampposts, apologizing for the loudspeakers strung up beneath them in readiness for any air-raid warning. So far, the speakers have been silent.

He spots Sophia waiting for him at one of the tables set out under the lindens, a low trellis separating her from the people passing along the pavement. Someone has tied their dachshund to the fretwork and the trellis moves each time the hysterical little dog jumps, ears flapping like limp propellers.

She can't help but look relieved when she hears of Misha's lack of success.

'Everyone's saying it's all bluster on Hitler's part. He'll never dare attack Poland, not with Britain and France our allies.'

Misha puts his gas-mask case on the table. 'He's annexed Austria and most of the Czech lands without a fight. So what is he planning to do with the tonnage of weapons he's amassed just over the border?'

'Don't let's be gloomy. It's a lovely afternoon. Let's walk down to the river.'

The boardwalks are filled with people in wide sailor-style trousers, elegant chiffon dresses, white summer caps. Couples are dancing to a band with a clarinet and accordion playing the latest jaunty tango. It's Misha's day off so they stay out late, eating dumplings at a café on Szucha Street. They come out into the moonlit streets and Misha walks Sophia home to Grzybowski Square in the mild night. The blackout feels like some romantic ruse for the sake of lovers, the war very far away. They linger in the courtyard archway, embracing, reluctant to part and give the night up to the next day.

Misha walks through the almost total blackness back to his narrow room in the orphanage, hoping that Sophia is right. But he can't escape a fear that follows behind, something about to break.

In the early hours as it gets light, Korczak sits up in bed, woken by loud booms. He's not dreaming. He really can hear a series of muffled explosions going off in the distance.

Abrasha appears at the door. 'Pan Doctor, they're bombing the industrial areas in Praga.'

'It will be more troop manoeuvres.'

'But the radio says it's begun. Hitler's coming.'

Stefa appears in his doorway, her face drawn.

'Is it true?' Korczak asks her.

'Yes, Germany's attacked us. No formal declaration of war, it seems. They've crossed the border in the north and sent planes to bomb the oil refineries just outside Warsaw. What should we do?'

'Carry on as normal. Hitler will steal Danzig, perhaps, but he'd never do more than that or he'll have our allies, France and Britain, declaring war on Germany. I'll be down in a moment. Abrasha, go with Pani Stefa and tell the other children not to worry. I'll be with you in the shake of a dog's tail.'

Korczak rattles through his few coat hangers and pulls his military officer's uniform from the back of the attic cupboard.

The braid is a little worn but this is an officer's jacket that has been through the Great War. It's seen the Germans retreat from Warsaw after they lingered on in Poland following the armistice in

1919. And then two years later, the war of Polish independence. If you include the Russian war on Japan while he was still a medical student, then this will be Korczak's fourth war.

And what has he learned? That it's always the children who suffer first in a war.

He pulls on the trousers, a tug to fasten them around the small paunch he has acquired of late. The jacket hangs emptily over his skinny chest.

'Well, what did you expect?' he tells his reflection in the little shaving mirror.

An old soldier looks back at him defiantly, a white beard, fierce violet-blue eyes in bursts of kind crinkles. He fastens the silver buttons up to his chin and pats them.

'At least we begin to fight back against this Hitler madness as one now, Poles and Jews together.'

He's too old to go back to his post as an army medical officer, Major Korczak, but he takes out his bag and checks through its contents, adding some bandages and a case of morphine vials. He clatters down to the hall in his old officer's boots.

Another series of booming explosions somewhere in the distance. The children look up from their milk and bread in alarm.

'Well, well, so Hitler's got up in a bad mood,' Korczak tells them, striding through the dining hall, giving out hugs and smiles to the children who run up to him to be reassured. Now that the Doctor's here, things surely can't be so bad.

'Pan Doctor, isn't it true that the Germans' planes are made of cardboard?' asks Chaya.

'And their clothes are made of paper,' shouts Szymonek.

'Absolutely,' replies Korczak, 'even their underpants!'

Erwin calls from the doorway. 'Pan Doctor, you're wanted on

the telephone. It's the manager of Radio Poland for you.'

In the office, Korczak answers briskly. He well remembers the last conversation with the radio manager, a bruising and embarrassing affair when he had gone in to propose his new idea for a programme only to be told his weekly talk had been terminated.

'I was wondering, would you have time to come in today and do a broadcast to the people of Warsaw, Dr Korczak? People are panicking and there's nothing like the voice of the old Doctor to calm people down. You've always had a way of speaking to the heart.'

For a moment Korczak's silent. The manager rushes in with an apology. 'Of course, I would have defended you. It was all pure revenge for your criticism of some of the politicians, you know. Ridiculous that some people feel a Jewish citizen should not comment on affairs. But one's hands are tied, you see.'

Korczak's voice is thick with emotion. 'Of course. Only too happy.'

Korczak sits behind the microphone. 'Today we stand together, united against a great madness. Today every man, woman and child in Poland has a part to play to overcome the darkness together.'

In the lobby outside the studio, the radio manager grips Korczak's hand.

'I should have been firmer, stood up to them when they sacked you. If only I'd—'

Korczak stops him, grasping both his arms. 'All that's in the past, my friend. It's the future we have to look to now. And have any fresh reports come in on how our army's doing?'

'We're not allowed to broadcast all the bad news that's coming in, but I can tell you that the German army are travelling at remarkable speed, wreaking havoc as they go. The Polish army is more or less in retreat.'

'You're sure of this? We were told Poland was ready to repel any attack. But things will be very different, when Britain and France come into the war. No news of a declaration?'

'Nothing yet, I'm afraid.'

All through the next day, Misha, Korczak and the other teachers keep returning to the office to listen to the radio bulletins. When the announcement finally comes, Britain has declared war on Germany, Korczak leaps from his chair. 'I knew it. I knew our allies wouldn't let us down. We must go to the embassy to show our thanks.'

Korczak and Misha join the crowds thronging the narrow street leading to the British Embassy. France has also declared war on Germany and the French and British ambassadors both stand on the balcony of the embassy. With one deep voice, the crowd begins to sing the Polish national anthem. When the crowd then takes up the Jewish national anthem, Korczak lets the tears flow, one arm around Misha and the other around the Polish man standing next to him.

Sophia looks down on the street below from the window in Rosa's apartment. For the last couple of days, Warsaw has been going about its business as if the war can be swatted away quickly, shops open, people dressed as elegantly as ever. But today the shutters are closed, people hurrying away in the direction of the bridge looking as if they've dressed in a panic or as if they're leaving for a hiking trip with boots and carrying backpacks. And as many people are heading into Warsaw, refugees from the rural areas to the west and north. No one knows what to do.

All the news is of defeat after Polish defeat as the Germans advance and the Allies do nothing to stop them.

Could the Germans really make it as far as Warsaw?

It's meant to be a celebration meal for Misha and Sophia's engagement but now the dishes have been moved to one side and a map is spread out on the table. Around it, Sophia and her family, Misha and his sisters watch with anxious faces as Rosa's husband, Lolek, traces a route across the Bug River into eastern Poland.

'When do you think you will leave?' Misha asks Rosa.

'In the next few days. Before it's too late to get out. If Poland falls, we'll have to live with the kind of restrictions you see in Germany.' She looks across at Lolek. 'The young men taken away for labour with no warning.'

'If Poland falls. What kind of talk is that?' says Mr Rozental.

Mrs Rozental looks at her girls poring over the map. Sabina is dark-eyed and too thin, holding her baby; there's no question of her travelling. Krystyna is too young to go. But if Misha goes with Sophia, looks after her, then should they let her go?

Niura pulls Misha to one side.

'I'm going to take Ryfka and go with Rosa, head back to Pinsk and Father. I know it's a risk but you could come with us, please, Misha?'

He can't reply. Should he and Sophia leave too? But how can he? He can't leave the children. He feels torn in half.

Outside, the speakers hung on the lamp posts buzz and crackle into life. A strident mechanical wail cuts the air.

'It will only be a drill,' says Rosa's mother firmly.

Moments late, the room vibrates and lurches palpably. An explosion out in the street.

By the time they are down in the cellars, the scores of planes fill the air across Warsaw.

Day after day, the carpet bombardment continues.

Erwin looks up at the sky through the branches of the tree in the middle of the yard as he helps usher the younger children towards the doors to the basement once again. At the last summer camp Erwin, Sammy, Abrasha and the other boys played Poland against Germans. Sometimes the Germans won, sometimes the Poles. But they are not playing any more. Day after day Hitler has sent his planes to bomb Warsaw. As soon as the siren sounds they help Szymonek, Sarah and the other smaller children down into the basement. Korczak watches proudly as the children calmly file down again and again. More sensible than many of the adults he's seen around Warsaw.

And every day, Korczak takes his medical bag and threads through the smoke and fire of Warsaw, past the broken buildings and the horses lying on the road, giving first aid, picking up children stranded in the smoke. On Marszalkowska Avenue he finds a boy with no shoes standing on a pavement covered in broken glass.

To Hitler's fury, in spite of the terrible bombing onslaught, Warsaw refuses to surrender. The city is determined to fight on. The Allies will come to Warsaw's aid any time now. All they have to do is stand firm, and sooner or later the Germans will retreat.

Then Zalewski comes into the dining hall, his face white.

'Is it true, Pan Doctor? Do you think it can be true?'

The Germans have reached the suburbs. The Polish government, however, are no longer there to defy them. They have fled the city, promising to reconvene in Krakow. 'And the army too. The Polish army have pulled out of Warsaw. How can they desert us?'

They switch the wireless on and the teachers gather round. Korczak grips the chair. He shakes his head slowly in disbelief. It's only a matter of time now before the Germans reach the very heart of the city and swarm along Krochmalna. Stefa looks at Korczak's major's uniform.

'My dear, shouldn't you take that off now? If the Germans arrive?'

He stares over the top of his glasses. 'Are we not at war?'

'Why do I ask?' says Stefa. 'You'll wear it. You'll wear it until they leave. Of course you will.'

Misha stands with fists clenched in frustration. What is he doing here? He should be with the Polish army, fighting, helping repel the invaders from the edges of Warsaw.

A new message comes over the airwaves. He moves closer to the wireless, listening intently as it's repeated over and over again. All able-bodied men are to reconvene in the east on the other side of the river. The teachers look at each other. Is it genuine? Is the army really reconfiguring in the east? Is this a call to join up? Or is it a trap?

Misha stands up. He knows what he must do.

CHAPTER EIGHT

WARSAW, SEPTEMBER 1939

It takes Misha a moment to work out where he is. He's so bone tired he can barely remember his name. He can feel Sophia's warm weight along his side and hear her breathing, regular and soft. He presses his chin against his chest and looks down so he can see if she's really there.

So they've slept together all night? Then he feels the bars of the delivery cart pressing into his back and remembers. It's no dream. They've been on the road with thousands of other refugees for two days now. This open-sided wooden cart has become their home, their world.

And yet he's content, happy. He passes his hand tenderly over her fair hair, not quite touching it but feeling the compact warmth of her head, and she sighs and moves her forehead against his chest, her breath warm through his shirt.

If he has Sophia, then he has everything.

He doesn't want to wake her. Let her sleep a little longer before she has to face what the day will bring. How many times did they have to run for the cornfields yesterday, the crowds spilling out like ants either side of the road? First the scream of the engines, then the Stuka planes appeared out of nowhere, suddenly swooping low and sowing death and mayhem along the route. An old man with a military bearing stood shaking his fist as the planes rose into the blue sky, vanishing once again. 'This is no way to wage a war. On children. Women. Not how a gentleman wages war. Preposterous.'

Later, Misha had come across him lying among the stubble in the field, neat holes in the fabric of his coat, red stains blooming around them, his family trying to gather him up.

How long before a bullet finds Sophia, or his sisters? They are lying asleep near to Sophia, curled up together in the way they used to when they were little girls after Mama died.

When Niura asked him to help them leave Warsaw and head for Pinsk and the safety of their father, he had had no idea that the Germans might machine-gun the civilians as they fled Warsaw.

At the far end of the cart, Rosa and her husband are also still sleeping, dressed in their expensive hiking gear. It was Rosa's father who got hold of the cart.

All around he can hear muffled coughing, children crying, the first argument as the hundreds of people camped among the trees begin to wake to the chill of early morning. The air is thick with the tobacco smell of leaf mould. He rolls his head, his neck aching, his clothes damp from the forest air.

He needs to pee, but he doesn't want to move.

Two days since they left Warsaw, two days on the road in a long procession of thousands moving at walking speed. Six days now since the strange message came over the Warsaw's airwaves calling for every able-bodied man to go east. It wasn't spelled out in the message, but everyone had understood that the Polish army must be regrouping somewhere beyond the Vistula. They were calling for recruits, reinforcements. It was all the call-up papers Misha had needed. But leaving Warsaw, the children, that would be like tearing himself out by the roots.

After he'd listened to the wireless announcement again, straining for more clues, he had gone down to the courtyard to speak to Korczak. He'd found a group of young men clustered around him. He wasn't the only one planning to go east to find the army. Sammy Gogol and Jakubek Dodiuk, boys he used to care for when he first came to the home, were now young men of eighteen. They had run back to Krochmalna Street to say their goodbyes before setting off.

'All my fledglings are flying the nest,' Korczak had said as he kissed the head of each of the young men.

He'd turned to Misha, saw his grave expression.

'And you too. So you're leaving me too.'

'I heard the message. But if you want me to stay . . .'

'I can't tell you what you should do. But in the last two wars it was me who had to go to war and leave Stefa to manage here. So now it's my turn to stay while others go. It's not the first time we've lived through a German occupation here – and seen the end of it. So from an old soldier to a young one, I salute you.' Korczak had stood to attention in his old major's uniform, then held out his arms and embraced Misha. 'Ah, but it's always hard to see one's sons go.'

Erwin had come running across the courtyard at full pelt.

'They say you're leaving, Pan Misha?' His blue, birdlike eyes were bewildered in his round face. 'When will you come back?'

'Soon. It won't be for long.'

At the gatehouse Zalewski, the Polish janitor, had come out to shake Misha's hand. Like Korczak, he'd also fought in the Great War and then the War of Independence.

'Don't you worry, Pan Misha, me and Mrs Zalewski here, we'll be taking care of the children and the Doctor for you.'

Sara and Halinka, Abrasha and Sammy, and little Szymonek and so many of the children that Misha had cared for over the past seven years had crowded around the gate, calling out goodbye, arms waving through the railings.

He'd waved back, giving one last look up at the large building that had been his home for the last four years and set out for Grzybowski Square to tell Sophia he was heading east to join up. He was going to fight for Poland, but he felt like a deserter.

Of course, Sophia had already heard the message too, already knew that he would decide to try and join up.

'If you're going east, then we go together,' she'd announced the minute she opened the apartment door. The wireless was on in the kitchen. He could hear the same message being repeated.

'But . . .'

'I don't mean I'm going to join up. I'm going to finish my degree in Lvov. Hitler will never get that far east. If the Germans get here, then you know life will be over for us. We won't be able to do anything. If I can get to Lvov, then I can graduate and by the time this is sorted out I'll be able to get on with life. If Hitler stops us doing what we need to, so we can make the world a better place one day, then he really will have won.' She'd held his gaze steadily. She hadn't said, and we won't be able to marry, but it was there in her defiant look.

Her mother had objected at first, but during the night the apartment block had been hit. The family escaped but lost almost everything. They could just about squeeze into Sabina and Lutek's place.

Suddenly Sophia's idea of going with Rosa to free Poland in the east began to look like a sensible idea. So Misha would go with Sophia as far as Lvov where she could stay with friends. By then he'd have found out how to enlist, help make the war a short one. They would travel with Rosa and her husband – a stroke of luck that they hadn't yet left – as her father had come up with transport and supplies. He knew a deliveryman travelling back to his village on the River Bug. There would be room for Misha's sisters in the cart too.

The German land grab of Polish territories would never stretch as far east as Lvov or Pinsk. There, his sisters and Sophia would be safe.

That was days ago and now the deliveryman is curled up under a rough brown blanket at the head of the long cart near his enormous white dray horse. Misha moves Sophia carefully and pushes a rolled-up coat under her head without waking her.

He really has to pee. And it would be good to see if there's any drinking water nearby. The flasks are almost emptied.

There's a yellow cast to the light slanting between the trees. The cloud of dust that followed the long line of refugees over the past two days has stayed with them all night, thickening the damp, turning the figures among the trees into yellow shadows in the morning light.

By the side of a swampy pond, a group of Polish soldiers are milling around. The first soldiers he has seen on the road. At last. They will know where he should report to join up. He notices that they have no tents, sleeping in the open like everyone else. They look dishevelled and defeated. Some don't have full uniform as if they rushed off to fight in a hurry and no one had time to give them adequate kit.

Misha goes over. Nods. 'So where are you men heading? Where's your regiment based?' he asks. 'I heard the message on the radio. I want to report to enlist.'

A soldier with a bandaged arm is watching a can of water set on a fire of sticks. He huffs. 'Another one who's heard the famous message. You tell me where my regiment is. We got mown down. This is it. We've been going from place to place trying to find a regiment, any regiment to join.'

A small man with dark hair and a dark shadow of stubble on his chin looks at Misha's eager face. He wears an army kepi pushed back on his head, a civilian jacket with a rifle holder slung across his shoulder.

'Polish army's gone, mate. In pieces.'

'So where are you heading?'

He shrugs. 'We've just come from up ahead. If you're going east, don't go through Siedlce. Place is full of Germans looting and firing on people.'

Misha walks back to the cart, frowning at what he has heard. A woman in an expensive fur coat and a man in a tailored suit stop him. 'You don't have a car, do you? We have money. Whatever you want. We need a car.'

He shakes his head. He hears her asking the same question to the next people and the next.

*

By the time he gets back everyone is out of the cart, discussing something. Sophia sees him and relief breaks over her face and she runs over. 'Where did you go? I didn't know where you were.' She hugs him for a long moment.

'I'm sorry. I didn't want to wake you.'

'Always wake me.'

She holds his arm as they walk back. The deliveryman is examining the horse's hooves while the others listen to him.

'This girl can't go any further,' he says, patting her neck. The horse is his most precious possession. 'She's gone lame. I'll have to walk her over to a village to see if anyone can do something. It's a fair way to the river, but you young people can do it on foot.'

Misha opens the map. It's two hundred miles from Warsaw to Lvov, a few hours by train normally, but it's turning into an odyssey of days. The deliveryman shows the best way, tracing out invisible tracks with his thick finger.

Their bags are too heavy. They take out all they can and leave it in the cart. A few more objects added to the discarded possessions that now grow along each side of the long road: abandoned cars out of petrol, doors left open; half-unpacked cases, clothes spilling out; an expensive fur coat now too heavy to carry that no one picks up; books that litter the roadsides like grounded birds, their pages fluttering in the breeze.

Carrying what they can, they walk across the open fields under a flawless blue sky. Misha tries to take Sophia's rucksack from her back but she won't let him. There's a rank and catty smell on their bodies but at least they are making progress towards the river. They come to a small track of sandy dirt leading through dark green woods and walk in line between the tall tree trunks beneath the canopy of dappled shade, listening to the sound of birds.

Faint at first, there's the sound of an engine and before they realize what it is, a motorbike with a sidecar has appeared on the track in front of them. It's steel grey, German helmets, and it's too late to hide. They're standing in front of two German soldiers wearing beautiful grey tailoring with black and silver details, handsome and blond and young. Nice boys.

One of the fresh-faced soldiers gets out of the sidecar and comes over to them. The birds carry on singing in nets of song.

Misha's eyes follow the man as he walks around the group, the soldier's eyes travelling over the girls, over the suitcase that Niura grasps with two hands. It's leather and cost far too much, a present from a Polish boyfriend with an aristocratic background.

The soldier says something in German. He grips the case expecting Niura to let go, but inside is her precious photo of Mama in a silver frame, everything that she owns. In the same moment, she tugs back hard. The soldier stumbles forward, looking foolish.

Everyone freezes, breath held. Red-faced, his hand goes to his gun, but the man still on the bike guffaws with laughter and shouts something in German. The soldier lifts his rifle and hits Niura in the face with the butt. She staggers back, her hand to her face where the skin has split. He gets back into the sidecar and the men roar away.

'He could have shot you,' Ryfka says crossly, dabbing at the blood.

'He wouldn't,' says Niura. 'He was being greedy, yes, but Germans aren't monsters who shoot in cold blood. I was quite in the right. You just have to let them know it.'

She picks up the case and they carry on.

'I still say you should have let him take it,' says Ryfka, following behind her, still pale with shock. 'Tell her, Misha,' she calls out to him.

'It's Niura who tells me what to do these days.'

'Oh, you.' But Niura doesn't sound displeased.

'All the same, you took a risk,' Misha chides her in a low voice. 'Don't scare us like that again.'

They carry on along the sandy path. The split on Niura's cheekbone is drying over but is surrounded by a red bruise turning to violet.

At dusk, they reach the village. It's just as the deliveryman described, a small wooden synagogue among low peasant cottages now black silhouettes against the gloom. The ferryman's cottage is a one-storey, tar-roofed house a little further along the riverbank.

But there's something going on. Across the narrow river, headlights, loud voices. They stand in the shadow of the trees and watch. They can see a jeep. Men in uniform. For a moment Misha's heart rises, thinks he's seeing men from the Polish army. Then he realizes the voices are Russian, loud and relaxed and confident. The headlights of a jeep show two men in green-brown uniforms.

'Russian soldiers. What are they doing here?' he whispers. 'Why are Russian soldiers this far over the border, miles into Polish territory?'

'They must have entered the war,' says Sophia in an excited whisper. 'On our side.'

The gruff ferryman soon explains that their optimism is mistaken.

'Where have you been? Under a stone? Don't you know that the Ruskies have got into bed with Herr Hitler? All happened yesterday. Russians get east of the Bug River, Hitler gets the west. That's the end of Polish Independence. A sweet twenty years and it's over.'

They stand on the riverbank in silence, the cold night slowly chilling them now they are motionless. Sophia and Niura are both crying. The news is like a lead weight on Misha's chest. He's been hurtling himself towards fighting alongside the army for the past two days, and now defeat settles over his body, draining his limbs of any strength. So his dream of finding a valiant regiment of Polish soldiers to fight alongside is just that, a dream, their hopes of finding a tranche of free Poland ended. Between the Germans and the Russians, Poland is once again entirely battened down under foreign rule.

'Stalin's almost as much of a monster as Hitler,' said Rosa. 'Perhaps we should go back.'

'But at least we're not second-class citizens under the Russians. We can walk the streets, work, study,' says Niura.

The ferryman coughs. 'So what do you lot want to do?' he asks. 'You going on or going back?'

'We don't have a choice. We're going on,' says Sophia, looking at the others.

Warning them to keep quiet the ferryman leads them towards a rough jetty where his rowing boat is tied up. He's not going over there himself, not till the soldiers have moved on. They can take the boat over and tie it up on the other side for him to collect later.

'Can you handle a boat?' he asks, doubtful.

'We boat on the Vistula all the time,' Rosa tells him. A vision of weekend picnics with the gramophone playing rises up and fades away.

He pulls the boat further along, away from any lights and Russian voices. There's no jetty here, only a slippery bank, the river deep. As they climb in one by one holding their suitcases and bags, the boat rocks wildly in the darkness, the current kicking against its side. At the moment when Misha holds out his hand for Sophia and she steps forward, the boat swings wide.

With a yelp and a splash she's gone, vanished beneath the black water. Misha plunges his arms in, scanning his eyes over the surface, waiting to hear the gasp of her rising, the thrashing of her breaking the water. Nothing but swirls of light from Niura's torch on the dark surface. In a moment Misha tips over the side and begins to dive into the darkness, his feet catching in the muddy weeds. Again and again he comes up without her, nothing but water and air in his arms.

'There,' calls out Rosa. 'Misha, I see her.'

Downstream, he glimpses the pale shape of her head and arms in the darkness, clinging to the branches of a low-slung willow in the swirling stream. He runs along to pull her up and brushes the wet weeds of hair from her face and holds her tight.

'Don't do that. Don't ever leave me again,' he says, his mouth on her cheek, her ear, breathing her in.

She's shivering violently. In the boat he sits with his arm round her, keeping contact with her body in the darkness. The others begin to pull on the oars, moving towards where the shadows are deepest.

On the other side of the Bug River they step out onto Russian-held territory.

They make good progress walking through the night, and at daybreak come into a hamlet of wooden cottages. Shivering with cold they share a small breakfast of salami and water in the shelter of a wood. It's time to split up, Rosa and her husband continuing east with Niura and Ryfka towards Pinsk. Misha and Sophia will go south towards Lvov. They eat in silence then clear away the paper; they stand in a group, not wanting to have to part.

'It's time to go,' says Rosa gently. Ryfka and Niura hold Misha in a hug for a long time. Ryfka breathes in the smell of Misha's jacket. Then she steps back, pale and looking so much younger than eighteen.

'Take care of each other. And tell Pa and the aunts, I'll see them soon, yes?' said Misha.

Niura gives him one last hug and nods, biting her lip. 'And you'll come to Pinsk and see us as soon as you can? You promise?'

'As soon as this is over.'

The girls begin to walk away with Rosa and her husband in front. They grow small and disappear between the creaking trees.

The road is empty. Picking up their suitcases, Misha and Sophia set out on the track south. They've been to Lvov once before, as part of a group of students attending a summer school where Korczak was lecturing. They fell in love with the pretty city with its Viennese cafés and red and green roofs. They had planned to return there one day, together, but never imagined it would be like this. He takes Sophia's hand and she looks up at him, feeling small and lost among the creaking pines. It's just the two of them now.

Later in the day they hear a distant hubbub of voices, growing louder as they come out of the forest onto a route that leads from a bridge across the river into what has been until recently eastern Poland. The road is packed with hundreds of refugees and soldiers, people who have hurried east across the 'green' border into the Russian zone while they still can. A lot of the faces look Jewish.

He takes Sophia's hand and they merge into the procession edging slowly towards Lvov. No one knows what they will find there now under Soviet rule.

CHAPTER NINE

WARSAW, SEPTEMBER 1939

K orczak comes up from the orphanage cellars holding Sara by one hand, Szymonek by the other. The rest of the children follow, Abrasha with his violin, Sammy, Erwin, Halinka, everyone grubby and blinking. Three days in the dark breathing the sooty air tinged with miasmas of burning sugar or paint, depending on which factories have been hit. Candlelight and muddy-tasting well water.

The sudden silence makes Korczak's ears ring. Out in the courtyard once again, the little ones are jumping to catch feathers.

'Look,' says Szymonek. An enormous cloud of feathers is undulating in the wind above the rooftops, made from the contents of thousands of burst eiderdowns and pillows.

In the distance there's the hoarse thrum of an engine, the roar growing louder. A military motorcycle with sidecar passes by the gates in the smoky air. Two grey steel helmets.

'Stay here children, stay here.' He joins Zalewski at the gate and they watch along the road as the motorbike comes to a halt at the top of Krochmalna Street. A soldier jumps out of the sidecar and begins to manhandle an industrial-looking machine gun into the iron trestle on the back of the bike.

A machine-gun emplacement at the top of Krochmalna.

Zalewski turns away, wiping his eyes.

'We didn't surrender like Vienna. They took Warsaw from us, but we'll stay Polish in our hearts.'

Korczak nods grimly, keeping his eyes on the two soldiers. Then he locks the gate and they take the children inside.

The Germans rapidly bring in the Nuremberg laws with a long list of restrictions on Jewish life. It hurts to have to explain to the children that they can't go to Saxon Park any more, can't go to the cinema. Erwin is incensed because after waiting in the Germans' bread queue in town, a friend has denounced him as a Jew and now Erwin's come home empty-handed.

It won't be for ever, Korczak tells the children. Hitler is a sad and spiteful little fire that will burn itself out in time. Sooner or later, the Germans are going to come to their senses again and leave.

Korczak knows how to survive a German occupation. He's done

it before in 1918 – although this spiteful mania against Jews, the insane Nazi theory of a secret Jewish conspiracy against the Reich, is something he hasn't experienced before.

For now, Korczak's main problem is to keep funds coming in – not easy when Jews are not allowed bank accounts and when all those who had the money to leave have left.

As the months pass, he makes a study of these delinquent conquerors. He notices that the German Nazis ignore anything illogical. He makes sure to be the doddery old man, possibly a little drunk, any time he runs into German bully boys in a café and they leave him muttering to himself in a corner.

He even – and here is the miracle – he even manages to cajole the German Kommissar in charge of the area around the summer camp into letting the children spend the summer of 1940 at Little Rose. The Kommissar is so charmed by Korczak's philosophy of childhood that he sends his own German soldiers out to repair the camp's huts damaged by the invasion, and even – though there's a death penalty for helping Jews under the occupation – he sends wagons of food for the children, courtesy of Wehrmacht stores.

'You see, there are no more bad Germans than there are bad Jews or Poles,' Korczak tells Stefa as they walk through the gardens around Little Rose once again, letting the summer sun soak into their skin.

Sooner or later, they'll have to return to occupied Warsaw. Korczak orders the gardener and cooks to pack up every last bit of food from the kitchens and vegetable beds to take back with them.

'But Pan Doctor, aren't we leaving some of the potatoes for next year, to grow the new ones?' asks Szymonek, who loves the garden and growing green things.

'Not this year,' says Korczak as he and Zalewski secure the tarpaulin on the cart. 'This year they may well be needed for soup if this German occupation is anything like the last. We'll start again with new ones when we come back next year.'

Korczak stands at the end of Nalewki Street; the Jewish commercial district with its towering apartment blocks is packed with families and small businesses of every description, each courtyard a small city in itself. He looks up at a new wooden board hanging on one of the lamp posts. The black gothic script warns non-Jews to keep away; Jewish districts are typhus zones. Yet he knows from friends in the Warsaw hospitals that no such cases have been reported.

The Poles are treated a little better than the Jews but not much and so far the mood has been to band together. It seems clear to Korczak that the typhoid warnings are some Nazi attempt to isolate the Jews from the Poles.

Looking towards Dluga Street he can see one of the sections of wall that have begun to spring up all over the city, cutting across roads and through buildings and courtyards. How far would the Nazis go to isolate the Jews?

He goes to see his old friend from teaching days, Adam Czerniakow, now head of the Jewish Council. If anyone knows what the wall is about, Czerniakow will. Korczak and he both come from the same circle of educated Varsorvians where Jews and Poles mix freely as friends and colleagues. They are both proud of the Jewish heritage they hold, but also speak Polish as their first language and treasure Polish literature and culture as their own. And like Korczak, Czerniakow's a passionate believer in unity. Now, to his consternation, Czerniakow is the main point of connection between the Germans and the beleaguered Jewish community, passing on the orders of the conquerors to the conquered.

His head as bald as an egg, a bow-tie and a well-tailored suit over his bulky torso, Czerniakow adjusts his round spectacles as he sees Korczak come into his office.

'At last, a ray of sunshine in a bleak day.'

'I've been called many things, but never that. But now here's a puzzle. What are all these sections of wall for? Yet more madness?'

'All I know about them is that the Jewish Council has had to pay for them and supply the labour.'

'Do you think it's possible that they intend to move us all into a Jewish district in Warsaw? They have a Jewish ghetto in Lublin now.'

'Warsaw is a completely different situation. Lublin's now part of the German Reich and subject to their jurisdiction while Warsaw is part of the German Generalgouvernement, and I've been assured that there are no plans for a ghetto here. Some Jewish districts possibly, but not a segregated ghetto. What is bothering me at the moment, however, is this situation with all our Jewish children forbidden to go to school. Mind you, the Poles are not faring much better, having to leave education at ten.'

Czerniakow taught for many years in Warsaw's schools before being elected to the senate and the Jewish Council. Like Korczak his heart remains with the children and their welfare.

'We are teaching the children at home now. And I might tell you about how Stefa and I have been giving lectures at the young people's commune on Dzielna Street, helping them set up an underground school. They have some excellent young people training to teach.'

'Ah, Yitzhak Zuckerman and his friends at the Dror commune. I know nothing of that, of course.' Czerniakow leans back in his chair, crosses large workman's hands across his suit jacket. His black eyebrows and thick lashes hint at how he once looked as a student, before middle age rendered him portly and bald. 'Strange how history repeats itself. Remember dodging the Tsar's police in the days of the underground university, never holding classes in the same place twice it seemed?'

'And we both know the inside of Pawiak prison. Of course, it's what the young people really want to hear about, the days of the flying university.'

'Well, just remember we're not so young any more, my friend.' Czerniakow looks down at the armband with its blue Star of David fastened around his meaty forearm, then at Korczak's coat sleeves bare of any band. 'You know the risks you're taking, going round town like that.'

Korczak looks at him sternly from over his wire-rimmed glasses, speaks quietly. 'And let the children see me treat the Star of David as a badge of shame? Never.'

As summer turns to autumn the sections of wall grow taller, but since nothing further happens people get used to seeing them, then almost forget about them altogether.

It's Yom Kippur, the holiest day of the Jewish year, a day of forgiveness and new beginnings. Korczak likes to take the children to the great synagogue to hear the poetry and faith of their tradition.

But later that day, as the children gather for the celebratory main meal in the hall, a van with a loudspeaker blares past. It takes a while to make out the message, then absorb the meaning. All Jews must move into a designated district. One of the teachers runs out and brings in a copy of the afternoon paper.

Stefa hurries over to study it with Korczak while the children continue eating, the room buzzing with a hum of conversation. She looks around the crowded hall, fifty new orphans since the siege. A deep crease between Stefa's eyes, new lines across her forehead.

They study the newspaper's map. The borders of the ghetto are inked over the map of Warsaw, a jagged black line scored around the main Jewish areas like pieces of a puzzle that can be excised from the city's heart.

'And we're outside the ghetto.' Stefa shakes her head. 'Surely they won't make the children leave their home.'

'Leave it to me,' says Korczak grimly, pulling on his coat. He winds a muffler around his neck to hide the military braiding on his jacket collar.

He's thinking of the kindness of the German officer who helped them spend the summer in Little Rose, but this time Korczak's charm falls on stony ground.

For the next two weeks, Warsaw is in an uproar as Polish families move out of the ghetto area and Jewish families move in, everyone trying to make exchanges. Businesses are lost, bribes change hands and there are deals and swindles from Sienna Street to Muranow. And in the meantime, the Germans continue to strip the best Jewish apartments of anything that takes their fancy, evicting entire families so they can move themselves into the best apartments around Theatre Square and St John's Cathedral, places where the architecture has a suitably Germanic feel.

Far away, pinned up on the wall of an architect's bureau in the German Reich, there's a new blueprint for Warsaw, for a provincial German town of a few thousand people, all Jewish and Polish architecture erased.

*

He wanted to make it cheerful, a circus troupe on the move with music and ribbons and drums, but there hasn't been time in the end. The children line up in twos in the courtyard wearing their winter coats and good shoes, carrying what they can – everything that Korczak thinks will be essential inside the ghetto, pots of flowers, pictures, toys, books. There's a cold damp soaking through to the bone.

Korczak takes out the new orphanage flag. On one side is a blue six-pointed star on a pennant of white silk, for the children to carry proudly. He still refuses to wear the obligatory armband, the Star of David treated like a symbol of shame. At least the children are not expected to wear the armband, there's that mercy.

On the reverse side of the pennant is a green silk chestnut leaf.

'To remind us of the tree in our garden. To remind us of home,' Korczak tells the children.

Sara pulls his sleeve. 'And Pan Doctor, it's like little King Matt's flag, in your storybook.'

He smiles and nods. 'You are right, Sara, clever girl. You see, everyone needs to try to make the world a better place, just like little King Matt, and even if it doesn't work out as well as we hope to begin with, we must never stop trying.'

He hands the flag to Erwin with instructions to carry it high and straight.

Now old Zalewski stands in the front yard saying goodbye to the children, his blunt soldier's face cut and swollen, a split lip. The day before, Zalewski applied to Gestapo headquarters for permission to go with the children into the ghetto.

'Don't you know it's against the law for a Pole to work for Jews?' the Gestapo officer screamed at him.

'But the children are my family,' Zalewski protested before the first blows fell on his head.

One by one, a hundred children hug the old couple, their grandparents. Mrs Zalewski dabs at her eyes every so often with her apron.

'And drive that cart carefully,' Zalewski tells Henryk Sztokman gruffly. He hobbles over to check the ropes on the tarpaulin. 'That's four hundred pounds of potatoes there to last the winter.' He takes his hand away from the horse reluctantly.

At the front Erwin holds high the green flag of King Matt and the Star of David. The children file out through the gate, passing through the fragile fog of their breath in the cold air. Someone tries to sing, but it's too sad and the song dies out.

Korczak won't look back, but Stefa glances one more time at the gracious white building where they have lived for almost twenty years, at the little oriel casement in the roof where he wrote each afternoon, at the generous windows that flood the house with light. How often had she heard visitors tell her that it looked more like a mansion for someone important than a children's home?

'This is a house for important people,' Stefa would always remind them.

They walk quietly along Krochmalna Street through the chill air, feet shushing against the wet cobbles.

At the ghetto entrance on Chlodna Street the children wait quietly while their papers are checked. They look up at the ten-feet-high mesh gates with interest, at the German guards, at the walls topped with sparkling broken glass that stretch away on each side. A German guard, a long coat buttoned over his thick middle, circles the potato wagon and looks under the tarpaulin. He orders Henryk down. He signals to the young guard to lead the horse away.

Korczak runs over.

'Is there a problem? We have permission to take supplies through.' He shows the guard the papers but the man shrugs.

'Permission cancelled.' He turns away. The children begin to file in through the gate, but Korczak isn't letting the matter drop, furious because can't the man see with his own eyes that he's stolen the very food meant for children? For children. What kind of black heart does the man have?

Korczak draws himself up in his uniform, every inch the Polish major, yelling. 'I shall be reporting you to your superiors. This is disgraceful.'

Unperturbed, the German guard waves him away. 'Go and see the Gestapo if that's what you want.'

It's not hard to leave the ghetto the next day – after all, it's a district not a prison – and Korczak sets out early for leafy Szucha Avenue. The building for Polish Religious Affairs and Education has been repurposed as Gestapo headquarters. Red-and-white sentry boxes with armed guards now flank the entrance with its rational, square-cut columns.

Korczak has heard plenty of rumours about the brutality that takes place inside the Gestapo headquarters. He can't escape a chill of fear as he marches defiantly through the courtyard, his army boots ringing on the marble flagstones. He demands to see the officer in charge of ghetto affairs.

He's shown politely into an office and left to wait. On the desk there's a row of paperwork lined up with exactitude next to a telephone and an anglepoise lamp. An officer's hat with its skull insignia hangs on a coat stand, two arms branching behind it like horns. To Korczak's right is a glass-fronted bookcase. It takes a moment for his eyes to register not papers but iron manacles, a bullwhip, blunt hammers and metal knuckledusters.

A Gestapo officer in a brown uniform enters. Korczak explains in his best official bluster that it is essential the supplies of confiscated potatoes be returned to the children immediately.

'You speak excellent German, Major,' the officer remarks cordially, casting his eyes over Korczak's Polish officer's uniform, narrowing his eyes a little at the threadbare braid on the cuffs.

'Thank you. I spent a year studying in Berlin at the Medical Institute and gained a great respect for the humane and efficient methods of the German doctors.'

'Indeed. But I don't understand why you're so concerned about these Jews, Major, or why you've been put in charge of what are Jewish orphans.' He reads through Korczak's papers for a few moments. Suddenly the Gestapo officer's face flushes. He rises up, his face filled with hate, the chair scraping back. 'But it says here you're Jewish. What are you doing, impersonating a Polish officer? Where is your armband?'

Korczak also stands tall, defiant and belligerent. 'There are human laws which are transitory, and higher laws which are eternal—'

The furious officer grabs Korczak by the collar, rips off his officer's insignia and begins to beat him about the head. It's only when Korczak is lying on the ground, a boot blow in his stomach, in his ribs, in his back, that the Gestapo officer's temper is finally sated.

'You will be transferred to Pawiak prison for infringement of regulations regarding hygiene and the quarantine of the Jewish Community.' He scribbles a note and drops it by Korczak. 'And here is a receipt for your potatoes.'

Bleeding and semi-conscious, Korczak is bundled into a black van and driven back into the ghetto. They pull him out in front of a squat building with rows of barred windows, Pawiak prison.

Looking up, he's not too dismayed. He's been here before, twice, for anti-Tsarist activities. Under the Tsar's regime a little money to the guards could buy extra food, the right to bring in blankets, even books to carry on studying. But as he hobbles down to the subterranean entrance and the iron bars are unlocked and he enters a corridor rent with screams, Korczak begins to understand that Pawiak under the Nazis is a far darker place.

CHAPTER TEN

LVOV, SEPTEMBER 1939

Hungry, cold and exhausted, longing to wash in hot water, Sophia and Misha reach Lvov the day after the Red Army take the city. Sophia is limping. They've taken days to travel the last fifty miles, sleeping in the open, walking most of the way, and now the blister on her heel has burst.

They wander through the old town. Red flags with black hammers and sickles hang from balconies, bristle around lamp posts. Soldiers in brown padded jackets and sheepskin hats are distributing blankets and soup and leaflets. Soviet marching songs blare from loudspeakers, interspersed with messages in Ukrainian and in Russian, congratulating the Ukrainian working people of Lvov. They are now freed from the oppression of their Polish overlords by the Soviet army.

Taking their bowls of soup, they listen to a soldier stationed nearby describing life in the Soviet Union to the sullen crowd around him. It's a paradise. A group of Polish soldiers are sitting at the edge of the square, smoking and looking lost. A Soviet truck draws up and begins to load the soldiers.

There's a tang of snow in the air, the light fading. They spend the rest of the evening trudging around a town already packed with refugees and displaced people. Thousands of Jewish families have fled across the border towards Lvov in the last days to avoid the German regime.

It's late by the time they find a small room to rent.

'Name?' asks the woman at the desk. A brief glance between Sophia and Misha.

'Mr and Mrs Wasserman,' Sophia says.

This isn't what she imagined for the first time they shared a room. There is one narrow bed. She looks around the wallpaper stained with rings of damp, at the bed with its worn covers, the grubby netting at the window. Sophia draws the curtains and Misha lights the oil lamp, covering the room with a subdued golden light.

'I'll sleep on the floor,' says Misha.

Sophia looks at the bare boards. They need a good scrub. 'There's no point getting cold and sick.' She sits down on the bed, the iron springs creaking. 'We're both tired. Sit down by me.'

Misha joins her. The bed groans again. He sits with his head bowed, weighted by responsibility. He turns to her and takes both her hands. She's cold and shivering.

'No matter what happens, I'll always look after you.'

Hollowed out, too exhausted to move, they lie close together, saved by each other's warmth, listening to the unfamiliar sounds of the city. This far up on the fourth floor it feels as if they are nothing but a small island, adrift on the cold air above a city of strangers.

'We'll both sleep here. Anything else is ridiculous. We're almost married anyway,' she whispers. 'I love you so much.'

There's no response from Misha, out cold. She gets up and pulls a cover over him. She goes to the window and lifts the curtain material. It's so dark outside. The only light comes from the snow that has started to fall out of the black sky. It covers the cobbled pavements with a white scrim, the cut-outs of dark figures hurrying past.

She takes off her coat and dress and gets under the cover next to Misha's sleeping form, pulls his heavy arm across her shoulders.

She lies awake, wondering what is happening in Warsaw.

CHAPTER ELEVEN

WARSAW, DECEMBER 1940

The Jews must adjust to all conditions and we'll do our best to make it very difficult for them . . . The Jews will perish from hunger and poverty and only a graveyard will remain of the Jewish question.
Ludwig Fischer, Governor of the Warsaw District

After two months crowded into a freezing cell with thirty other men listening to the gunfire in the prison yard each day, the cell door opens and Korczak is called out.

So his time has come to be marched out into the yard, or down to the torture cells.

He's shown into a clean bright office.

'Undress over there,' says a tall German in a white coat.

Korczak stands stiffly by the door as if he has not heard or does not understand German.

'Dr Korczak, please, I have heard your lectures in Germany as a student and your German is excellent. Please, I need to examine you for your release. You have a friend, I think. Harry Kaliszer?'

Korczak's eyes flicker towards the German doctor. Harry is one of Korczak's past pupils, grown up now with a boy of his own. Has Harry managed to pay the Gestapo a bribe to get him certified as medically unfit for prison – the Holy Grail that means release rather than death?

Korczak grudgingly lets the doctor place a metal stethoscope over his heart, his lungs, his back. The doctor folds away the rubber tube and looks grave.

'You do realize that you have a serious heart condition?'

'Nothing that's enough to stop me going about my business as usual,' Korczak answers curtly in Polish as he buttons up his grubby shirt.

'You need to take better care of yourself, Doctor. I have read your book in Germany, *The Child's Right to Respect*. Excellent. You have many friends here who value you greatly. You shouldn't be here in the ghetto. Really, there's no need.'

He hands the certificate to Korczak and moves to shake his hand. But outside, the sharp crack of gunfire cuts across the courtyard and Korczak's hand draws back instinctively.

The German doctor looks down, embarrassed. He has seen the bruises, new and old, across Korczak's body.

*

Korczak can see in Harry's face that he barely recognizes this gaunt, elderly-looking man with a bluish nose who has come out of the prison gates. The battered major's uniform with its ripped collar is filthy. Korczak has to lean on Harry's arm for support as they walk to the tram stop slowly, barely enough breath to thank him.

'You took a risk, running round the ghetto trying to contact the Gestapo to get me out, Harry. And expensive, I think.'

'A lot of people who love you helped, Pan Doctor.'

The bitterly cold wind carries a fine sand of snow. The Muranow tram appears through the stinging mist. Korczak sinks down onto the wooden bench and watches the street flicker by. But why are so many children out in the snow at this hour, huddling by the walls of the buildings? He glimpses an entire family sheltering under a blanket.

The light is leaching from the sky, curfew not long away. At Chlodna Street the tram goes no further.

'I'm sorry, we have to get out here, Pan Doctor. The prison's in the main part of the ghetto, the big ghetto and there's an Aryan road cutting off the rest of the ghetto, the smaller area. We have to wait here until there's a gap in the Aryan trams so we can cross over and join Stefa and the children in the small ghetto.'

They join the huddled crowd in armbands at the gate waiting to cross over into the rest of the ghetto. After the beatings he has seen and experienced in Pawiak, the German guards at the gate stand far too close for Korczak's liking. He feels a sweat prickle down his back. They are bored and pick out a man on crutches to dance to a busker's accordion, the man's eyes glazed with terror as he stumbles around.

There's a sudden commotion to the left. The sound of a child crying. To his horror Korczak sees one of the guards beating a small boy. Korczak starts forward, but Harry pulls him back sharply.

'You can't. It's too dangerous.'

The guard signals for the crowd to cross. Bicycles and rickshaws surge across the street, past the Polish policemen barring the way into Aryan Warsaw to the right and left, and behind them follows the hurrying mass of people.

He knocks on the front door of 33 Chlodna Street, until recently a Polish technical school. A boy he's never seen before opens it, takes one look at him and runs away shouting for Pani Stefa.

Little Szymonek appears in the hallway. His face lights up.

'Pan Doctor is home,' he yells at the top of his voice.

For once, Stefa does nothing to calm the chaos. The children crowd around him, calling out their news, jumping up and down. What a joy to see their dear, bright faces.

Stefa sits down at a table, her shoulders sagging with relief.

'Why are you crying, Pani Stefa?' asks Sara. 'Aren't you happy to see the Doctor?'

Stefa hugs the child. 'I'm crying because I'm so happy. People can do that. We have Pan Doctor home.'

Clapping his hands high in the air so that all the children join him in the steady beat, Pan Doctor begins what has become the home's anthem over the past year. 'Black and white, brown and yellow, we are all brothers together.' The children sing out, eyes shining, smiling at each other.

'Was it boring? What did you do in prison?' asks Halinka.

'When the thugs and robbers in my cell found out that I was the old doctor from the radio, they made me sit on a straw bale and tell them all the fairy stories that their mummies used to tell them.'

He acts out how he taught the men to catch the fleas that plagued them day and night while the children yell with laughter.

'I'm glad you are back, Pan Doctor. Now everything will be all right,' says Sara.

Stefa's eyes shine with a sad elation as she stands at the back, watching the commotion. It's true, now Pan Doctor's back, somehow, everything will be all right.

But does he understand yet how things are?

After a hot bath, his razor and clean clothes, Stefa makes him drink soup by the stove in the kitchen, her eyes with their soft pouches barely leaving his face, making an inventory of the damage inflicted by the past weeks. A bruised cheek, painfully thin ankles. She hovers close as if someone might spirit him away again.

'Sometimes, I honestly wondered. The things you hear about Pawiak, so many people disappearing . . .' Her voice breaks.

He reaches out and holds her hand in his. 'This old dog's not so easy to keep down. But Stefa, first thing tomorrow we must brick up the main entrance. We don't want guards wandering in off the street, looking for trouble. We'll use the side entrance in the courtyard. It's less obvious.'

'But who lives with their front door bricked up?'

'Tomorrow, Stefa. We must brick it up tomorrow.'

She's never seen him so nervous and agitated. 'I'll ask Henryk.'

'And we can't let the children out on the streets unless someone goes with them, the things that are happening out there, the risk of bringing back typhus.'

'I agree. They hardly go out as it is. But shut away from the world, how will they cope with normal life when the war's over?'

He thinks for a moment, frowning. 'We must bring the world to the children. We'll invite people here, from every walk of life, to come in and talk to our republic of children.'

'It would certainly be good for the boys to see more men here. There's our cook Roza Sztokman's brother, Henryk, but of course he's more like one of the boys. Hardly makes sense now he's decided he's in love with our medical intern, Esterka. And now we have you.'

'Your most troublesome child, I know. What would I do without you, Stefa? In spite of everything, you have the home up and running in here, with the same spirit as the old place.'

'The children still understand fairness and kindness in spite of living in this place. They remember what you taught them. But we are low on everything.'

'Medical supplies?'

'A vial of morphine and one syringe, a sock filled with warm sand for earaches, salt water for inflamed throats, and that's it. And Esterka has been wonderful. She may only be a student doctor, but she's so bright and the children love her. As for the rest, the children have enough clothes. But with the potatoes gone our remaining food won't last much longer.'

'And funds?'

'Mostly from within the ghetto, but really, what can people do? The rich are becoming poor. The poor are becoming destitute. I haunt the offices of the aid agencies.'

'Time for me to start getting out, making my rounds again, visiting friends.'

'Not yet. You need to recover your strength before you face going out. It's too dangerous.'

Outside there's the whine and clank of Aryan trams passing through the middle of the ghetto. Korczak lifts the blind and looks down on the familiar red trams, people going home from work. Stefa joins him, looking down on the wall that runs along each side of the Aryan cut-through.

'A sealed ghetto. Who could have imagined?'

'I didn't know how to explain it to the children when they sealed the gates. It was panic in here. None of us expected that. I'll never get used to not seeing all our Polish friends.'

'But they're still our friends. And the Germans are good people at heart. Once the German people realize what the Nazis are doing here in their name, they'll be horrified. They'll soon put a stop to all this madness.'

'Perhaps. And perhaps the rest of Europe will hear about us soon and do something.'

He takes her hands. 'Until then, our children have only one childhood and we'll do all we can to make it happy and safe.'

For the next few days as he recuperates, he stays in the home with the children, sometimes sitting outside in the weak sun as they play. Around the central courtyard is the main school building with several apartments taking up the other side. A German widow, a young Hebrew teacher and several other families live there. It's reputedly the best-kept and cleanest block in the ghetto. A little world within a world.

With Michael, the Hebrew teacher who lives across the courtyard, as his guide, Korczak makes his way through an enormous bazaar of people hawking the most pitiful possessions, so many beggars bundled up in rags. A cacophony of shouts and street singers, the signs of starvation clear in people's faces.

He passes endless musicians and singers busking on the street. In Tlomackie Street he pauses in front of the Great Synagogue. The synagogue doors are chained shut and the cantors are singing on its steps for pennies.

Karmelicka Street is a bottleneck, so crowded that Korczak is knocked off the pavement as the crowd suddenly surges in a panic. Michael pulls him into the shelter of a doorway as a black prison van barrels along the street in the direction of Pawiak, the guard beating people from the window. Afterwards, a woman staggers up from the road, her head pouring with blood. The truncheon was studded with nails.

So this is the ghetto, a square mile of hell containing half a million people slowly dying of hunger. Leaning against the wall, Korczak catches his breath, then he and Michael make their way back towards the little oasis of the republic of children on 33 Chlodna Street.

CHAPTER TWELVE

LVOV, APRIL 1941

One should not put any obstacle in the way of efforts at self-cleansing arising in anti-communist and anti-Jewish circles in the territories to be newly occupied. On the contrary, one should provoke these, leaving no traces, intensify them if necessary.

Reinhard Heydrich: Telegram to
Einsatzgruppen leaders 29 June 1941

Sophia comes down the steps of Lvov University to a cold dusk running with birdsong. Looking up at the trees around the square, it feels there's a hint of better days at last, but she huddles into her coat and sets off quickly along the narrow street towards their apartment.

Perhaps there will be a letter from home waiting for her today. It's been so long since they had any news from Warsaw.

A boxy black van approaches along the narrow street. Her palms grow hot and sticky but she makes herself carry on walking at an even pace. No good can come of attracting the attention of the NKVD, the Soviet police.

She quickens her step, almost there, the white spire of St Anna's rising up at the end of their avenue. Soon she'll be running up the stone steps of their apartment block, opening the door, safe inside.

The trick is to get into the tiny apartment before their Ukrainian neighbour, Mrs Yelenyuk, appears on the landing, peering inside the door, asking questions.

As Sophia puts her key in the lock, sure enough, Mrs Yelenyuk comes hurrying out.

'Having something nice for supper?' says Mrs Yelenyuk, craning to see in Sophia's bag. With her yellowed skin and pale blue eyes, a faded brown woollen scarf wrapped around her shoulders, Mrs Yelenyuk is like an old print that has lost its colour.

'Cabbage and potatoes again.'

'I'll show you how to cook my mother's stew one day, a proper Ukrainian dish. I always cooked it for my brother.'

'Have you had any news of his release?'

'Any time now. They have nothing to charge him with,' she says angrily, her face old and crumpled suddenly.

'You'll hear soon,' Sophia says.

Inside, Sophia leans against the closed door and breathes in the calm. Its pine-clad walls varnished a deep brown, olive-green tiles on the tall chimney stove, the little apartment is gloomy but she's made it a home, covered the shelf in the corner with a lace cloth, added a pretty oil lamp and two frames for their pictures of family in Pinsk and in Warsaw.

She picks up a photo taken in Warsaw on Sabina's wedding day. There have been no letters from Warsaw, and little news from Misha's sisters in Pinsk, although they've at least heard that the girls reached there safely.

Misha will be back from the oil refinery soon. He's wry about how his engineering degree has come in use after all, supervising the laying of new oil pipes for the factory, but at least it's paid work.

She's running water in the tin bowl to wash the potatoes when he comes in. Three strides to cross the room. He puts his long arms around her waist, his chin resting on her hair.

'I have two presents for you. First . . .' He holds out a letter.

Seeing the ghetto postmark, she snatches it from his hand.

'I hope the parcel's arrived safely. Not that I'll know with so much of the letter inked out by the censor. You'd think it was all state secrets. And it's taken so long to get here.' She goes silent, reading and re-reading the letter.

'What's the matter? What is it?'

She can't speak. He takes the letter from her hand and scans it. Sophia has crumpled onto a chair, her face drained.

He reads the letter again. Sabina is dead. Died over a month ago. There's nothing to say how or why, most of the letter cruelly inked out by the ghetto's censor.

*

Her eyes heavy from so many tears, Sophia lies curled up on the narrow bed, staring at the panelling in the evening gloom. Misha has lit the lamp, turned the wick down low. He's getting ready for bed when she suddenly turns, raises herself up on one elbow, her face tense with apprehension.

'Misha, what was the other thing you had to tell me? Has something else happened? What is it?'

He's quiet for a moment, then sits down on the bed next to her. He takes a small pouch from his pocket and tips something onto his palm. A narrow circle of pale gold.

'Oh.'

'I didn't want to ask you like this.'

She watches the last of the evening light run around the gold band as he tips his palm. 'It was what we meant to do once we arrived, but if you'd rather wait . . .'

She moves closer, puts her head on his knee, her hair spilling out like someone pulled from the water. 'I love you so much. All I've wanted since the day we met is to be with you.' He bends down and they stay wrapped together, silent and still, for a long time.

Sophia wears her good summer dress – dusky pink with puffed sleeves and a row of little pearl buttons. Misha looks handsome in a white shirt and dark jacket, his hair combed back from his brow, his amber and green eyes crinkled with smiles.

It's May and Lvov's many trees are in bloom. They walk through the white city with its green domes and red roofs. It could almost be a time before the war when Lvov was a little Vienna, before the red-and-black Soviet flags appeared.

She feels his hand press hers tightly for a moment.

'I'm sorry, darling. I wanted family to be here for our wedding day. I wanted flowers, dancing.'

She stops in her tracks, faces him. 'Never, never say sorry when we have each other,' she says, fierce and sure.

Inside the building they wait in a scuffed green corridor that echoes with Russian voices. The light from a high window casts a rhomboid of butter on the unwaxed linoleum. A woman in a beige skirt and a blouse with epaulettes comes out and calls their names. She has thick features, greying blonde hair pinned back; she is mannish, indifferent as she squeezes her chair up to the desk and shuffles out a form with her nicotine fingers. Next to her, the clerk takes their details, scolding Sophia when she corrects herself over a date.

'This is an official document,' the woman tells her crossly. 'And it will go into police records so don't make any problems for yourself, that's my advice.'

The first woman lights up a cigarette, a strong tarry odour of ships and rope. 'I got a good deal on herrings yesterday.'

'Haven't found good herring for a while now. How much?'

'Expensive, but if you buy it by the barrel, it's much cheaper. Do you want me to give you his name?' She flicks ash on the floor and turns her attention back to the marriage certificate. 'So you've filled in all your details?' She takes the form and asks them some abrupt legal questions. They both answer yes.

'I'd buy a barrel. Herring keeps and who knows when you'll get the chance again. Sign here, both of you, Mr and Mrs Wasserman. Here's your duplicate copy. And you pay the fee at the desk.'

They leave the office, the two women still discussing herrings. Misha wafts the form in front of his chin. 'Is it my imagination or does this whiff of fish?' He's trying to make a joke of it, but her throat hurts and she doesn't manage to laugh.

They come out to the blessing of the May sun dazzling across the square. For a moment Sophia sees a white carriage decked with flowers, Sabina's veil fanning over her shoulders as she and Lutek ride three times around Grzybowski Square on their way to the little white synagogue, waving and blowing kisses. She stands immobile on the steps. How can Sabina be gone, beautiful Sabina who passed by laughing and waving and so alive?

Misha takes Sophia's hand. 'But you're so cold.' He puts it between his palms to warm it.

They walk down to an elegant old Viennese café and order glasses of tea with a plate of cream-and-jam pastries.

Misha places a flat parcel on the table.

'A wedding present from me.'

'I didn't get you a present.'

'It's to both of us,' he said. 'You'll see.'

She unwraps the white tissue. Inside there's a copy of Korczak's book, *How to Love a Child*.

'I know you've read it many times, but when this ridiculous war is over, that's what we'll do. We'll make the world a better place, for the children.'

Her hand folds over his, holding on tight. 'You miss them terribly, don't you?'

She loves waking next to Misha each morning as his wife, Mrs Wasserman. She feels changed at some molecular level, as if bound together they have become more solid, able to endure anything. The sunlight streams in through the thin net curtains. The bells of St Anna's mix with the electric crackle of trams and the echo of horses' hooves.

It's early but she wants to go out and fetch fresh bread for breakfast. Misha's still sleeping. His workman's overalls hang empty on the back of the bedroom door.

Outside, the air has the clarity of a new summer's day, the white steeple clear against a blue sky. Later, she plans to walk to the market in the Jewish quarter where apples and bread are so much cheaper, where buskers play boisterous Klezmer tunes on clarinets and fiddles and women in white aprons shout out in Yiddish as if she might be back home in Grzybowski Square.

There's already a queue outside the bakery. She tips her face up to feel the warmth of the sun. A woman is leaning on the rail of a balcony, a gramophone playing.

Suddenly the air is split by the piercing wail of a siren. The queue outside the baker's immediately peels away, heading towards the houses. She stumbles and begins to run home, the unrelenting din clawing at her back.

Mrs Yelenyuk stops her in the stairwell, grabs her arm.

'Mrs Wasserman, such news on the radio!' Sophia can smell her mustiness, a kitchen where the window is never opened. 'When the Germans get here, we'll see the Ukraine respected again.'

Misha is already on the way down to find her. He's wearing a vest and pyjama trousers, his hair sticking up.

'We should go to the cellars,' he shouts above the raw ululation of the siren. They clatter down as a roar of engines passes above. A series of explosions shakes the building.

'It's true then,' says a man in a long black coat as they stand in the cellar. 'The Germans have broken the treaty, attacked the Russians. That's Hitler's first mistake. The Russians will soon see Hitler off.'

*

The town fills with the noise of Russian trucks and jeeps pulling out, retreating east. They set explosives, burning and destroying anything that could be of use to the incoming Wehrmacht army. From the NKVD prison a few hundred yards along the street, there's the sound of gunfire and shouting.

By dawn the next day, a fearful silence hangs over the city in the already simmering heat.

There's a hammering on Sophia and Misha's door. Mrs Yelenyuk is beside herself.

'Not a word from my brother. What have the Russians done to him? We've been outside the prison all day, crowds of us relatives, calling up to the windows, but no one's answering us any more. Ah, you wait till the Germans get here,' she rages; her face is streaked with dust and tears. 'Then we'll see who pays. Oh, yes. We've suffered long enough, we true Ukrainians.'

She grabs Misha's arm, her hand thin and hard. 'All I know is, better the Germans than the Russians, Mr Wasserman. I have family in east Ukraine. We know what Stalin did there in thirty-three. Sold the peasants' grain to feed Moscow, and you never saw such sights. Millions died. People were cannibals back then, Mr Wasserman, for the hunger. I am telling you, people walking like dead bodies, and it was Stalin and his communist Jews who did that to us. Ah, yes, the Jews. You Jews.'

She leaves them stunned. And uneasy. The heat mounts as everyone stays inside and waits for the Germans to arrive. A terrible smell begins to seep along the street from the direction of the NKVD prison.

'What should we do?' Sophia says, looking out over the deserted street below. 'Should we pack? Where would we go?'

The air begins to quiver with the approaching noise of heavy tank tracks, the roar of motorcycles. It's too late.

The German units roll into Lvov as if for a summer camp, young and tanned and healthy in pale green uniforms with black-and-silver decorations on the collars. At their head, the Ukrainian SS Nightingale regiment. They smile and sing Ukrainian anthems as they ride in on Panzer tanks, a homecoming of Lvov's own handsome boys.

From their window, Misha and Sophia watch women in summer dresses and old grandmothers in white headscarves hand them flowers. Men salute with emotion, thinking no doubt of happier and more civilized days under the Austrian Germans.

And all the while a terrible stench continues to seep from inside the prison along the street. Leaning out, Misha can see crowds now gathered outside the walls. The heat mounts, the stench is becoming intolerable.

Something terrible is waiting inside to be discovered.

That night there's a sudden commotion out in the stairwell. A woman crying as someone is dragged down the stairs.

'It's the Cohens,' says Misha.

They're being expelled from their large apartment on the top floor and out onto the street.

Misha gets up and checks the apartment door is locked.

In the morning they find a hysterical Mrs Yelenyuk in the hallway, eyes red with weeping. She puts her face into Misha's. He can feel her spittle on his cheek. 'You should know what the Jews have done in the prison,' she hisses. 'Piles of bodies. A priest nailed to a wall in the shape of a cross. Thousands of innocent men murdered by those NKVD Jews. Animals. My own brother. There's no place in Lvov for Jews now,' she said. 'No place.'

When she's gone, Sophia's face is white. 'Is she warning us? What does she mean?'

'I don't know but I think I should find out.' Misha pulls on his jacket.

'Don't. It's not safe.'

'It's not safe if we don't know.'

There's an angry crowd milling along Kazimierza Street towards the Brygidki prison, people talking animatedly. Posters have appeared on the walls during the night. 'Ukraine for the Ukrainians. Say no to Moscow, to Poles, to Armenians, and Jews.' He reads them with incredulity. Do the Ukrainians really believe the Nazis are going to allow them to rule themselves, under a benign Nazi protection?

Outside the prison gates, people hold handkerchiefs over their mouths. The heavily planked prison doors stand wide open. Misha covers his mouth with his sleeve to block the smell and moves forward. He can see rows of bodies lying in the courtyard under the baking sun. Women in summer dresses, men in suits, are carrying more bodies out of the prison, lifting out corpses from shallow graves in the dirt. There's Mrs Cohen, her face terrified, brushing dirt from a dead body with a branch.

He looks around in a daze. Groups of women in peasant headscarves stand wailing over the muddy, sunken-eyed corpses.

SS soldiers stand in the shade, casually holding their unused rifles while a hysterical man with a blue-and-yellow armband yells at a Jewish woman. She cowers and pleads as he slaps her repeatedly. A tall, immaculately dressed man with a white embroidered tunic is beating one of the startled Jewish men, strips of flesh flying from the man's face with the force of the rough metal rod.

Misha backs away from the gates. The air crackles with anger. Outside, a running riot has erupted along the street. Jewish civilians outnumbered and chased by furious Ukrainian relatives baying for blood and revenge. Boys with blue-and-yellow armbands, sticks held aloft, are beating them to the ground. A woman, her clothes half torn off, is being dragged along by her hair.

Trapped against the wall by the crowd, Misha pushes himself along, trying to get back to the apartment. People pay him no attention. They're watching a crowd move away from a man lying motionless in the road, dark blood pooling in a grid between the cobblestones. There's a naked teenage girl sitting on the kerb, shouting back at the jeering crowd while her mother tries to put a jacket around her. Other women are being stripped of their clothes, pushed and shoved, noses bloodied, fleeing the crowd.

The Nazi guards stand watching, faces dispassionate.

'The Jewish Bolsheviks had it coming. They say three thousand good Ukrainians were murdered in the prisons, and that's how many Jews are going to die before this is over, you mark my words,' a woman tells Misha, her eyes glazed.

Misha nods politely, finally frees himself from the crowd and walks on. Once he's out of reach of the mob, he begins to run, praying that Sophia has stayed safe inside the apartment.

She opens the door as soon as she hears his key. He holds her tight.

'What's happened? Misha?'

He doesn't want to tell her, but she needs to know how things are.

'They are murdering Jewish people, humiliating them in terrible ways. I can't tell you, a woman with no clothes, her face bleeding. It's not safe here any more. Sophia, we have to leave.'

'But where?'

'We could only go east, but the Germans will surely follow the Russians. Perhaps south, towards Syria and Palestine, but it would be risky. I don't know. If we go west back to Warsaw . . .'

'We go home.'

'We can't go back and enter the ghetto.'

'At least we can be with family in the ghetto, with Korczak and the children. I know they say the ghetto's more or less a prison, but the walls keep people out, keep people safe. And Jews have lived in ghettoes before.'

He shakes his head, but he knows they have no alternative. 'We'll try to go before it's light, when the town is quieter. But are you sure?'

'I'm sure.'

All night, the town rings with screams and shots. They hear feet running up and down the stairs of the apartment block. Misha puts a chest against the door and sits up in bed watching it. The Cohens are well off. Up on the top floor in the Cohens' apartment, they hear crashes, heavy things being carried and dragged downstairs. Before dawn, everything finally falls quiet.

For the next few weeks as the Germans advance eastwards and hundreds of German troops pour through the area, they lie low, trapped in a battle zone, waiting for an opportunity to return to Warsaw. As soon as the Germans begin to establish some kind of order and trains start to run again – with a possible connection running to Warsaw – they decide to make their move.

The town is silent as they walk through the dark streets, keeping to the shadows. The station, however, is brightly lit and already crowded with people trying to get home to Krakow or Warsaw now that Lvov is part of the Reich and the border is gone.

As the buildings flicker past in the grey dawn and they pull away from Lvov, Misha sees for a moment the blur of white skin, a woman chased by boys with sticks, blood running from her nose, hair ripped and flying, her face a mask of dazed terror.

Nothing, nothing can be worse than the horror of Lvov.

His seat faces east, towards the sunrise that dazzles through his closed eyelids. Father, and Ryfka and Niura, will be waking soon in Pinsk. What if the Wehrmacht's advance reaches that far? As a boy he once saw Polish soldiers in Pinsk ducking a Jewish schoolgirl in a freezing horse trough, laughing that they were baptizing her, but he can't believe that the horrors he's just seen in Lvov could ever be repeated in his home town. No, something odd and isolated happened in Lvov, a specific conflagration of fury and revenge.

As the miles between them and Lvov increase, he feels Sophia's body lose its tension and her dark blonde head rolls against him trustingly in sleep. The train stops for hours for no reason, starts again, all day to get back home to Warsaw. He's bone tired, but a grey apprehension of the unknown life in front of them won't let him sleep. Again and again, Misha asks himself if he is doing the right thing. But what choice do they have? Life will be difficult inside the ghetto, he's sure of that much, but at least there she will be safe.

CHAPTER THIRTEEN

WARSAW, SEPTEMBER 1941

The sun is beginning to set, its red light flashing between the iron slats of the Kierbedzia Bridge, as Misha and Sophia cross back into Warsaw once again. In the old town people are walking briskly past the cleared bombsites and damaged buildings. Red banners with black Nazi insignia hang from the palace in Saxon Square – a new name now, Adolf Hitler Platz.

At the ghetto gate by Krasinskich Gardens they get out their identity cards. Sophia looks up at the white-rendered walls and the plank gates over ten feet tall. A wooden board is attached to one side warning people to keep out, typhus zone. Two well-fleshed

German guards with rifles over their shoulders stand next to a small brick hut on the Aryan side. She looks anxiously at Misha.

'Once we go in, there's no going back,' he says. But the reality is that they have no choice. To survive as a Jew outside the ghetto takes contacts and an inordinate amount of money, neither of which they have to hand as they stand in the street.

'We'll be with Mother and Father, with Korczak and the children. It's time,' she says.

Holding hands, her heart beating fast, she and Misha approach the guards and explain that they wish to go into the ghetto and join family.

The German gives them an odd look as he checks their papers. He taps Misha's forehead, and waves them in. Inside, a Polish policeman in a navy uniform also has to examine their papers before he too motions them on. Last of all, a Jewish policeman checks through their documents, staring at them with a quizzical expression. Sophia waits, noticing that no one has bothered applying white render to this side of the wall, just dried mortar oozing between the rust-coloured bricks.

From Sophia's mother's letters, they expected to walk into an area of Warsaw that was enclosed, but still recognizably the old streets that they had known so well. Nothing, however, could have prepared them for what they now find inside the ghetto walls. How can this be Warsaw? The streets are so crowded, they advance with difficulty. Even the air is different here, a persistent smell made up of rotting rubbish, unwashed clothing and sewage. Along each side of the street, thin and listless people in shabby clothes stand by little piles of redundant-looking items – battered saucepans, broken bits of clocks, an armful of old underwear – hoping for a sale. A sallow woman watches over a table of stunted bread rolls guarded by a barbed-wire cage. Two haggard children bundled in rags come swaying towards Sophia on stick legs, each holding out a hand and chanting as if in a dream, 'We are hungry, please give us bread.' Sophia gives them a coin and stares as the children carry on past, still swaying and chanting. An emaciated teenager with a rope around his frayed coat is stretched out on the flagstones, his sunken face as grey as putty, his eyes closed. Is he alive? He groans and opens his eyes as Sophia bends down.

There are so many beggars, wandering through the crowds or propped against the walls, their faces resigned and almost apologetic in their quietness. And there's no end to it. The terrible bazaar stretches on as far as they can see in a loud clamour of voices and snatches of buskers' songs.

At 26 Ogrodowa Street Mr Rozental answers the door, his face fearful. His expression changes to joy and amazement. Mrs Rozental follows close behind.

Sophia blinks. How they have aged.

'It's you. It's you. Dearest Sophia. Misha.'

'You can call us Mr and Mrs Wasserman, Papa. We're married. I sent a letter.'

Her mother takes her hand and looks at the narrow gold band. 'But the letter never came. So you're married and we weren't there, didn't even know.'

'Don't cry, Mama.'

'That we should see you again. Oh, but you shouldn't have come.'

Krystyna squeezes through and kisses them both. She's holding a little boy. The child hides his face in Krystyna's shoulder.

'Thank goodness,' she says to Sophia quietly. 'If you only knew . . .'

Sophia holds out her arms and takes the little boy.

'Sabina's child. He's beautiful. But Mother, I don't understand. How could it be? What happened to Sabina?'

The little boy struggles and goes back to Krystyna. Mr Rozental sags, deflates as if punched. 'We should sit down.'

Mother puts a kettle of water on to boil, concentrating on this small task, keeping her back turned to the table. Holding Misha's hand, Sophia waits; Father nods distractedly to himself before he finds the words to begin.

'Sabina and Lutek moved into their own flat, a tiny place but a godsend, given to them by a good friend. People here, you know, they're having to crowd in six, eight, to a room.'

'I should have kept her with me,' interjects Mrs Rozental. 'I should have seen how she was, may her soul rest in peace.'

'My beautiful girl, she never got over the shame of being sacked from the couturier's. The wrong hair, the wrong nose, the posters of ugly Jews with lice in their beards: that was the beginning. Sabina was never strong like you girls. It hasn't been easy. Often we're hungry. Yes, that's the truth. I have to tell them, Mother. One night, Sabina came to us. She wanted us to sell everything, have one last good meal together and then kill ourselves. We didn't take her seriously. Everyone here has those thoughts now and then. She seemed to calm down. The next morning she went out to sell her watch to buy carrots for the baby, for the vitamins, but while she was in the market, someone stole her wallet. All the money from the watch was gone. That afternoon she asked us to take care of the baby. We didn't know it then, but she went up to the roof. She took the ribbon from her hair and put it around her eyes. Then . . .' Mr Rozental pauses.

Sophia's hand flies to her mouth. 'She killed herself?'

'She's buried at the edge of the cemetery,' says Mrs Rozental thickly. 'A suicide. Away from everyone else. My girl.'

They sit around a table in a shared silence. A scratchy noise of voices comes in from the street outside.

'I don't understand. I don't understand anything. If things are so very bad, then how are you managing in here, for food?' Sophia asks.

'To begin with we sold razor blades. You remember Sammy? He was sweet on you, Sophia. He closed down his razor-blade factory before he left Warsaw and gave us the rest of his stock. It's been like gold. Lutek's printing firm made new envelopes for single blades and we all sat round night after night putting them in the packets. Then we sold them. They lasted a while.'

'And now?'

'Krystyna works as a waitress on Sienna Street. Lutek lives with a school friend who gives him work. You can see there's no room here. He comes and brings some food when he can, for the little boy. We have things left to sell if we need to.'

Mr Rozental brings out a card with neat rows of black stars and puts it on the table. 'It's nonsense but you'll have to register for one of these. It allows you enough food rations so you can starve to death, two hundred calories. It's only the smugglers bringing in food who are keeping people alive in the ghetto.'

Mrs Rozental's eyes fill with tears. 'And a lot of them are only children. It's a beating and prison if they get caught.'

'But I saw some people who were well dressed, with smart clothes just like outside the walls. How do they live?'

'Yes, how do they live with themselves?' mutters Mr Rozental.

'Oh, if you're rich, if you've got deep pockets and you're happy for the Nazis to put their hand in, there's nothing you can't bring in here. Brandy, furs. There are little restaurants with champagne and fancy women, all with the shutters closed, of course. You'll hear two big names in here, Kon and Heller. Two of the biggest crooks in Warsaw.'

'They're Jewish?'

'Oh, yes. They live in the ghetto but they live in style.'

'That's enough for poor Sophia and Misha for today, Father. They'll see it all soon enough. It will all be there in the morning.'

'And Dr Korczak?' asks Misha. 'Have you had news? How is he?'

For the first time Mrs Rozental's face breaks into a smile. 'Korczak, he's like a ray of light in the ghetto. You see him everywhere with a sack on his back, looking for food for the children.'

'And are the children well? And Stefa?'

'Yes. Yes, they are all here. They say his orphanage is almost like being outside the ghetto. Poor of course, but clean, the children happy. A little oasis.'

'They're down in Chlodna Street,' adds Krystyna.

'We can go and see them first thing in the morning,' says Misha, squeezing Sophia's hand.

'First you must go to the Judenrat and register for your cards, as soon as it's open. If you were stopped on the street . . .'

Mrs Rozental glances at her husband. 'Oh, Sophia, why didn't you stay in Lvov?'

Sophia has no words to describe what they have left behind in Lvov.

'Well, you are here now and I'm so thankful to see you. All we have to do now is stay together until this is over,' says Mr Rozental.

The Rozentals sleep in the tiny main room, Krystyna in the kitchen. There's just room for Sophia in the bed, the little boy in a cot next to them. Misha tries to sleep on two chairs in the small gap between the window and table but he's too anxious and flooded with adrenalin. What terrible place has he brought them to? How can so many children be going hungry, left to beg on the street?

Are Korczak and the children suffering in the same way?

His long legs cramp in the small space, he sleeps fitfully. He's ready to get up now and begin looking for some way to earn enough to survive in this unimaginable place.

He's walking with Sophia by the Vistula, a blue sky and endless space. He opens his eyes and the ghetto returns. It's early but outside on the street there's already a thin cacophony of voices echoing between the buildings. No sound of car tyres. No tram passes along here.

He's stiff and needs a hot shower. He washes his face and armpits at the kitchen sink, quietly. He doesn't want to wake Sophia and Krystyna, both still deeply asleep in the bed against the wall. Marianek is sitting up, watching Misha cautiously. The child begins to cry at the sight of this tall interloper. Sophia wakes and lifts Marianek next to her, cajoles him into a smile. She crosses the room in her nightdress, kisses Misha briefly and cuts a piece of bread from the loaf in the metal bin for the little boy

She holds up the remains of the loaf, barely enough for three, and all there is for breakfast.

'We won't eat it. We can buy more on the way to Korczak's, perhaps. Soon as I'm dressed, we can go straight there. They'll all be up and having breakfast at the home by now.'

Misha smiles at how well she knows him. 'Just to see how they are. Then we'll get our papers sorted out at the Jewish Council offices.'

*

A body is lying on the pavement outside the apartment, naked and emaciated. The few sheets of newspaper covering it are lifting and blowing away.

'But why is no one doing anything?' To her horror Sophia sees more corpses along the street. People walk past, eyes averted.

A long black handcart comes squeaking along the street, iron rims of the wooden wheels clattering against the stone cobbles, one man pushing, the other pulling between the black shafts like a horse. They stop and collect naked corpses, stacking them like firewood on the cart, the bodies juddering when the cart moves forward over the uneven cobbles.

The cart stops in front of Sophia and Misha. The men begin lifting the body.

'Why have these people been left like this?' asks Sophia angrily.

The man eyes her quizzically. 'And this is news? Where are you from?'

'We came here yesterday, from Lvov.'

'You should have run away in the other direction while you had the chance.' He rubs his cheek and looks embarrassed. 'You have to pay to bury a body in the Gesia cemetery, so they leave the bodies out, may they rest in peace, on the street. People need the clothes to sell for food.'

'I don't understand. Yesterday we walked through Warsaw and there were markets and shops selling plenty of food. It's madness.'

He shrugs, gets back between the cart shafts and the wooden hearse rattles away, the lifeless heads bouncing against the boards of the cart.

*

It's the right address but the front door has been bricked up. Children's voices float over the wall. And laughter. Misha realizes it's the first time he's heard laughter since they came in through the ghetto gates. They knock on the side gate; the jalousie cover opens and Mounius with his bright red hair appears behind the grille. He lets them in, giving Misha a deep hug, yelling out that Pan Misha and Pani Sophia are here. Misha takes in the scene. The side gate opens into a yard with walls of apartment windows rising on three sides like the courtyard of a castle, the wall cutting across the back. Children are playing quietly, pale but healthy. Korczak is sitting on a bench in the afternoon sun talking with a group of children. Misha is shocked to see how the flesh has fallen away to leave his face thin with large rheumy eyes, pouches underneath. His hair completely white. He's wearing his Polish major's uniform, the insignia gone from the collar.

The moment Korczak sees them he breaks into a delighted grin, stands with his arms wide open.

'And so you've come home to us.' He embraces them warmly.

'How are you, Dr Korczak?'

'Fit as a fiddle, as you can see. Oh, yes, we do very well here, very well. Not a sick child among us.'

A band of children with familiar faces but thinner, so much taller, gather around to greet Pan Misha and Pani Sophia; Sammy, who's now almost as tall as Misha, with his harmonica; Abrasha with his violin in his hand; little Sara who was once hit with a stone on the way home and still has a silver scar on her forehead; gentle Halinka holding her by the hand. Squealing and shouting their news, the children pull Misha and Sophia away on a tour to see their new home.

Inside, a wistful, scrubbed-clean poverty hangs over the place, but the children's paintings are everywhere. Korczak's beloved brave red geraniums are growing on the windowsills. The same white duvets neatly folded, the pristine bathrooms, the library corner and the notices on the wall with the children's news.

'Pan Misha, are you back to stay?' Erwin comes running down the stairs, now a tough wiry thirteen-year-old, with his fair hair, his small beak of a nose and round, startled eyes. He has the pugnacious stance of a little boxer. 'Will you come and read our Saturday news out to us again?'

'Yes. Yes, I will. But this can't be Erwin. So tall.'

'Not so tall, and I don't live here all the time now, Pan Misha.' He leans in. 'I go out to smuggle bread over the wall for Pan Doctor and for Halinka.'

'I'd go too,' says Sammy, towering up behind him, 'but what can I do?' He covers his long and handsome nose with a hand, a habitual gesture.

'Sammy, you have an emperor's nose, like Caesar,' Misha tells him. 'Be proud.'

'It's killing me.'

Pani Stefa hurries over, as ever in a brown dress and white collar. She's gone completely grey and her face sags with age and fatigue but her beautiful smile is still the same.

'It's good to see you both again. I can't begin to tell you.' Stefa gives them a clearer picture of how serious the situation is as they walk back down to the courtyard. 'Korczak is out all day seeing people about donations but I don't know how he can keep it up. He's not well. It will do him so much good to know that you are here.'

'I see you have almost all female teachers here.'

'After the siege, the men went east as you know. But we manage between us. Esther is here now, the student doctor. She helps a lot with Korczak's rounds. He's very fond of her. As is Henryk, though in a more romantic way, but what can you expect from a boy of seventeen? So you see, apart from young Henryk, we don't have any male teachers living in the home, and some of the boys who come in from the ghetto streets, they've seen too much.' She bites her lips together.

'You know I'll be back to help, as much as I can.'

Stefa's face breaks into a relieved smile. 'I didn't like to ask now you're married but it would help so much. We can't pay you, Misha, of course, but we have meals. If you could help with the night shift in the boy's dormitory sometimes.'

He glances at Sophia.

'Of course, you must,' she says.

'It's so good to have you both back. I can't tell you.'

They leave the children playing in the courtyard, Korczak watching over them. The sound of children's laughter follows them for a few steps, and they are back in the world of the ghetto. Sophia draws closer to Misha and holds his arm, but it's impossible. She has to let go as they thread their way through the crowded pavements, following close behind him.

People are hurrying up and down the steps of the Jewish Council offices on Grzybowska Street, but Sophia carries on walking past, her feet heading towards her old apartment block, following the route that she has taken since a child. Misha takes her hand and walks with her, understanding where she is going.

Sophia turns around, looking for a landmark from her childhood. Her apartment block is gone, an empty space leading through to the next street, any remaining bricks swept into slopes of rubble and scree. The church is still there. The people going up its steps all wear armbands with the Star of David: Christians sent into the ghetto for their Jewish parents or grandparents, some of the families not even aware of their Jewish heritage until contacted by Nazi officials.

Yes, it's Grzybowski Square, but it's hard to recognize. Instead of the generous clamour of the market with its overflowing baskets of bread rolls and flowers, there's an assortment of desperate people selling next to nothing from tiny stalls or from trays hung around their necks, kindling, scraps of meat. The cobbles are filthy with mud and straw. A tiny child with eyes too large, legs like bare bones beneath its coat, begins to do a dance in front of Sophia. Sophia empties out her purse and buys the child a large bread roll. A flock of more children gather around.

Nothing left in her purse and a ring of hungry children's faces. She reluctantly follows Misha to the Jewish Council buildings.

The Jewish policemen who guard the tall double doors have the air of louche imposters. Their uniform is nothing but a police armband, a belt and cap over shabby civilian clothes, grown men playing a sinister version of a child's dressing-up game. They look out above the crowds, uncomfortable, supercilious. They each carry a rubber truncheon.

Inside, she and Misha begin queuing beneath a poster of a large louse with instructions in German to keep clean.

'Not that you can get soap,' mumbles the man next to them, nodding at the poster. He removes his glasses and rubs his eyes. 'Sorry, my dear, it's just that I'm a doctor and one gets tired.'

'Are there many cases of typhus in here?' said Misha. 'We've just arrived.'

'What do you think? Half a million underfed people crammed

into a square mile, in these conditions. A quarter of the population gone, I'd say. Try not to touch anyone as you go down the street. The lice.'

Sophia can feel herself shrinking into her jacket at the thought.

The man looks down at Sophia's wedding band and then fixes her with a sad look. 'And my dear, be careful not to risk a pregnancy, not in this place.'

When they come out, one of the Jewish policemen is beating a beggar with his rubber truncheon. The man cowers under the blows.

After days of seeing nothing but buildings the colour of dirty sand, only a narrow channel of sky visible between the terraces of apartments, it's a shock to come into a place where green grass and flowers grow: the cemetery. Sophia and Misha follow Krystyna beyond the rows of stone slabs towards a rough and greener acre. Young people are weeding new onions and cabbages in the sun – a farm in a graveyard.

Far away from the entrance, at the furthest boundary wall, they find the wooden marker for Sabina's grave. This is where the suicides are laid to rest. They stand in a half-circle, listening to birds singing, breathing the almost forgotten scent of trampled grass and wild flowers.

Sophia closes her eyes, trying to see Sabina again, a girl sitting high in a white droshky filled with flowers on the way to her wedding, so hopeful and so beautiful.

But Sabina's gone. Sophia opens her eyes and gulps air arid with grief. She feels a hand creep into hers: Krystyna folds herself against Sophia's shoulder and they weep together for their sister.

CHAPTER FOURTEEN

WARSAW, SEPTEMBER 1941

Korczak sees the guard kick the boy to the ground. He winces at the steel boot in the child's ribs, feeling every blow from the rifle butt. Runty parsnips and carrots lie scattered across the cobbles in front of the gate. When the German guard has sated his temper, when the little smuggler is no longer screaming or moving, the guard orders the vegetables to be taken to the guardhouse and then loses interest in the child. A younger guard signals to a man to come forward and remove the boy. The terrified man scoops the boy up and walks away, the child's arms and legs dangling, head flopped back, his mouth open.

Korczak hurries to catch up with him.

'Where are you taking him?'

'I don't know. To the hospital, if they'll have him.'

Korczak frowns. The hospitals are full of typhus cases, a bed there is more or less a death sentence.

'I'm a doctor. Bring him with me.'

'Of course. Dr Korczak, isn't it? I used to listen to you on the radio, sir.'

At the home on Chlodna Street, the man decants the child onto a bed in the sickbay.

The boy is barely conscious. A faint snore of breath. Korczak examines the lesions on the child's head. A baggy jacket with the hidden inner sack ripped open. Cut-off trousers are tied with fraying rope round a skinny waist, his arms and legs like sticks. He might be around eight but it's hard to be sure with so many children undernourished. He's fine-boned, with small clever hands and face. He looks like a child who in another life would be destined for the Yeshiva school, have a mother who made him wear a scarf in the cold. Korczak unties the string on the boy's too-large boots and releases a smell of damp and rotting cloth.

The man at his side looks around the calm, clean home with wonder. 'It's like you're not in the ghetto here.'

'I can assure you we are,' says Korczak, taking the boy's pulse. 'But that does not mean that we live like monsters.' He holds the child's wrist, counting faint beats with concentration. Glances up at the man's once good coat, his white skin and grey veins standing out across his forehead, the smell of hunger on his breath. 'Go down to the kitchen. Tell them to give you a meal. I don't know what it will be.'

*

'You can stay here now,' Korczak tells the child when he comes round. The boy is puzzled to find himself lying on one of the beds in the sickbay, a large bandage on his leg.

'Why would I want to?' he asks Korczak suspiciously. 'And where's my boots?'

Korczak points to the boots lined up by the bed. 'There. Quite safe. We always respect children's property. Tell me . . .' He pauses.

'Aronek,' the boy says. 'My name's Aronek.'

'So tell me, Aronek, do you have parents in the ghetto, some family?'

The boy's eyes are hard and defiant, a thousand years old.

'I look after me.'

He speaks well enough, educated, yes, but the logic of the ghetto has taught him to trust no one.

'Commendable. But if you do stay . . .' A smell of lentil soup with a hint of sausage from the hallway, a loud gurgle from the boy's stomach. 'If you want to stay, I will need to shave off your hair, you understand. If you can be very brave.'

The boy's hand flies to his head.

Korczak says he'll make a map of Warsaw in the boy's hair with the clippers. Marshall Street, Jerusalem Street – did Aronek know he had some very swanky shops above his left ear, a sausage shop above his right? Last of all he sits Aronek in front of the mirror and the clippers polish his head like an egg. Behind him, Sara and Abrasha and the others clap. Aronek frowns at them in the mirror. Doesn't like them crowding around him. He leans forward with a scowl and doesn't recognize the mean little whippet boy in the mirror. Hunger has taken every last trace of childish fat from his face. The sharp nose and jug ears protrude painfully. He touches the blue-and-red bruise that the guard's boot has imprinted across his temple, admires his scabbed cut. It hurts.

He looks down. He's not been so clean since – since before the ghetto. He pushes away a memory of his mother filling a zinc tub with hot water in a room with lace curtains, a tiled stove in the corner with soup on it.

In the dining room the chattering children pass him a large bowl of soup and a basket filled with hunks of bread, asking so many questions. Aronek ignores them all, his arm around his bowl, scooping up the lentils before anyone can swipe them from him. He's seen the grabbers in the street who snatch the parcels from people's hands and gobble down the contents so fast they sometimes don't even stop to check it's food. Who's to say that drippy boy with the big eyes won't do the same?

When no one's looking, Aronek slips a piece of bread from another child's plate and hides it away for later.

Someone is looking, of course. Korczak decides to say nothing about the bread. It often takes a while for children who have known hunger – and he's known many such children – to believe that there will be bread at every meal. Best not to notice the stolen bread for now. Korczak's eyes rest on Aronek with sadness. This is a child hungry for his mother. A child in pain.

But the swearing. Aronek has made himself master in the special kind of Jewish curse that comes from the Yiddish slums of Warsaw, long and poetic, and filled with everything from the gutter. Korczak has learned a few choice curses in the army, but he honestly wonders if Aronek couldn't outdo him. The children stand around aghast. Or they come screaming to tell him that Aronek is swearing again.

The child doesn't seem able to stop himself, swears just as he breathes.

And all the children know there's a penalty for swearing. They'll expect Aronek to be treated like everyone else. This could be a tricky one.

Korczak leads Abrasha to stand in front of Aronek.

'This is your new big brother.'

'What's he want then?' Aronek eyes Abrasha warily. He doesn't like this thin, girlish boy. One push and a boy like that would cry.

'I don't want anything,' says Abrasha. 'I can tell you all about what we do here, how things work.'

'Don't need no help from a big cissy like you,' Aronek says, scanning Abrasha's sensitive musician's face, his long hands and almond eyes.

'Everyone has a big brother or sister here,' explains Korczak mildly. 'It's normal. Smart people take advice from time to time. Why don't you listen to Abrasha? And if you still don't want a big brother by the end of the day, then so be it.'

Korczak leaves Abrasha beginning the tour of the home and its ways.

'What do you mean there's a court for children?' asks Aronek. 'You mean the teachers can send the kids to prison if they want?'

'No, it's the children who are the judges. I was a judge three times, you know. Even Pan Doctor was told off for speaking crossly to a girl. All the teachers and children here have to abide by the same rules, respect each other. That way it's fair. Say if somebody's mean to you—'

'Then I'd thump them.'

'But then they'll hit you back. You'll have a war. No, here you say, I'll sue you, and the court will listen to your case.'

Abrasha stops in front of a tall cupboard.

'And each child has a drawer in this cupboard to keep your things. No one ever touches them. The little ones just keep buttons, string, but people still respect their stuff. They really respect children in here, you know.'

Aronek shrugs. Face pinched. Nobody's fool.

The two boys come to a mop and bucket left out in full view like a beautiful ornament. 'And we all help with the chores.'

'Not me. Catch me mopping the floor.'

Later, when all the children are ready for bed, Korczak settles down in the chair in the boys' dormitory to read them a story from Little King Matt.

Aronek turns away, pulls the sheet up over his head. He's too old now at eight for babyish stories, after what he has lived through in the ghetto.

He doesn't believe in childhood any more.

Korczak reads on, his sad eyes returning to the sharp shoulder blades moulded under the sheet that stick out like the stubs of wings.

A few days later, as Korczak sits on the bench in the courtyard while the children play, letting the sun warm his closed eyelids for a moment, he feels a small presence at his side.

He knows if he looks down he will see those wide ears and the beginning of a pale regrowth of blond hair on the shorn and scarred scalp.

At least the fetid smell has gone, the decay of pre-death that he's noticed the starving carry with them.

'Pan Doctor, do you have another of those stories?'

'I might. Let me think. Do you know the one about the flying ship in the forest and the boy with nothing to save him but his kind heart?'

A hand slips into his.

CHAPTER FIFTEEN

WARSAW, SEPTEMBER 1941

Sophia raises her head, stretches out her arm. Misha's side of the bed is empty, but the sheets still feel warm. She can hear him in the kitchen, brewing something on the stove. She breathes out with relief. He's here then.

He's away at least three nights a week, caring for the children at Korczak's home, which she absolutely wants him to do, but that doesn't make it any less difficult. She hates it when his side of the bed lies empty all night.

Misha pushes aside the chenille curtain and hands her a cup.

Behind the curtain, the wives from two couples who share the tiny flat have already started their first argument of the day, food that's gone missing, who should go first at the stove.

She can feel Misha's pent-up nerviness as he sits on the narrow bed and drinks his coffee, a vibration in his long limbs.

'What is it?'

'Nothing.'

'Tell me, Misha. I'm not a child you need to protect.'

'The last of the money we've brought from Lvov will be gone by next week. And what I'm earning giving rickshaw rides, it's just not enough, not with food so dear . . .'

Sophia looks at his skinny arms with veins like ropes, the loss of flesh alarming.

'You eat more than you earn heaving people around on that bicycle. It can't be worth it. And I am earning a little from tutoring my nieces.'

He leans back and squeezes her hand. 'The main thing is that we're together. We can get through anything if we know we have each other.'

In the kitchen, a pot crashes to the floor. The curtain is rudely pulled back and a woman with unbrushed hair stands gesturing at the other woman.

'A louse,' she shrills. 'There's a louse on her. Doesn't she understand how dangerous that is with half the ghetto dying of typhus? How can I cope if she doesn't even have the decency to keep clean? I can't stand it, I tell you.'

The curtain falls back.

At the tiny flat on Ogrodowa Street Sophia finds her mother sitting at the table, watching Marianek play with his wooden blocks on the floor. Marianek holds out his arms and Sophia picks him up.

'Where's Father?' Her mother looks around the room absently.

'Oh, you know your father, he's taken something to sell, though goodness knows what we have left.' She picks up the purse on the table, opens it, then closes it again with a blank expression. 'I should go out and buy something for supper. I don't understand how potatoes can be so dear now.'

'I'll go, Mother. It's a while before my next pupils come for their session. I'll see if I can get some eggs.'

'That I should come to a day when I worried if we could afford an egg.'

'At least, I'll see if I can get one for Marianek.'

She goes out into the street with the empty basket, wondering if you ever get used to feeling a little hungry all the time.

As curfew approaches, Erwin walks along one of the blank-faced streets that run along the ghetto walls. During the day they are deserted, guards passing on patrol. But after dusk almost all of the Germans leave the ghetto and the border street fills with a scuffling and pattering of feet, children running across the cobbles to squeeze under the wall through the drain openings.

Erwin stops at a section of the wall and Isaac appears from the shadows. They check no one is about, then begin to loosen the bricks around the drain opening. Erwin squeezes through, Isaac remaining behind, waiting in a doorway.

The street on the other side is empty. Erwin stands up cautiously. The light is beginning to fade, the street is empty, but there's the sound of German voices on the main street a few yards away, convivial laughter. He waits for the soldiers to pass by, then walks out into Aryan Warsaw.

With his snub Polish nose and fair hair, no one gives Erwin a second glance as he hurries to a small bakery, the first he'll visit tonight. He buys a loaf of rye bread, so warm and sweet that it's all he can do not to tear it apart there and then.

Back at the wall he gives a low whistle. A reply from Isaac, and Erwin passes the bread through the hole. Now he must wait, hiding in the shadow of the wall, ears alert to every sound. Later, another low whistle and Isaac's back. Fingers slide some zlotys through to Erwin.

In the ghetto, bread sells for twice its Aryan price, so he'll buy two more loaves, then take those back to sell. He'll need to make several trips before the boys have enough to buy bread to eat and also to keep enough zlotys to begin again tomorrow.

He's on his last trip, skirting the walls along Rynkowa Street, when he comes across three Polish men throwing sacks over the wall, fast as they can. Harsh voices shouting in German, the pounding of boots. He draws back around the corner and runs, the sound of gunfire behind him.

He hides in a doorway until all is quiet, then makes his way back to the wooden fence, his heart still thundering, listening out for the sound of soldiers' boots.

Misha is woken by stealthy footsteps across the wooden floor. He sits up, his skin prickling, senses alert. A short, stocky shape is moving over the other side of the dormitory, the jacket oddly bulky.

Erwin. Misha turns up the carbide lamp a little.

The teenager comes over to Misha's bed. He opens the flap of his jacket. Inside, there's a rough canvas knapsack sewn with big, childish stiches. He rummages and pulls out loaves of black rye bread, his eyes bright in the light of the lamp.

'It's the real thing, Pan Misha, not the gluey stuff full of sawdust they send into the ghetto shops. And look.'

He hands Misha a tiny hand soap wrapped in thick paper. Misha takes a sniff of the sugary lavender scent.

'You're going to smell very good, Erwin.'

'It's for Halinka. She's my best friend, Pan Misha. When we grow up I'm going to mend cars and we'll get married and go to America and have three children. And they will all have milk and white bread every single day. As much as they want.'

'It's a good plan.'

Erwin nods and puts the soap away carefully in his jacket.

'But listen, Erwin, you do understand, don't you, what could happen if you were caught?'

'I can take a beating.'

Misha lies down, thinking. His own trips over to the Aryan side, using one of the courtyard clothes dryers as a ladder to get over the wall, have provided a pitiful amount – some potatoes, a couple of loaves. A child could have done better. Little children do, since it's easier for them to squeeze through the sluice holes. Many parents now rely on children as young as six to bring food home.

What Misha desperately needs is to find a way to join one of the bands of men smuggling in significant amounts of food. These are the people keeping the ghetto alive. He's heard of houses straddling the ghetto boundary where hundreds of sacks are brought in every day through attics or cellars, tales of a hole in the wall where gallons of milk are poured in through a pipe.

You need the right contacts before you can hope to be invited into the kind of smuggling enterprise that can bring in enough food to make a real difference.

But for every man risking his life to smuggle in food to feed the starving ghetto, there's a man willing to profit from the ghetto's misery, charging extortionate prices, men who mix with the Gestapo in seedy nightclubs and are happy to sell you out to them for the right price.

How do you make contact with smugglers without ending up in Pawiak prison?

Misha lies awake worrying, the intractable wooden hunger prodding at his stomach.

CHAPTER SIXTEEN

WARSAW, SEPTEMBER 1941

J ust had the fright of my life.'

Mr Rozental puts down the books he's been trying to sell on Nowolipki Street. 'There I was, standing with my books and a Polish policeman comes over, heading straight for me. Then I saw who it was. You'll never guess. Stanislaw Zymkowski. Remember, Mother? We were at the gymnasium together, years ago. So, what do you think? He tells me he's smuggling food into the ghetto. Says he can let us have bread at a good price. And there's more. He's looking for a good man to help them on this side of the wall. So I told him about Misha and now he wants him to meet the Jewish man he works with, Jakub Frydman. What do you think of that? Isn't that good news? He wants Misha to meet him at Zglinowicz's café.'

'Misha is not getting involved with any smuggling ring. Do you realize how dangerous that is?' Sophia tells him angrily.

But when Misha hears about it he won't meet her eye.

'It could be the answer to our problems,' he says quietly.

'What if this meeting's a trap to sniff out smugglers? We can't let you risk it.'

'But it's a risk to carry on like this, food getting more expensive, money so short.'

She lies awake listening to the hungry cries of children out on the street. She knows Misha is right. They've no choice if they're to survive in here.

Misha sits a couple of tables away from the plate-glass window of Zglinowicz's café. It's on the lower floor of a smart new apartment block, built in a time when the world was modern, when the world was getting better. From here there's a clear view of the ten-foot wooden gates and the guards that check everyone as they go through, delivery trucks, a horse and carriage, people on foot. There are three kinds of guards, the Germans with rifles, the Polish blue police with their black patent caps and the Jewish police with their rickety uniform of belt, cap and truncheon over civilian clothes.

Misha's already checked out that he can slip away through the back exit if he needs to. He tries not to fiddle with his glass of tea.

A tall, broad-shouldered man wearing the cap and belt of the Jewish Order Police walks smartly past the window and turns in at the door. He surveys the room, walks over, and takes a seat at Misha's table. So this is Jakub Frydman.

A coffee arrives, a friendly word with the barman. Frydman's evidently well known in here. Liked even. The barman was quick to bring his order.

Frydman's tall and healthy, no sign of hunger. He has an open, well-proportioned face, the sort that inspires confidence, handsome enough to make women's heads turn, but he wears the requisite gleaming white shirt of the Order Police beneath his civilian suit – who else can afford to wear such pristine linen? – and Misha's eyes go to the policeman's cap Frydman places on the table next to a pair of expensive leather gloves. Some of the Jewish police now seem to believe that behaving as brutally as a Nazi makes them a Nazi, privileged and untouchable. Not to be trusted.

Frydman sees where he's looking.

'So you don't like talking to a policeman.'

'Can you blame me?'

Frydman lights a cigarette, offers one to Misha but he declines.

'You're taking a risk. I'm taking a risk. The question is, what are you prepared to do to survive in here?'

'I'm not prepared to work with anyone who works with the Gestapo.'

'There's something we agree on. But are you prepared to run the risk of being caught by the Gestapo?'

Misha keeps his gaze steady. 'If it means I can get supplies through, for Korczak, for my family, I am.'

'Naturally. For Korczak especially we'll do what we can. A good deal on the price.'

Misha tries to control a look of gratitude in his face. He still has questions. 'And you're sure your Polish connections can be trusted?'

'These are good people. They need to make a living but they don't do it just for the profit. The Poles are beginning to realize what's happening in here, talk of piles of bodies. They hear it from across the wall, smell it on the wind, and they know the scent of death is blowing their way too. You should know, for every Pole out there who'd blackmail a Jew or turn him in there are twice, three times as many who would – who do – risk their lives to help a Jew. These Poles I work with, I trust them like my brothers.'

Misha studies Frydman's even, admirable face a moment longer. He seems genuine, capable. And there's something about Frydman's energy, his will to take a risk and beat the odds in here, that chimes with Misha's own restless drive to do more. His instinct is to trust Frydman. A friend perhaps – in time.

'So what do you need me to do?'

To begin with, Misha's only job is to wait near the phone in the café opposite the gate. Frydman works with a Polish couple, Tadeusz and Jadwiga Blazejewski. When they are ready to come in through the gate they phone the café and ask for Misha – the barman gets his cut. Misha answers with a code word to let them know if the right guard is still on the gate – the one who will take a bribe – and the young couple drive in, the supplies hidden beneath the cart's false bottom.

'I don't know where you get it, and I don't want to know,' says Stefa as Misha carries the impossible into the orphanage kitchen, boxes of lard. 'But thank you. We sorely needed fat for the children, for the vitamins. And tell those friends of yours thank you. But you will be careful, won't you, Misha?'

Sophia worries too.

'Darling, I'll be careful. I promise,' he says as they hold each other in the cramped bed, that way she has of pulling his arm over her shoulders like a tent, of making a world in that small space just theirs with her love and her closeness.

And he wonders how to tell her that Frydman has already asked if he's prepared to go out of the ghetto into Warsaw and help load up the cart at the Wola warehouse.

CHAPTER SEVENTEEN

WARSAW, SEPTEMBER 1941

Today Korczak is sitting in on a session of the children's court, perched on one of the rows of chairs where the children are gathered to listen as Halinka explains the crime she's bringing before the children assembled behind a table to hear the case.

It's a tricky matter. To Halinka's left Aronek is sitting sulking, his arms crossed tightly across his chest as if no one will ever be able to prise them apart and find out what's going on inside his heart, his face shut down into an expression of anger and bitterness.

'I put the chocolate in my drawer. It was a little bar, a present' – Halinka colours a little – 'from Erwin. I didn't want to eat it straight away. I wanted to keep it because it was special. And I thought it was safe in the drawer, of course, until it was time to share it. But I went to look at it yesterday and it was gone. And Sara says she saw Aronek closing my drawer. He went off holding his arms over his jumper in a funny way.'

'Is that true, Sara?' asks Chaya. Black hair, deep brown eyes and a serious face, she's the judge for the day's court.

Sara nods, eyes wide with the gravity of what she has to report.

'What do you have to say?' Chaya asks Aronek.

Aronek folds his arms tighter, glares at Chaya. 'What does she want keeping the stupid chocolate in her drawer anyway? What good is that?'

There's a little gasp from the children assembled around the court table. It's more or less an admission. Erwin starts up, fists clenched, but Misha by his side gently pulls him down into his seat.

'Let the court finish,' he whispers to the furious boy. Misha knows that the chocolate will have come in from the Aryan side on one of Erwin's trips over the wall. And he knows that this is no ordinary chocolate bar, it's a small rectangle representing how much Erwin cares for Halinka, and the risks he will take for her.

There's a defeated sigh from Korczak a few feet away. He's put so much time and love into helping Aronek trust the other children and begin to make friendships, play with them like a normal child. Aronek has even stopped the spectacular cursing.

And he has become especially devoted to his big brother Abrasha.

So why this sudden stealing?

'Do you have nothing to say in your defence? No explanation for why you ate Halinka's chocolate?'

'I didn't eat it.' Aronek scowls back.

'So where is it?'

'How should I know? I sold it.'

Another outraged gasp.

'And are you sorry about it?'

Aronek shakes his head, eyes still on his boots.

'So where is the money?

'Gone.'

'Gone where? What did you buy with it?'

'That's my business.'

'Do you have nothing to say in your defence?' Chaya looks troubled. 'Stealing is a serious offence. If you have three serious offences, you can be asked to leave the home.'

'I didn't ask to come here in the first place. I can go any time.'

A sigh from Korczak again. Aronek does come and go, although he's too young to be out on the streets at barely nine. A few days ago the child went missing for a whole day. What has he been up to? There are some children who have been so badly affected by the neglect and harshness of the streets that they never manage to recover. It's rare, and its heart-breaking, but sometimes it happens.

Szymonek is standing. 'Chaya, I think Aronek might have taken something else?'

'Are you sure, Szymonek?'

'He opened Abrasha's drawer this morning. Very fast, then shut it again. Maybe he took something else.'

Aronek's face is bright red. He stares at the floor as if it has just insulted him. Arms locked.

The court confers. 'This court thinks Pan Doctor and Abrasha should go down and look in the drawer.'

The cupboard is on the floor below. It's a while before they hear footsteps coming back up the stairs. Abrasha bursts in holding up a small square envelope, a big grin.

'It's a new string for my violin. The one I couldn't replace when it snapped. Did you put it there, Aronek?'

Aronek looks caught out, guilty, accused of being soft and girlish. And it proves he was the thief, sold the chocolate to buy the string.

And where did he manage to find the string when Misha has already scoured the ghetto for one? That explains where Aronek went last week. He made a trip over the wall to buy it.

He shrugs. 'So?'

The court confers excitedly. Aronek glares at them. Finally they have a verdict.

Chaya reads it out. 'This court declares that since it was for a kind reason, and since Aronek has not been here very long and he probably did not know that he could have talked to Pan Doctor about how to get the string in an honest way, then this court will issue a warning this time, and order Aronek to replace Halinka's chocolate when he can one day in the future.'

Abrasha hardly hears. He's run to fetch his violin and is already tightening the peg, listening to the note the new string plays, plucking and tuning until the string thrums in harmony with the others. He takes out his bow and, eyes closed, he begins the first notes of 'Night in a Forest', and for a brief second his eyes open and rest on Aronek with a soft thankfulness. As the music threads through the room and the children are carried away to a still night among the tall pines, Aronek's arms unfold, the anger in his face unties – a child's face again. A boy with short hair and big ears, lost and hopeful.

CHAPTER EIGHTEEN

WARSAW, SEPTEMBER 1941

Back at their room on Leszno Street, Sophia finds a note but no Misha. He's doing an extra night duty at the orphanage.

She sits down on the bed with a thump, disappointed almost to tears. Of course she wants him to help with the boys at the home – it's essential to all they believe in – but she hates him being away. When he is there, she and Misha have to speak in whispers, every creak and moan from the other couples audible.

Then there's the rent on this terrible little room, money they need to use for food, for the family, for the children. And Sophia worries more and more about her parents. It gets harder each day to leave them. They seem to have gone into collapse, distant from reality. An accident with the stove has left Sophia's mother with a burned arm. She worries about Marianek.

She knows what she needs to do. She should move in with her parents and help them care for the little boy. But there simply isn't room for another couple in the tiny flat at Ogrodowa Street. It's unthinkable.

No, she can't bear to go back to being apart.

And she knows that sooner or later, they will have no alternative.

She lies in the dark in their cramped little space and wonders how to begin to talk to Misha about them living separately.

Tears run down the sides of her face as she thinks of saying the words.

The following afternoon Misha comes to eat with them at the flat in Ogrodowa, potatoes with a little margarine and a small portion of herring.

Lutek's there too, his little son on his lap. Lutek has brought potatoes but only a few. He doesn't look well, hasn't had any work for a while. He's sold his winter coat, he says. He'll get another when it turns cold.

As Sophia and Misha walk back to the flat on Leszno in the late sunshine, Misha looks across at her with concern.

'You've been very quiet this evening. What is it?'

'Why don't we pretend the war never happened, just for a few minutes? We're walking along the river, and we're going to stop and buy ice cream, or perhaps we'll go to the café in the park again, the one with the little dance floor under the trees. The new songs will be playing.'

They walk on in silence, past the same desperate beggars and street hawkers, the same stuffy air and filthy pavements.

It's not until they get back to their apartment block that Sophia finally stops under the archway and turns to Misha.

'Darling, we've tried and we've tried but it's impossible. We can't afford this room any more, not when food is so expensive.' She pauses, not wanting to talk about the shadow of hunger that has settled on their stomachs. 'And I need to be with my parents to help look after Marianek. I know what it means. There won't be room in the flat for both of us, but you're staying over at the home so much now. And we can still see each other every day.'

Misha closes his eyes and holds her gently against his chest. 'I know. I was thinking about it too. I should go back and stay with Korczak. They desperately need more help there.'

In an apartment above someone is playing music on a gramophone, an old Warsaw dance tune. She rests her forehead against the warm place in the crook of his neck. She can smell the comforting odour of his skin, a little goaty with no chance to shower. Her hair's the same, no doubt. They listen to the music for a while. She feels as though she's breaking apart.

'I'm not sure I can bear it, Misha, not to be with you every day.'

He brushes his cheek against her hair. 'It will only be for a while, darling. Till all this ends. It's the right thing to do.'

They stand holding each other for a long time, Sophia's tears making a wet patch on his shirt. He rubs the back of his hand across his eyes, and she can feel him moving to take something out of his jacket.

He shows her a picture from his wallet. It's a photograph of them arm in arm on the steps of the wooden dacha at the last summer camp at Little Rose.

Sophia stares into the picture. There they are, smiling like people who know it will always be summer and the future theirs, white clothes dazzling in the full sun. Sophia is still a teenager with plump, rounded cheeks. She's standing one step up so she is level with Misha. He's holding her arm as though he's won a prize. Two years ago.

An older Misha with hollows around his eyes now takes out his ink pen and carefully writes on the back: 'Darling Sophia, let us believe that we will be together again one day soon, and as happy as we were that day at Little Rose.'

They don't sleep all night, holding each other, talking in whispers until the dawn arrives.

In the morning, Misha has to leave early, some urgent errand for Frydman. Later, he'll make the arrangements to move back in with the children at the orphanage.

Sophia needs to pack up their few things ready to move in at Ogrodowa, a matter of moments, but she sits on the bed looking at the young couple in the picture confidently linking arms in the sunshine. Her eyes prickle with tears, as if the sunlight in the picture is too bright to bear.

Time in the ghetto is going backwards, unmarrying them.

CHAPTER NINETEEN

WARSAW, SEPTEMBER 1941

P an Doctor, can you do my laces up?' Szymonek, the youngest in the home, is standing in front of Korczak with his boot flapping open.

'I can do better, my son. I can teach you how to do your own laces. It's never too soon to learn how to do things for yourself.' He puts down the hessian bag. 'This goes over there. Now you try. Again. You have it. Well done.'

Szymonek goes away proudly looking at his feet.

Stefa has asked if Korczak can get something with oil in it today. She might as well ask for a few packets of gold. It's possible he can get a little sausage, however. He sets off to see if the sausage promised in the Judenrat note has come in at the shop.

The woman behind the counter is yelling at a man. 'So the lard's a bit off. If you don't like it, then why don't you leave? I've got plenty of other customers waiting.'

'Madam, what sort of shop is this?' the man replies. He's thin and studious, wearing an old coat. 'You'd cheat a customer out of his money?'

She waves the ghetto note in her hand as though it's something distasteful and sighs with her whole body. 'He thinks it's a shop. This is not a shop, and you are not a customer. I don't sell anything, and you don't pay me since these scraps of paper they call money in here are worthless. Why would I cheat you when I never make a profit?'

When Korczak reaches the head of the queue, he watches his small section of sausage being weighed out.

'It's so expensive, are you sure it's not made of human flesh?' he jokes.

She looks at him flatly. 'How should I know? I wasn't there when it was made.' All humour leached away.

He stows the stub of salami in his canvas sack and heads for the Jewish Council building to see the head, his old friend Adam Czerniakow.

Korczak climbs the stairs to Czerniakow's office to deliver an invitation to the home's Yom Kippur celebration. Czerniakow's fleshy face is haggard, a man being slowly crushed by the responsibility of his postion as intermediary between the ghetto and the Gestapo.

'Still no armband then,' says Czerniakow, not raising his eyes from the ledger he's reading. He takes the glasses from his long nose and rubs his heavy jowls. Statesmanlike, always in an immaculate suit, Czerniakow never smiles. Behind his glasses, however, his tired eyes are kind and humorous.

Korczak sinks into the chair opposite and stretches out his old boots. His fingers tap on the armrests, still showing the faint nicotine stains of the beloved cigarettes he used to smoke. No question of wasting money on smokes in here, but his fingers still search for the comfort of those little paper sticks.

'I don't understand. Why is it that everyone here hurries off when they see me coming along the corridor these days?'

'What can you expect, Korczak? You're breaking their hearts. Everyone dreads seeing you. Whatever we give you, it's never enough. No wonder they run off.'

'Is it so much, a couple of sacks of potatoes, for my children? And I'm not always asking for something. In fact, the reason I dropped in is to give you something. This.' He places an invitation for a concert at the home in front of Czerniakow.

'Thank you. You know, I still think about your play at the Athenaeum, nearly ten years ago, the insane general stomping around the stage who wanted to burn everything, burn books, burn Jews. The critics panned it for being too gloomy, and now it seems prophetic.'

'It was all set out in Hitler's little book if people cared to read it. But Hitler is not the German people, remember. When the German people realize what is being done in their name, they will soon put a stop to it.'

'You may be right. At least I have some good news, some real cause for hope for the ghetto. We've been given permission to open schools in here at last. Six of them.'

Korczak looks over the announcement from Bruhl Palace and hands it back. He doesn't look impressed. As Czerniakow knows, he's been running a school in the home under the guise of recreation activities, diaries, lectures, reading library, all along – activities that will pass a Nazi inspection to check that no Jewish minds are being educated.

'Don't you see? If we have formal permission to educate our children now, then it means the Nazis must see a future for the ghetto.' Czerniakow takes off his glasses to clean them with his neat square of handkerchief and fixes Korczak with his haunted eyes. 'I know that people make up songs about me, about my fat belly, how I work with the Germans, but someone has to try and get the best deal we can for our people in here.'

'My friend, if you hadn't accepted the post, they would have simply shot you and gone on to someone else, someone who didn't care about the fate of the people in here, perhaps.'

'I try. I try to demand better conditions. Mostly I fail, but all I can do is keep trying.'

He walks over to the bureau and folds a small square of paper from a stack, adds a dose of headache powder and tips it into his mouth, takes a sip from a glass of water. Czerniakow has a constant migraine.

'I'll be frank with you, Korczak. I'm not going to pretend that I believe everyone in this prison will survive the war. The death toll from hunger and disease in some of the refugee shelters is unthinkable. Unthinkable. Yesterday I left the doctor with a packet of headache powder and a woman snatched it out of my hand, ate the lot in front of me, desperate for food, starving.' Czerniakow looks up with hollow eyes. 'But so long as we can take care of all our children, so long as we can protect our little ones, then we still have hope as a people. And so long as we have hope, then I'm willing to keep on going to the Bruhl Palace day in, day out, and try and get some concessions for the ghetto, anything to help our people come through this.

'And listen, I'm going to write a chit for potatoes. Tell them downstairs to let you have two sacks.'

'Thank you. Thank you, my friend. If you could possibly make it three . . .'

CHAPTER TWENTY

WARSAW, OCTOBER 1941

Misha buries his chin further into his muffler, turns up his collar. The Wola backstreet behind the two grey factories is deserted but he keeps watch in both directions. Standing here on the street corner in Aryan Warsaw, he feels unreal; his skin prickles as if he has stepped down into a forbidden underworld, a ghost out of his time. The gloomy afternoon light is seeded with droplets of fog rendering the buildings indistinct and ghostly. For people who live in the ghetto, Warsaw has become nothing but a legend now, a dream.

If he's caught, he'll never return home.

From here he can see Tadeusz and Jadwiga, hurriedly loading sacks of kasha onto the cart that's waiting just inside the warehouse gate. The horse's hooves scrape and clop, the beast made nervous by the tense atmosphere. If Misha sees anyone coming, he's to remove his cap and the brothers will immediately pull down the canvas cover over the buckwheat and melt away inside the warehouse.

Inside, there's the sound of the false bottom being hammered down, not too well since it will all have to come up again soon. Tadeusz comes out and hands Misha an apple. Short and round-faced, Tadeusz seems little more than a boy. In spite of the cold his face sweats with the effort of loading sacks.

'Some time we should go for a beer.'

'We should.' Misha gives him a wry smile.

The cart covered over with refuse, Misha climbs up behind the horse and clicks to it to move forward, just another Polish workman ambling home through the streets.

As they approach the ghetto gate, Misha's stomach knots. He has enough cash to pay the bribes and he can see that the right guard is there on duty as usual but his palms sweat and slip on the reins as the German starts walking over towards him, continuing a conversation over his shoulder with the other German next to the guardhouse. They are laughing about the fat goose dangling from his belt.

He checks Misha's papers absently, removes the notes inside and pockets them.

Misha clicks to the horse and they begin to move.

His heart lurches. Just inside the gate, seated on a stool and having his boots shone, is another German guard, Frankenstein, short and apelike, face hewn from rough pieces of wood, eyes glassy as a man without a heart. He's vowed to shoot a Jew a day, can't eat breakfast until he's murdered one. He's famous in the ghetto for his savage beatings of any smuggler children he catches and for killing people at random, through windows, on street corners. Today he's sated, dozing with legs apart on the stool as the cart rumbles in and past him.

But Misha's not clear yet. He has to stop a second time. The Polish policeman in his navy uniform holds up his hand, checks the papers, and looks over the refuse bound for Gesia cemetery. He hands the papers back, keeping the newly added banknotes, and waves the cart on.

A few coins to the Jewish policeman and he's almost through, but the Jewish policeman keeps hold of the horse's reins, beckons Misha to bend closer.

'You tell your Korczak now. Looks like he's going to have to move.'

'What do you mean?'

'They're shrinking the ghetto. Thousands are going to be thrown out on the street any day now. He'll need to get a move on to find somewhere decent.'

Misha lets the heavy hessian sack slide onto the table in the kitchen but there are no smiles from Stefa today. She looks lost and worn down, examining a copy of the *Jewish Gazette*.

'Oh, Misha. Have you seen this? It's utter madness. They're going to make us move again. Where?'

Misha reads the notice. All properties bordering the Aryan side are to be excluded from the ghetto. As he studies the new map it dawns on him what the Germans are doing. There will be no more buildings straddling the wall, just a clear strip of cobbled road around the ghetto blocks for the guards to patrol with ease, to shoot any tentative smugglers at their leisure. No more sacks of flour passed through attics and basements. It's going to make it harder than ever for people to bring in food.

The ghetto is being squeezed in a noose of hunger.

'And only days to find somewhere,' Stefa continues. 'He's gone out already to make enquiries. I don't know how he'll cope. He's not well as it is, hardly sleeps at night writing his diary, up all day tramping the streets and now this. Oh, there. There he is.'

A wan-faced Korczak, skin lined with fatigue, comes in and sinks onto the stool by the stove, his coat and muffler still on.

'The officials at the Jewish Council say they can do nothing. It seems we must move again.'

'But can they tell us where?'

'No. But we do have other friends who can help us, people with influence.'

'You haven't been to see that gangster Gancwajch? He's always circling, wanting you to take his money and help whitewash his reputation. The ghetto's worst collaborator.'

'Stefa. Please. No, our saviour is a little angel in an apron. Your sister-in-law, Misha – Krystyna. But she says we must go and see the place now.'

It sounds hopeful, an empty businessmen's club on Sienna Street, one of Warsaw's best addresses before the war. Here, there are still people with money left. They pass a woman in a small hat walking her dog, ignoring the new barbed-wire fence that has been rolled out down the middle of the road.

The club is on the top two floors of a grand apartment block. Krystyna is in Tatiana Epstein's café on the floor below. She unties her apron and fetches the key from the board at the back.

'We've been telling everyone it's taken,' says Tatiana, 'but we can only hold them off for so long.'

The street entrance to the businessmen's club is impressive, double doors, a balcony above the portico but inside . . . oh, dear. So run down and grubby. The first floor has a raised stage with old scenery in scuffed oil paint propped up at the back.

'Not ideal for children,' said Stefa, looking at the empty room, the dust-ingrained boards. 'Perhaps the top floor will be better.'

On the floor above they walk through a mirrored ballroom with marble pillars. The tall windows let in a brisk draught through the damaged panes.

'An architect's school used it in the summer, but once it got cold they went elsewhere,' Krystyna says.

'I'm not surprised. It's going to be impossible to heat in winter,' says Stefa as they walk around gloomily.

'Perhaps the older boys could sleep up here when it gets warmer.' Korczak's making the best of it, but anxiety grips his heart. What he sees is the kind of large unsuitable building, a synagogue, a redundant factory, used to house refugees in squalor – where you return a few weeks or days later to find that hunger and typhus have emptied the hastily constructed plank beds.

No. It's not going to be like that. This is Stefa walking by his side. They'll make it a home for the children, a good home.

He sits down on a dusty chair and taps the parquet floor. 'Just needs a scrub.'

'But one grimy lavatory for two hundred children and staff.'

'So we'll buy buckets, empty them each morning.'

'The first thing we must do is give everything a good clean,' says Stefa.

Krystyna returns with brooms and mop from the café downstairs.

Korczak takes off his coat and jacket and rolls up his sleeves, holds out his hands.

'Oh, no, Pan Doctor. Let me,' says Krystyna.

'It's what every noble thought or idea comes to in the end – how many sweeps of the broom did you give, how many potatoes did you peel?'

'You,' Stefa tells him, 'will only get in the way. Go down to Tatiana's and see about the lease. And drink something hot.'

He sets off but suddenly turns and comes back, takes Stefa's hands in his, says unsteadily, 'We'll manage, Stefa, dear, won't we?'

'We'll manage,' she tells him. 'We always do.'

CHAPTER TWENTY-ONE

WARSAW, DECEMBER 1941

A dim December afternoon in the large hall in Sienna Street. The children gather round as Halinka lights the last candle in the menorah. The small flames grow, chasing away the encroaching gloom at the edges of the high ceilings.

'See how even a small candle is stronger than the darkness,' Korczak tells the children. 'Just as we must never stop believing that every act of kindness is stronger than the dark.'

Sammy plays the first line of a Hanukkah song and the children begin to sing softly. Standing at the back with Misha, Sophia slips her hand into his. Sara is holding tight to her other hand, resting her head against Sophia's arm as she gazes across at the candles.

Korczak has always loved this season. The rhythm of the year has always been first the lighting of the candles for Hanukkah in the Jewish home and then candles on the Christmas tree in the Polish home. The Polish children would come to the Hanukkah play. The Jewish children would sing with them around a Christmas tree. Don't the children have a right to be part of each other's Warsaw – to know and respect each other's traditions?

Before the war there would be special food for the Festival of Lights, fried potato cakes, fried doughnuts with jam, but it's simply not possible this year, so little is coming into the ghetto now. It's been all they can do to get the children safely installed in their new home and fed each day.

They are coping well enough, mostly. At night the room is packed with rows of beds and the shapes of sleeping children under the white duvets, barely enough space to walk between the rows. Screens run down the middle of the room dividing the boys' and the girls' sides, giving the place the air of a hospital ward at night. The stage now serves as a dining room. The painted scenery at the back, a forest and a cottage under a moonlit sky, add to the unreal, impermanent air of the place, although the children like the feeling of living in a play. And perhaps they are living out a scripted drama: written by Nietzsche and produced by Hitler.

By day the beds are pushed back; a corner for reading, a handicrafts club, a sewing circle and the puppet workshop. The choir and drama club, the children's court and the newspaper all carry on as before.

But it's not as before.

It's been weeks since he's seen a Polish face. Now that there's a strict death penalty for leaving the ghetto, reprisals for Poles trying to enter without a permit, the ghetto has become even more isolated. Even children caught on the Aryan side are no longer sent to prison but coldly gunned down on the spot. The steady stream of old Polish friends coming to spend the afternoon in the home has entirely stopped.

Maryna and some of the Polish teachers such as Ida and Newerly have sent what they can for Hanukkah, smuggled in by Misha, but things are hard on the Aryan side too now.

The song is finished. The children stand and watch the candles. Korczak looks round at their faces, too thin and serious for children.

From over the wall, faint sounds of a passing car. Stefa claps her hands softly and the children take their places at the tables for supper, bowls of boiled buckwheat and slices of black bread.

'So there's a new edict,' she says to Korczak as they watch the children eating. 'The Germans want us to hand over every bit of fur, on pain of death. Every coat, every boot lining.'

'But this is good news, Stefa.'

'He calls this good news. I have to pull the collar off my coat and he calls that good news. In this cold.'

'Don't you see? It means things aren't going so well for the Führer if he needs to steal the ladies' fur collars. The Russian winter did for Napoleon and it will do for Hitler too, you mark my words.'

CHAPTER TWENTY-TWO

WARSAW, JANUARY 1942

They can take absolutely no more children. It's agreed.

This time it's Stefa who's relented, a friend of a friend's child. The address Stefa has given Korczak is for one of the refugee shelters on Nalewki Street, a disused workshop with rows of hastily thrown-up rough wooden platforms covered in straw to serve as beds, litter scattered around them.

Of all the misery in the ghetto, the refugee shelters are the most wretched places. People arrive on trains from the surrounding villages and towns, robbed and exhausted, nothing to cook with and no tools to carry on their trades. They are lodged in synagogues, in churches or workshops, and very quickly, hunger and typhus begin to decimate the population. The building committees of various apartment blocks do their best to raise funds, Korczak has held concerts in the home in aid of the refugees, but such efforts are a drop in a bucket compared to the need.

Korczak looks around, searching for the woman. A stove made from an iron barrel burns in the middle of the room, giving off an acrid smell but little heat. It's clear from the half-empty sleeping platforms that disease and cold have already begun to do their work here.

He finds the mother greasy with fever, her skin tinged with blue. Her child, a boy of nine, is busy trying to warm water on a trivet over a fire of kindling on the concrete floor by her bed.

If the boy is going to survive, then he needs to leave now, before he too succumbs to the fever.

When the woman sees Korczak her face relaxes into a look of peace. 'My boy will be all right now. Thank you, Doctor. Zygmus, I want you to go with Pan Doctor.'

'No. No.' His face says how could she think he would leave her?

She moans, puts her hand on his hair. She's close to death but won't let herself be released while the child needs her. And the boy's determined he won't leave her while she needs him.

He won't lie to the boy. He won't pretend that his mother will not pass away if he goes. 'But she will die peacefully, Zygmus, if she knows that you are well cared for. Can you be very brave and do something very difficult but beautiful for your mother?'

'Go with Pan Doctor, my Zygmus. It's time.'

The woman's eyes follow them as they leave, burning like the last flames of a fire.

One child. One child saved.

On the way back to the orphanage he passes scores more, hungry, emaciated, dying. All night he listens to the whimpers out in the street, children crying for a little bread.

First thing in the morning, Korczak bursts in at the Jewish Council offices. He has a plan. A shelter. If they could just let him have a building, anywhere where the children close to death can die with someone to care for them, a little soup to save those that can still be saved. No child should die alone. It doesn't have to cost much, a disused shop perhaps. He can put the children on the shelves for beds.

'I'm sorry, Dr Korczak.' They lead him out of the building. 'We are doing what we can. There is nothing more we can do.'

He marches back to the home. He won't give up. He'll find a way to help at least some of these children.

A few days later, walking around the Dzielna Street children's refuge, a thousand babies and children dying of hunger and neglect, their food stolen by the staff, he decides enough is enough. He storms back to the Jewish Council and demands that the directorship of Dzielna be given to him. He writes letters in the ghetto paper exposing the scandal – since he's such a big rogue himself, annoys everyone he meets, he'll fit right in with the staff there. He's perfect to run the shelter. A few weeks later, Czerniakow gives him the Dzielna shelter to run.

'A thousand more children!' Stefa says, almost in tears, not sure if she's more cross or proud. 'You're too old to do this. How?'

He shrugs. 'I'll go to war with the staff there,' he tells her. 'Make sure they care for the children properly. You know as well as I do, Stefa, a beautiful life is always a difficult life.'

'Yes, yes. If you don't kill yourself first.'

Her words are cross, her eyes worried, but there's only ever love in Stefa. From the day he met her, a plain nineteen-year-old with a beautiful smile, dedicated to the children, there's always been Stefa.

In the sickroom where he watches over the children Korczak is sitting at his father's old desk. Two in the morning. The carbide lamp fizzes with a sharp, sulfurous smell, casting an uncertain circle of light. He has a pencil in his hand, his diary waits. He wants to write it all down, bear witness to what's happening in here, but he's exhausted by another day spent trudging from building to building with his canvas sack, asking for donations for the children. How easy it would be to give in to the pain in his chest, the anger at what he sees each day – to give in to despair.

He closes his eyes, turns his palms upwards, and lets the kindness of the world come to him, soak through his soul. He's walking in the fields around Little Rose, a summer's day, a concert of crickets. His heartbeat slows. The pain in his chest eases. Suffused with calm, he opens his eyes, blessed enough to bless the world again.

CHAPTER TWENTY-THREE

WARSAW, FEBRUARY 1942

Sophia comes in from the kitchen, wearing her dusky pink dress. Misha applauds as she gives a small twirl, but fear pinches his heart. It's the dress she wore on their wedding day, but when did her apple-like cheeks fade away to reveal the plane of her bones beneath?

She bends down to look in the small mirror on the cloth-covered chest and pins up a stray strand of hair.

'So that's the best I can do.'

'You look beautiful.' He takes her hand and she lets it rest there almost shyly. Now they're so often apart, time together has become both precious and unsettling.

Mr Rozental is back from the street, his spare trousers still folded over his shoulder.

'My, you look lovely. Is something happening?'

'Misha's taking me out to the Sztuka café.'

'Ah, the Sztuka. So who's playing? We might be short of food in here, but we're not short of top-class musicians.' He pulls the brown suit trousers from his shoulder and lets them fall on the table, his expression despondent. 'Hours in the Gesia market but even the smugglers who come in to buy old clothes to sell on the Aryan side turned their noses up at these today. And look, plenty of wear left in them. Almost good as new.'

'They don't want to sit here talking about your old trousers.' Mrs Rozental folds them away. She puts an arm around Sophia and begins to turn her towards the door. 'You young people should go, make the most of your afternoon.'

Sophia pulls on a cardigan and coat, winds a scarf around her neck.

'And Mother, remember, there's a little of the butter left for Marianek to go with the potatoes and—'

'Stop, stop. For once, don't think about anything but each other for a few hours. Goodness knows you deserve it. The rest of us will all be here when you get back.'

The Sztuka Arts Café on Leszno Street keeps its shutters permanently closed against the ghetto streets. Sophia and Misha pass beneath the clock that hangs over the doorway and enter a magical space, a bubble of time from before the war. The room is packed with young people crowded around small tables. Everyone is wearing the best clothes they can muster, all the mends and substitutions hidden by the lamplight that spreads a smoky atmosphere of glamour over the room. On the raised podium, a girl in a black lace dress is singing in front of a backdrop that's painted with a Chagall scene of floating girls dancing among stars and flowers. The singer's arms rise and fall with the melody, as if she's joining in with them.

The only jarring note is the white band on the arm of the violinist beside her.

Misha manages to find two empty rattan chairs at one of the little circular tables. Sophia takes off her coat and cardigan and checks her hair. The menu is shockingly expensive, and short. A small beer for Misha. When it arrives, he keeps his hand on the glass, the return of a much-missed friend. For Sophia, a coffee. She closes her eyes and first savours the smell, then slowly takes little sips. Almost real coffee. It will need to last all afternoon.

One thing Sophia is sure of, she won't be able to enjoy the music in the way she once did. After these long months in the ghetto, she's become aware of a slow numbing of emotions. She wonders if she will ever be able to feel anything deeply again.

Pola Braun enters, her hair swept up, a green satin gown. She sits down at the baby grand to play a wistful tune with her graceful hands. She begins to sing, calling for the mountain winds of faraway Zakopane to reach into the ghetto, her clear alto undulating like a soft breeze. The music hits Sophia like a sideways blow, catching her off guard. For a moment she's left the ghetto, standing on the mountainside, the pure, cold winds stroking her face. Sudden, hot tears stream down her face and all the things her heart has forbidden her come flooding back in a rush.

She feels ashamed, dips her head, and hides behind her hand. It's bad manners to break down when everyone's trying to have a moment of happiness.

It's a while before she dares look around the room. Misha's face is broken with emotion, almost everyone else in the room openly crying. She moves her chair a little closer to lean in against his side and he wraps his arm around her shoulders in reply. There's so much they don't have in here, so much lost or threatened inside the terrible prison of the ghetto, but if they have each other, if they have love, then they have the victory over anything the Nazis believe or try to do to them.

After Pola leaves there's a lull. The room rustles before the most anticipated act of the evening comes on, Wladyslaw Szlengal, poet and comedian. Short and well built, wearing round American spectacles with thick tortoiseshell frames, he has the room in stitches, nothing off limits to his mordant black humour. Sophia and Misha exchange wry glances as he delivers jokes about two couples trying to share one room.

Then Szlengal takes out a poem. 'For those who have loved and lost Warsaw. "The Smuggler".

And I, when night falls . . .
I come to the window in the dark
And gaze, gaze with hunger in my eyes
And I steal extinguished Warsaw.
I steal the silhouette of the town hall.
At my feet lies Theatre Square.
The moon on his watch
Turns a blind eye
to this sentimental smuggling.
Warsaw, answer me.
I am waiting.'

Silence follows, then the rupture of applause. Sophia is startled by a familiar voice close to her ear.

'May I?' A gamine girl with a frizz of strawberry-blonde hair and freckles indicates the spare chair.

'Tosia!' cries Sophia. 'It's been so long. Misha, you remember, Tosia and I met as students? But I didn't know you were here in the ghetto.'

'I'm not here very often.' She leans forward, speaks almost in a whisper. 'I travel between youth movements in different towns, finding out what's happening in other places.'

'But isn't that terribly dangerous?' Everyone knows what happens to Jews outside the ghetto now, instant death or torture if the Germans think there's information to be gained.

Tosia shrugs. 'We have a network of places we can stay, our ways of getting out of the ghetto. And it's important. We know so little of what's really going on, shut up in here.' She shakes her head and gives a defiant smile. 'Anyway, turns out I've got what you call good looks these days. If you've got fair hair you can ride the trains without too much difficulty.'

Misha leans forward. 'So what is the news out there? Tosia, have you got any news from Pinsk? I've heard nothing from my family since the Germans invaded Russia.'

'Not about Pinsk specifically – I'm sorry – but you should know that there are a lot of bad reports from the east. We think the ghetto in Vilna has been completely cleared.'

'Isn't that just a rumour? But where have they taken them?'

Tosia doesn't reply for a beat. Her voice barely audible. 'Shot in Ponary Forest. Almost the whole Jewish population of Vilna.'

Sophia gasps. 'But there's almost as many Jews in Vilna as in Warsaw. No, I can't believe that.'

'No one can, but it's been verified by witnesses.'

'Tosia, that just isn't possible.'

There's a burst of laughter from a table by the bar. Two men in new suits are eating caviar with their overdressed girlfriends. Tosia looks at them in disgust. There's always good money to be made in the ghetto if you work alongside the Gestapo.

Tosia leans closer. 'Listen, I have something to ask you. Are you going to Korczak's lecture at the Dror commune?'

'Of course.'

'Then I'll see you there.'

Outside, the cold pinches their faces, their breath fogs in the early gloom. The ghetto takes them back in. Nothing has changed. They walk home in silence, curfew not far away.

'Do you think Tosia could be right?' asks Sophia.

'I just don't know. A new rumour every day. No one knows what to believe. I'll ask Yitzhak at the lecture. His family are from Vilna. He must have heard something.'

They walk on in silence, the huddled shapes of homeless people still there along the walls of the buildings.

Up in the Ogrodowa Street flat, the Rozentals have gone to bed early, Marianek sleeping in their room tonight. A note says Krystyna is staying over at Tatiana's flat.

A lamp burns on the table. There are two small glasses and a remnant of plum vodka in the bottom of a bottle. There's no fire in the stove, but tonight, the room and the falling dusk belong only to them. Misha takes Sophia's face in his hands and covers every inch in gentle and hungry kisses. She nuzzles into the base of his neck, the place that feels like home, as their hands map out each other's skin once again.

There is still love in the ghetto. And if you have love then you have everything.

CHAPTER TWENTY-FOUR

WARSAW, MARCH 1942

I t's a bitterly cold day, a clear blue sky. Sophia hurries past the rust bricks and verdigris spire of St Augustine's and turns into the archway of a large apartment block at 34 Dzielna Street. She always tries to make Korczak's Monday lecture at the home but today it's being held at the Dror commune's building. It's just a few doors down from the terrible shelter where Korczak is still trying to improve the conditions of a thousand children. She glances over, wondering how the building can look so respectable and municipal when inside the staff are still trying to do all they can to steal the children's food.

In the Dzielna commune it's a different story. Here the young people run an illegal school under the guise of a soup kitchen, giving what they can to help feed the children and young teenagers.

The courtyard is busy with young people, talking ten to the dozen, peeling vegetables or hanging out washing. Until war broke out the commune was secretly preparing to begin a new life in Palestine, learning to run a small farm near Warsaw in readiness. Now all their skills are used to support the 300 teenagers and young adults who live in the apartments around the courtyard.

Sophia goes up to the large dining room on the upper floor. It's packed, students sitting on every surface, on the floor, on cupboards.

Misha's at the back of the room, talking with an equally tall young man who looks the very picture of a dashing Polish pilot with a lick of curly blond hair over his forehead, a blond moustache, and bright blue eyes. Yitzhak Zuckerman is in charge of education in the commune. Today, he and Misha are talking with grave expressions.

Sophia makes her way through the packed room towards them, wondering what they are discussing.

Misha turns as she joins them. 'Yitzhak says he's had bad news about his family in Vilna.'

Yitzhak's eyes are seared with pain.

'It's been confirmed. My family has been murdered, along with the rest of Vilna's Jews.'

Her hands fly to her mouth. 'I'm so sorry.'

'And Lublin's been cleared. Everyone disappeared on trains. We think Warsaw could be next.'

'But how can you know that for sure? There are so many rumours.'

'The Germans confiscated our farm but they still send us out as labour and the Pole in charge is a good man. He lets us get couriers out through the farm. So we're sure. And we've decided to be ready to fight back if they come for us.'

'So they're going to stop the education programme,' says Misha as he turns to her.

'But why?' says Sophia. 'Korczak says that the school you run here is the best in the ghetto.'

'We're beginning weapons training.'

'Weapons training? What do you mean? Have you spoken to the Jewish Council about this? What do they say?'

'They say we're just frightening everybody. Putting people at risk of German reprisals. They don't want to know. But we think the Nazis are planning to eliminate the entire ghetto here. All ghettos. Nothing less than the systematic destruction of the Jews. And we have decided that we won't go like sheep to the slaughter.'

Tosia slips in and joins them. Her frizzy blond hair is thicker than ever, her freckles across her tomboy's face pale against her paler skin. She looks enquiringly at Yitzhak.

'I've told them.'

'But weapons training. Have you got guns?' asks Misha.

'A pistol.'

'One pistol?'

'It's a beginning.'

Tosia turns to Sophia. 'We got it through the Polish Workers Association. They're short of weapons themselves so they were reluctant to pass more than one on. They want to know if it will be used well before they send any more, so we're asking everyone affiliated and checked by the Polish workers to do the initial training and I know you were when you joined the union at college. Will you come and learn to use it, Sophia?'

Sophia looks doubtful.

'Perhaps it would be good to know how,' Misha says. He already knows how to use a gun after many summers shooting game in the Pripyat marshes as a boy.

Sophia's mouth sets in a firm line. 'When?'

'Tomorrow at four.'

Tosia whispers an address for Nowolipie Street and slips away before the lecture begins.

At the front of the room, Korczak stands behind the kitchen table, polishes his glasses and then closes his red-rimmed eyes as he begins.

'I want to teach people how to understand and love this miraculous and creative state of "I do not know" when related to children – so full of life and dazzling surprises.'

Sophia writes fast, trying not to think about what Yitzhak and Tosia have said, making herself concentrate on the talk. It's a theme she knows well from the book that Misha gave her as a wedding present. Korczak's call to respect each child represents an oasis of hope and human values in the middle of a desert of dehumanisation and cruelty. And what better protest than to carefully carry on the flame to the next generation – no matter what the Nazis do to try and exclude a class of people from humanity?

But Yitzhak's news refuses to leave her. Can it really be possible the Nazis have a plan to eliminate all Jews in Poland?

CHAPTER TWENTY-FIVE

WARSAW, APRIL 1942

Should Sophia get involved in learning to shoot a pistol with all the risks it would entail?

She thinks of Krystyna. Her little sister has been leaving the ghetto on a regular basis as part of a smuggling ring, taking the train out of Warsaw to bring back Jews stranded in the eastern towns now suffering terrible pogroms under the Reich.

How can she not go?

The address Tosia has given Sophia is for a tall and run-down building on Nowolipie Street. The stairs to the upper floors are in a barely usable state, the banisters and side treads stripped for firewood. She follows the stone steps down to the cellar, and calls out into the gloom. A door opens. Tosia is waiting inside with a handful of other people in their teens and twenties who Sophia hasn't met before.

They learn guerrilla tactics, street fighting, how to make bombs from bottles and petrol. Over the next two weeks Sophia becomes very familiar with the weight of the cold, dense metal in her hand, the way it smells of oil and of the metallic tang of blood on a cut lip as she learns to shoot, strip down and reassemble the pistol.

But each time she leaves the cellar and walks back to Ogrodowa Street, the hour she has just spent seems like an overreaction. It's warm weather now, the lilacs shedding their scent from across the wall. Recently, the Nazis decrees have become milder, curfew put back till later.

Are Tosia and the others right in thinking that the Germans really plan to liquidate the ghetto?

Perhaps the Jewish Council are right. It's a mistake to stir up trouble. If they can hold on, stay alive, perhaps the best thing to do is simply keep your head down, try and make it through to the end of the war?

CHAPTER TWENTY-SIX

WARSAW,
APRIL 1942

It's Sammy Gogol's last night in the home. His aunt has decided to pay a bribe to leave the ghetto and take the tall teenager with her to hide away at an uncle's farm in the south.

'Don't you think Sammy will be safest here with the other children?' Korczak asks. 'Surely it's a risky journey.'

He doesn't state the obvious, the inescapably Jewish nose on Sammy's face. No chance if he's seen. The horrible consequences if he is caught.

'We'll travel by night,' Sammy's aunt says. 'I've got enough saved up to pay off one of the guards to help us get out and then we'll have to take our chance.'

Korczak's not happy but he doesn't argue with her. In a time of peace, it's always the best outcome for a child to have the shelter of an extended family's watchful eye after they leave the home. And he can see that the rumours blowing through the ghetto have unsettled the aunt. Her instinct is that it's time to head south like a homing pigeon. She's taking Sammy with her, mind made up.

'It's your decision,' he tells Sammy.

'I'll go with her,' Sammy says. 'Make sure she's safe.'

Up in the ballroom the boys have swept the hall and rolled out their lines of mattresses. Erwin listens gloomily to his friend Sammy playing his harmonica for the dormitory one last time before the boys go to sleep, *Shalom Aleichem*, peace be with you. The two boys have been in Korczak's home together since they joined at eight years old. Abrasha joins in quietly with his violin, Chaimek on his mandolin. The rest of the boys sit up in bed, entranced and wistful, thinking of Sammy making his way through the dark forests of Poland, wondering if he will be safer, happier, than in here.

When the music stops, Misha walks around the room, checking they are settled. It's easy for an argument to break out between two boys with frayed nerves. But tonight the night is almost warm with distant promises of summer. They lie awake soothed by the music.

Misha settles down in the screened-off area that serves as his room. Night is almost peaceful here at the furthest edge in the ghetto. The occasional tramp of a patrol but otherwise the streets are largely free of Germans who still clock off promptly at five like office workers and rush out of the ghetto to their nice clean apartments and the Bruhl Palace.

Misha lowers the flame on the carbide lamp, stretches out on his bed and begins a prayer for Sophia sleeping a mile away. So much fragile air between them. He sighs and reaches out his hand to his right, where she always prefers to lie beside him.

Three sharp shots. Misha sits up, heart hammering. The boys too sit up on their mattresses and pallets, terrified, silently listening for what might happen next. An exhalation of breath from Aronek who has been too close to guns many times in his short life.

No further sounds of gunfire.

'It's all right, boys. Settle down,' says Misha. Creaks and rustling sheets as the boys shuffle down, eyes wide awake into the darkness.

A second burst of gunfire, a little further away. And then another. And another. Through the rest of the night, rifles crack and sing in the darkness.

No one in the ghetto is sleeping; they're lying awake listening to the gunfire, wondering what it can mean. The Germans never come back to the ghetto after dark unless it's to carry out some terrible scheme.

As soon as it's light the next morning, Misha goes out into the deserted street. Tatiana Epstein is standing outside her shuttered café, her apron over her mouth. A few doors down, people are sluicing bloodstains from the pavement, sweeping the dark water towards the drain with long scrapes of a broom.

'Oh, Misha, the old man and his son at number thirty were shot, their bodies left on the cobbles like dogs. An old man and a boy, what have they ever done? I'm not opening the café today. No one's turned up for work. And tell Korczak that he should stay at home today too.'

'I'll tell him.' He turns to go but Tatiana calls him back. 'You don't think the shooting last night means it's true, that it's the beginning of the Warsaw ghetto being liquidated like Lublin? A man came into the café from Lublin, looked like death. He said he managed to escape just before everyone there was sent away to the east to some unknown place. I don't know what to believe any more. A new story going round the ghetto every day, and each one worse than the last.'

Needing to know if Sophia is safe, Misha decides to risk it and make his way to her apartment on Ogrodowa Street. A sinister air of fear hangs over the ghetto, shutters closed, the streets deserted. No one else on the wooden footbridge over Chlodna Street. But outside the courthouse on Leszno Street a handful of people are reading a notice plastered up by the Nazis. Misha joins them and scans the black ink message.

The executions were necessary to cleanse the ghetto of undesirables. Loyal people have nothing to fear. Everyone is to open their shops again and go about their business.

By the time he reaches Sophia's apartment people are appearing on the streets again. The announcement has begun to circulate through the ghetto, reassuring people.

As he turns into Ogrodowa Street, he recognizes a boy from the Dror commune. Misha runs to catch up with him and ask if Yitzhak has heard anything.

The boy's face is white. 'Yitzhak? Haven't you heard? They came for him and his wife Zivia last night. Fortunately he'd already had a tip-off that he was going to get a visit, so he and Zivia had gone to hide at a friend's place. But the guards had a list, numbers to fill. They took a boy and his father from the flat below in their place. Just to fill up their numbers. And tell Sophia, training is cancelled.'

Sammy leaves a couple of days later. After he's gone, it's not just the children who are unsettled.

'Do you think we're doing the right thing?' Stefa asks. 'Should we split up the children and try and send them outside? There's the nice Polish nurse, Irene, who's smuggled children out in bags and toolboxes, coffins even.'

Korczak stares at her, unable to countenance shutting a terrified child up in a coffin, in the dark, alone. 'No, we keep them together. They are safest here with us until the war is over. It won't be the first time we've kept our children safe through a German occupation.'

Sophia waits to hear from her cell leader. After this, she feels more committed than ever to learning how to fight back. But no message comes.

Korczak carries on with his Monday lectures as usual at the home, although there are fewer people attending. She's surprised to see Yitzhak at the back.

Misha is listening as he talks, his face grave.

He turns as she joins them.

'It's bad news. This morning two of the cell leaders were arrested by the Gestapo,' Yitzhak tells her. 'They'll be tortured for the names of other people. I came to warn you.'

Sophia gasps. 'Those poor men.' The Gestapo brutality is well known.

'So you'd best be careful.' Yitzhak leaves. He has others to tell.

Misha won't leave her. He walks back with her to Ogrodowa Street and sleeps on a chair by the girls' bed all night. In spite of the fear that ends only when they sleep, washes in the moment they wake, they have never felt closer, blessed by each other's presence, never more in love. Krystyna wakes very early and slips out.

He slides in next to Sophia and wraps his arms tight around her as she sleeps.

When a knock comes at the door they freeze. It's the boy from the Dror commune. They've had word that both men have been tortured to death but not one name has passed their lips.

The danger of further arrests is passed, but now any hope of organizing resistance has been smashed.

And with all underground newspapers wiped out in the night of slaughter, from now on, the half a million people trapped inside the ghetto will know only what the Nazis want them to know.

The weeks pass. The first signs of spring returning, a change in the air. Faint scents of lilac from over the wall. A blue sky and a clean sun.

None of the black rumours about some unknown event falling on the ghetto have come true. With Russia and the US in the war, the UK bombing German cities, everyone knows that it's only a matter of time before the Germans are defeated and the war is over. The feeling in the ghetto is that so long as they hold on, they will come through the war. And as for the rumours about Warsaw being liquidated like Lublin, the terrible murders reported from survivors, such a thing could never happen in Warsaw, in such a large population. Unthinkable.

CHAPTER TWENTY-SEVEN

WARSAW, MAY 1942

On Korczak's suggestion, the children are writing a letter. A few days ago, crossing Grzybowski Square in the stifling heat, Korczak glimpsed the green of a tiny garden beyond the arched portico adjoining the Catholic church. Roses hung from a trellis. It was only a block away from the children's home. It wouldn't be too risky to take a few children at a time to play there, if they were allowed. He knew the priest. Father Godlewski had been a rabid anti-Semite before the war, but had changed his tune after witnessing first-hand the suffering of his congregation of Jewish converts to Christianity, still Jews in the eyes of the Nazis. He's now known for doing everything he can to help the Jews around him in the ghetto.

In the home, a group of children sit round one of the oilcloth-covered tables on the stage. Halinka and Abrasha, Sami, Erwin and Aronek pore over the empty piece of paper. What they write will be very important. It could make all the difference to whether the priest will let them play in the tiny garden next to the church.

'Say we long for some air and some greenery,' says Halinka to Abrasha, the scribe.

'Yes, tell him how stuffy it is in here, and crowded. I'd give anything just to spend an hour in Saxon Park again,' says Erwin.

'And pick flowers for Halinka. Remember when the park keeper chased you.'

'They were nice flowers,' Halinka whispers.

'And tell him we won't break the plants,' adds Aronek. 'Honest we won't.'

'After the war, you won't believe it, Aronek, you'll see. We'll all go to Little Rose summer camp,' says Halinka. 'The forests and the fields. We have campfires, and swimming.'

'Oh, and remember big skies,' says Abrasha. 'That go all the way down to the fields and the river. All we see here is little squares and strips above the buildings. I'm going to stand in the middle of the fields, no fences, and shout all the way to the end of the world.'

'Or just have some fresh air to breathe.'

They sign the letter, give it to Korczak, and hope.

Czerniakow too is determined to do something for the children of the ghetto, locked up with no parks or green spaces. One victory at a time, he is determined to improve conditions in here, even though most of his requests meet with refusal. But this time his visit to Kommissar Auerswald in the Bruhl Palace has paid off. He's succeeded in winning the right to open three children's playgrounds.

On a hot June day, Korczak, Misha and several hundred people wait around the edges of an expanse of cracked concrete swept free of rubble that wavers in the heat as lines of children in white dresses or white shorts and shirts stand to attention. In a white tropical suit, a pith helmet with a plume of white feathers, Czerniakow walks up and down their ranks while the Jewish police band plays 'Hatikvah'. Behind him are wooden swings and climbing frames constructed on his orders by a gang of ghetto workmen. A small area of new grass, yellowing already, clings on in the heat. The walls of the buildings each side have been painted with murals of open countryside. A dusty smell of broken bricks rises in the hot wind. Czerniakow lifts his hand to stop the band and addresses the crowds, his voice breaking with emotion.

'Our highest and our holiest duty is to ensure that our children survive these tragic times. Life inside the ghetto has become hard and difficult, as you know, but we, the Jewish people, must not give up. Every man, every woman and every child must keep on planning and working for our future. And this,' he cries, indicating the bombsite around him, 'is only the beginning of many new projects, playgrounds for our children, an institute to train teachers and a ballet school for girls.'

The crowd applauds and the children begin to march in a circular parade while the band plays a jaunty tune. The children are all given bags of molasses sweets fabricated in the ghetto. The smiling crowd begins to mill about and peel away.

Korczak finds Czerniakow at his side. 'What did you think?' he asks the doctor.

Korczak is wearing a beige mac over his army uniform. He cuts a poor figure next to Czerniakow's white splendour. He looks up at the pith helmet with the white plumes. 'Wonderful. Perhaps a lot of money to spend on a ceremony, some might say.'

'I know you don't like pomp, Korczak, but people need balm for their wounds. See how the street is smiling. It's good for morale.' Czerniakow allows his fleshy face to fall into a bleak expression. 'I have to tell you, my friend, there are days when I think I'm like the captain on the *Titanic*, telling the orchestra to play while the ship goes down. But I'm determined to steer this ship home at least with all the children safely on board.'

Korczak grips his friend's shoulder. 'I know. I know. And so did you have any reply to your request to get some of the children released from prison?'

'I tried, but the Gestapo aren't budging. But at least I've got some of the men released. They're being sent to do construction work at a camp nearby. It will be hard conditions, but it will be better than dying in Gesia prison. It's a new work camp called Treblinka.'

CHAPTER TWENTY-EIGHT

WARSAW, JUNE 1942

On his way to Zglinowicz's café opposite the gate on Leszno Street, Misha pauses to watch three Wehrmacht soldiers with a camera tripod. They are filming a dead body lying on the pavement beneath a shop window. Next to it is a skeletal child in rags. The shop window is remarkable, fully stocked with a display of caramels and chocolate. On cue a woman in a smart suit and a minute fashionable hat comes out, holding a parcel. The cameraman stops filming and asks her to go back into the shop, this time exiting past the starving child more quickly. Two more takes before the cameraman is happy. The terrified woman hands the parcel back and leaves as quickly as possible.

Outside, the withered child sits below the window display like a tiny sage, her sunken eyes watching the street as if from very far away. The Germans go into the shop and start clearing the window.

Misha realizes he's been standing and watching for too long.

He hurries on to Zglinowicz's café feeling unsettled. This mania for filming the ghetto is something new, evidently some scheme the Nazis are planning, but what?

In the café he orders a watery, ersatz coffee and sits down at a table where there's a clear view of gate number two.

The black phone hanging on the wall next to the bar is one of the few still working in the ghetto. With most phones disconnected, someone must be paying a lot in bribes to keep this one open. The barman turns his back and carries on wiping a glass. Misha opens a copy of the *Jewish Gazette*. Under lowered eyelids, he watches through the window to check that the guards who Jakub Frydman has bribed are still on duty inside the gate.

Over the months that Misha has been sitting in the café and watching the gate, he's seen a gradual evolution take place. The trees that once lined Leszno have now gone for firewood. The Aryan tram has stopped travelling in through the gate. The entrance has grown from a low, farm-style barrier through which people used to show their passes to go in and out to work, to a ten-foot-high brick wall surrounding a palisaded gate, and a death penalty for leaving the ghetto.

The wooden noticeboard is still there, however, warning Warsaw's Poles that the ghetto is a typhus zone. And the German guards still stay just outside the gates, afraid of infection, with a little brick guardhouse for them to eat breakfast or have a nap. The guards are in there right now, enjoying the bottle of brandy Jakub Frydman sent them. They won't bother coming out for a while.

Misha looks at his watch. Any time now his Polish contact,

Tadeusz, will ring from the Polish café on the other side of the wall and Misha will give the password to let him know it's safe to drive the cart in. There's a jukebox on duty at the gate, which is to say put the money in and the guard will play the right tune.

The phone rings. The barman studiously ignores it. Misha walks over to pick up. Tadeusz's voice. 'Your brother can't come for lunch today. A sickness in the family. Get home quickly.' The phone goes dead.

His hand shaking too much, Misha immediately puts some coins on the table and leaves as calmly as he can. Something has gone wrong. He hurries away down Leszno Street, cold sweat on his back, looking behind to check that he's not being followed.

At Sophia's flat she's tutoring her two nieces at the kitchen table.

'No messages came for me?'

'What is it?' she asks, seeing his face.

She takes him into her parents' room where the girls can't hear.

He tries to keep his voice even but try as he might he can't hide his concern from her. 'Some problem with the delivery. There's an atmosphere in the ghetto. Tense. Listen, I'm going to see if I can find Marek, so why don't I walk the girls back home for you now? And stay inside perhaps today.'

'If we stayed in every time there was an atmosphere in the ghetto —'

'Today, please.' No lightness in his voice.

'I'll stay here.'

The girls pack up. Sophia calls him back as they leave. 'You forgot something.' She kisses him. He finds he doesn't want to let go of her hand.

'I'll come back, before my shift.'

*

By curfew he's still heard nothing.

In the ballroom that night, Misha is reading by the light of a naphtha lamp. Dawidek comes over and sits on the end of Misha's bed, anxiously biting the skin on the side of his thumb, his tall skinny frame bowed over. He wants to talk about nothing in particular but Misha knows Dawidek's still upset by the brutal beating he witnessed by the gate that afternoon. Dawidek yawns, finally calm enough to feel the fatigue dragging his eyes shut and settles down in his bed. Soon Misha can hear that the boy is asleep.

The night is hot and the windows are open behind the blackout curtains. A little breeze tinged with sourness manages to make its way into the room, cooling Misha's bare arms in his vest.

The book is open but his mind drifts away. What's Sophia doing now? Is she sleeping or talking with Krystyna? Every moment that he's away from her he worries, relief only coming when he holds her in his arms again, safe and alive and warm.

This time, three years ago, they were at Little Rose, flying kites with the children. Summer was for dances in the park, for eating ice cream by the Vistula, for sleeping in the sun.

He listens for sounds from beyond the wall across the street, people talking and singing as they leave the café on the corner, cars and electric trams.

Another noise. A car is approaching slowly, its tyres sucking against the cobbles with a mechanical thrum, the noise echoing against the walls. This side of the wall. Only the Germans have cars in the ghetto and there's no good reason for a German car to be here at this hour. He listens, fear prickling his hands and feet, but the car continues to rumble past their building and he breathes again.

A few doors down it stops, the engine running. Boys are awake now, sitting up, listening. They hear running boots entering a building, a din of shouting, boots running down again, out onto the streets. Misha goes to the window, looks out obliquely from behind the blind. A bright light illuminates the street, car headlights. A harsh voice shouts out orders in German. Men begin to run along the cobbles in front of the car as the guards inside take shots. Laughter, then the car drives on, jolting and bumping unevenly over dark shapes on the cobbles, over bodies.

All through the dark hours shots resound through the ghetto. Another night of bloody slaughter, just like the night in April. In the morning, hooded bodies are found throughout the streets.

Misha gets a message to meet Marek in Sliska Street at the back of the home. Marek looks haggard, his hands sunk in his short blue coat.

'Have you heard from Jakub? Why was the delivery cancelled like that?'

Marek's face is hollow and grey. 'Jakub's dead. He was shot outside the ghetto walls.'

'They shot him?' All he can see is Jakub Frydman, so full of life, his dark hair and ruddy complexion, his way of being sure about everything. Misha puts his hand to his eyes to stem the tears that threaten to spring out. A senseless waste of a good life. But there's no time for tears.

'He was a good friend, to you and to me,' Marek says thickly, looking away as Misha wipes at his face. 'A lot of people relied on Jakub.'

'But what will we do about bringing supplies in now? For the home?'

Marek steps closer. 'We do nothing. Listen, you should know that Jakub was caught bringing in pistols. Someone blew his cover. How else do you think the Gestapo knew to look for the guns? It's over now, Misha. You don't know me, and I don't know you. Sorry. I know it's hard, the children . . .' He gestures towards the home. 'We give up now or we are the next to get shot. I'm sorry.'

He hurries away.

Deeply worried, Misha goes back inside the building and into the main room. The children are quietly reading or writing in their diaries. The younger ones are playing with bricks, building little houses. Another group are making a theatre from a cardboard box, a torch for a spotlight.

Korczak looks up and sees Misha's face. 'We'll talk more later,' he tells the boy next to him and hurries over to Misha.

'You look as if you have seen a ghost.'

'Frydman has been shot for smuggling.'

Korczak recoils. 'The salt dissolves and the manure rises in here,' he says angrily.

'We still have the rickshaw,' says Sophia that evening. Krystyna has borrowed some money from Tatiana to buy a red three-wheeled bicycle with a passenger seat. She keeps it in the courtyard behind the café and rents it out to pay off the loan.

'Krystyna lets the older boys take the rickshaw out to earn a little. You can still use that, Misha. And I can try and get some paid work again as a tutor from somewhere.'

Her voice trails off. Even the wealthy are beginning to starve now and her uncle has had to stop paying for the girls' lessons.

'But we still have Krystyna's waitressing. And then Lutek comes

by most days with a bag of kasha or something for Marianek,'
Sophia continues brightly. But that's the end of her list, and they
both know it won't be enough.

CHAPTER TWENTY-NINE

WARSAW, JUNE 1942

Misha finds Stefa saying grace at breakfast with the children on the stage, dark rings around her eyes. This time the Gestapo's slaughter has not ended after one night as it did in April. The shooting has continued night after night. Everyone lies awake listening, for the sound of a car drawing up, for the knock on the door.

And finally the reason for the slaughter is becoming clear. Most of the smugglers have been wiped out. Mass starvation has begun to set in.

'I've had to water the milk this morning,' Stefa tells Korczak as he joins them. Korczak's face is gnomish and withered, his collar too loose, his eyes grown large in the wasted flesh, bloodshot with fatigue. He looks nearer seventy than sixty.

'But surely that counts as a crime.'

'I don't know what else to do. Milk costs more than liquid silver now that Misha's unable to bring in supplies through Frydman.'

Misha watches Korczak slide the bread from his plate onto Aronek's who's been watching it with an unrequited love. It's gone in seconds.

'Somehow we need to find a way to get food in from the other side,' says Korczak. 'I may know someone.'

Korczak heads for the steep new wooden bridge over Chlodna Street that leads from the small ghetto into the large ghetto, a drab stream of people climbing up into the perfect blue sky above. As ever, the Doctor wears no armband.

He makes his way with difficulty through the crowds bottlenecked on Karmelicka Street, keeping close to the wall in case a prison car comes careering down the narrow gulley overhung with iron balconies, the guard clearing a way with his nail-studded truncheon.

On Tlomackie Street Korczak heads for the Great Synagogue. For a moment, standing in front of the wide steps and the enormous dome in the stuffy heat, he's a boy of seventeen again, following his father's hearse with the crowds of mourners in top hats or silk skullcaps and shawls.

Now, the Great Synagogue is being used as a shelter for the thousands of refugees recently arrived from Berlin. They are healthy and well dressed, in much better shape than the ghetto's long-time residents. And since they are able to lift a pick or shovel with vigour, and since they speak a good homely German, they are picked out first by the German guards for any labour outside the walls.

Work outside the ghetto in one of the gangs of prisoners under armed guard is now almost the only way to a regular food supply; not only does it give a tiny amount of pay, but more importantly, it gives the opportunity to buy food in Warsaw and smuggle it back in through the gates.

It's almost impossible for a Warsaw Jew to get a place on the work gangs.

Inside the Great Synagogue, the spiritual smell of wax candles and old books has been replaced by the odour of soil buckets and boiled onions. The ornate plasterwork is smoky with soot. The wooden pews on the ground floor and the balconies of the second floor have been partitioned with string and blankets to make living spaces for families. Compared to the other shelters – dying stations – it's clean and the people still look neatly dressed, but the strain of hunger and insanitary conditions is showing, men who haven't shaved, raised voices of women quarrelling over a pan, children crying. The start of a downward spiral.

In the corner, Korczak recognizes his old friend from his days as a medical student in Berlin, the widow of a German Jewish doctor.

She stands and takes his hands. She's sorry her son's not there to meet him, a fine young man of twenty, but he's out of the ghetto, doing building work at the barracks.

Yes, of course she'd be happy to ask if they could find space for some of Korczak's boys.

'And Dr Korczak, when do you think they are going to let us go home?'

*

Each morning after sunrise, Misha and three of the older boys, serious Jakubek, Mounius with his bright red hair, and little Dawidek, leave the ghetto under armed guard through the Krasinskich Gate. They pass the park where old men in wide-brimmed hats and side locks used to gather to discuss texts or read the paper, where women with boxy little baby strollers took the next generation for a walk in the fresh air under the green trees.

It's empty. Guards patrol the terraces of the palace in the middle of the park, now a German officer's residence.

Four abreast, their work unit walks along Dluga Street towards the familiar lanes of the medieval old town. No one greets these shabby men who pass like ghosts towards the bridge.

Crossing the river after so long, it's a shock for Misha to breathe the summer wind coming clean off the water, to feel it passing over his scratchy skin and old clothes. What would it feel like to bathe in the river again, or to lie in a hot bath? What would it feel like to put on new clothes and stand on the balcony of an apartment looking out over the river with a cup of good coffee, contented and hopeful about the day ahead?

They march through the streets of Praga to the old military barracks, now housing Wehrmacht soldiers. A man in a well-pressed uniform is leading a beautiful chestnut horse into stables with reverent care. The air rings with building work. The barracks are being refurbished and extended for their new masters.

Misha and the boys are put to clearing rubble and carrying bricks. The German guards who look after them are young and not without human feeling for the Berlin Jews who speak their home language. It's a relief to find that they are not vicious. They look the other way when the Berlin Jews take it in turns to slip off to do deals with Polish workers for food.

Misha knows the area well. After a while, he too slips out through the gate to buy bread and potatoes from a shop on November Eleven Street. Looking at Misha's battered clothes and armband, no one can fail to see he's not supposed to be there. The elderly Polish couple who run it take a risk serving him, but they are kind, add in a couple of extra carrots.

'You should come to the back door next time,' the woman tells him.

She looks at him with defiant eyes, fully aware that there's a death penalty for helping a Jew now.

'The Germans, they took my son away to a factory. They've stolen so many of our boys. That's what they use us Poles for, you know – slaves. Just enough food, just enough education for our children to do their dirty work. Whatever you need, come to the back door.'

Misha thanks her, then slips back into the barracks, warmed by the old woman's bravery. He knows that there are thousands of Jews living in hiding in Warsaw, all depending on the kindness of Polish friends.

But for every Pole willing to risk their life, there's another willing to sell one.

In the afternoon the men march back through Warsaw, the weather mild, the guards not especially vigilant. No one will try to escape. A wall of eyes surrounds the prisoners, Polish blackmailers waiting to rob and blackmail any Jew who might try and slip off their armband and escape into the streets of Warsaw. If you want to survive on the Aryan side, it takes a great deal of money to buy off the greasy palms.

At the ghetto gates Misha and the boys wait with blank faces and sweating hands. The smuggled food is in the bottom of their knapsacks under the tools they had to supply themselves to do the Germans' work.

They pass through and walk home exhausted in the hot and crowded streets.

Day after day, they walk back in through the gate unscathed, the food still there. Stefa has even designed flasks with false bottoms where Misha and the boys can hide valuable oil or margarine. But no matter how much they bring in, it's never enough.

Late at night, Korczak reads through his diary. He closes it, shocked by his disjointed thoughts. It's nothing like his usual lucid prose, but then who can concentrate in this state of perpetual hunger? People constantly drift off halfway through a sentence, forget what they were going to say. He lies down under his old army blanket. All he dreams about now is food, and so vividly. Raspberries and cream. Goose cooked in Marsala. He's only ever tasted champagne twice but after the war he intends to have it every day. And trifle and cakes for the children – their first meal as soon as they get home to Krochmalna.

CHAPTER THIRTY

WARSAW, JULY 1942

Misha wakes to the sound of sobbing. Aronek has had a nightmare almost every night this week. Misha goes over to find the child sitting up, fists in his eyes and his large ears pink in the lamplight.

A rifle retorts through the streets. Aronek's eyes lock onto Misha's, filled with fear and questions.

'I'll stay here until you sleep.'

'I thought Aronek's nightmares had stopped,' Korczak says sadly when Misha gets back to the ghetto the following afternoon. 'It's hearing rifle shots every night, so many deaths, it's taken him back to the terrible things he saw living on the ghetto streets before he came here.'

'But what can we do? With the arrests and shootings each night, what do we tell them about what's happening?' asks Misha.

'We can't lie to them. They're not stupid. Their diaries are full of stories of smugglers being shot, people fighting for bread. They need a philosophy to help them come to terms with the death around them, just as much as the adults do.'

Esterka, with her slender face and curly hair, her thick cardigan with its large buttons, a stethoscope always round her neck, is checking through the contents of the medicine cabinet nearby. Korczak turns to her and calls her over.

Esterka sometimes reminds him of his younger self, a newly-qualified doctor, dedicated to children. A difficult life, but a beautiful life. She also shares Korczak's love of literature and theatre.

'Esterka dear, didn't you say you'd seen the children's play by Tagore, the Indian poet?'

'Yes, *The Post Office*. I saw it in Warsaw a few years ago.' She closes the cabinet and comes to sit at the table on the stage with Korczak and Misha. 'I thought it would be morbid, about a child who dies, but it was poetic, uplifting.'

'Perhaps it might help the children.'

Esterka nods. 'I think it could. And we certainly aren't short of scenery here,' she says, gesturing to the oil-painted backdrops stacked at the back of the stage. 'Pan Doctor, you know I'd love to help organize auditions, even put the play on.'

'Who better than you? I'm grateful, dear Esterka.'

*

The lead part of Amal the orphan boy is given to Abrasha with his long-lashed eyes and sensitive musician's face. Halinka plays his mother, a poor peasant in an Indian village. The role of doctor goes to serious Chaimek with his glasses and a bow-tie borrowed from Korczak. The king's messenger is Jerzyk with his loud, clear voice.

Sophia comes to help make costumes and paper marigolds for Sara who is to play the flower girl. The rest of the children form the audience, watching the dress rehearsals and giving Abrasha advice on the most convincing way to die.

Szlengal the poet and star of the Little Review show at the Stuka café writes the invitations to an event that will be 'not so much a play as an experience and a mirror to the soul – being the work of children'.

The hall fills with guests: Yitzhak and Zivia from the young people's commune at Dzielna Street are there. Krystyna appears, taking off her apron, and joins Sophia and Marianek. She kisses his dark hair, so like Sabina's.

The lights dim. In a faraway village in India, orphan Amal meets his new parents and explores the forests and fields around his village.

But Amal becomes sick and must stay in bed in a tiny room with only a small shuttered window. He longs desperately to run through fields and forests once again. One night, as he struggles to finally open the shutters and let in the light of the stars, the passing watchman has good news for him: one day he will leave the room and find freedom again.

But instead, Amal gets sicker. As he lies in his bed, his head droops, his arm falls to the ground and Amal dies. As his family weeps, his little friend the flower girl arrives and places marigolds on his bed.

'Don't be sad,' she tells them. 'Amal is only sleeping. Soon the king will come and Amal will wake up. Then they will leave together for a wonderful land that no one on earth has ever visited before.'

The children in the front rows are very quiet. Perhaps they have forgotten that it is Abrasha and Sara in curtains and make-up, as they watch the sleeping Amal with thoughtful expressions.

Behind the children, the adults are also very still, many openly crying, everyone a little hungry, everyone exhausted. For several moments longer the room remains in a quiet hush.

Then applause. The lights come on. The children come back to take their bows, and the room fills with chatter and smiles.

Korczak joins Stefa at the back of the room, clapping hard. 'If only we could stay here like this, Stefa, in a new play, one of our own choosing.'

Czerniakow has arrived late and appears at Korczak's side, joining apologetically in the applause.

'I'm sorry to miss it,' he tells Korczak in a low voice, 'but I've been besieged all day, people wanting to know if this is true, if that is true. Are trains waiting to deport them somewhere? Are we going to be sent to the east, to Russia?'

'Are we?'

'Kommissar Auerswald assures me not. And only yesterday two Germans came to me, placing a very large order for boots. Would they do that if the quarter were being dissolved? The Germans are desperately short of labour now. They must need the Warsaw Jews to work for them, that's the only rational conclusion.'

'You know, some of the young people are convinced the Nazis mean to dissolve the ghetto and worse.'

'Yes, they came to me again. This talk of armed resistance from the youth movements.' He glances over at Yitzhak who is talking with Misha. 'It's madness. It would bring disaster on us all. I'm in the middle of some delicate negotiations to get more of the men released from prison. They will be able to live in the work camp, not far from here, Treblinka. The Germans need men for labour, you see, but as for clearing the whole ghetto . . .'

'I suppose that's all the Jews have become in this giant German enterprise of war,' says Korczak. 'Not people but a commodity. No need to give us sunbathing on beaches, or pleasant naps or games of bridge, just footwear, clothes, tools, a little food to do our work. We're hands and feet to keep the German machine functioning.'

Czerniakow nods lugubriously. 'But come what may, I'll make sure the children are safe. These little ones will see the future. I'll make sure of it. And now I have a meeting with these cameramen the Germans have sent in. They've brought in all sorts of things to my office from the synagogue – rugs, paintings, a menorah candle that dripped wax all over my table because they thought my office didn't look Jewish enough. They're not interested in filming the orphanages or soup kitchens. They only want to film pictures of wealthy women next to starving beggars. And now they want to stage a ball to show how we're living it up in the ghetto. We've been ordered to provide food and find women with long gowns, with me as chief guest. Well, I shan't be going to that, I can tell you now.'

Later, as the children settle for bed, Korczak walks through the halls and stops by Aronek's bed.

Aronek is sitting with his arms around his knees, rocking a little, a furrowed brow.

He looks up at Pan Doctor sitting next to him in the dark.

'Are you afraid of death, Pan Doctor?'

'Nothing ever dies. Even our physical body goes on to live another way, the same atoms in a new shape, as a flower, as a bird. And I believe that God loves us, and that love never dies.'

Aronek presses his lips together and thinks about this. He nods his head. 'My mother loved me,' he says gruffly.

'I know she did, Aronek.'

'If I had a father, he'd be like you, Pan Doctor.'

CHAPTER THIRTY-ONE

WARSAW, 20 JULY 1942

In spite of Czerniakow's official assurances, the rumours of deportations continue to fly through the ghetto. Is it true that trains are waiting to take sixty thousand people away to build fortifications, or to build a new work camp for the Germans? Is it true that if you have a certificate proving you have work in the ghetto you won't be taken?

Czerniakow wakes on Monday having slept little that night. First thing, he takes his chauffeur-driven car to the Gestapo headquarters in Szucha Avenue to try and find out what is happening. He's used to the Nazis' techniques of deception but if he can ask enough people, then at least some picture might emerge between the evasions to let him see what is really afoot.

Jews are no longer allowed to be on Szucha Avenue. Czerniakow feels apprehensive as he steps out of the car and walks past the sentries into the Gestapo building. Inside, he heads for the department in charge of the ghetto and is shown into SS Sergeant Mende's office.

In a bow-tie and a pressed suit, with a triangle of white handkerchief showing at a precise angle above his top pocket, Czerniakow stands at the required respectful distance from Mende's desk. A headache is already building behind his broad forehead.

'Sergeant Mende, the quarter is in turmoil as a result of wild rumours about deportations. May I ask if there is in fact any substance to the rumour that the Jewish quarter will be cleared today?'

Well built and tall, Mende has the mild face of a man who has never hurt a soul. His white gloves are placed neatly on his desk next to a stamp album. 'I can assure you, I have heard nothing,' he replies calmly. He turns to his aid, SS Lieutenant Brandt, a sour and obese man who is sitting in a chair, cleaning his nails. 'Have you heard anything about this?'

Brandt scowls and shakes his head.

Mende gives a definitive nod of his head to indicate that Czerniakow is dismissed but Czerniakow remains in front of his desk.

'Could such a thing happen in the future, Herr Mende?'

'I repeat. We know nothing of any such a scheme.'

Czerniakow walks along the corridor to the head of all ghetto matters, Kommissar Bohm.

'Is it true that deportations are to begin this evening, at seven-thirty?' Czerniakow asks.

Bohm too evidences surprise. 'I can assure you that if that were the case I would certainly know about it. You may ask Hohman in the political section if he has heard anything about such rumours.'

Hohman won't see him, but his deputy is also astonished to learn of such rumours. 'It's utter nonsense. You have the Gestapo's permission to issue a message through the Order Police that any such fears are groundless.'

Still not satisfied and sweating inside his immaculate suit, Czerniakow directs his chauffeur to drive to the Bruhl Palace on Adolf Hitler Platz to speak to the man in charge of all Jewish affairs in Warsaw. Kommissar Auerswald too reassures Czerniakow that the rumours are completely false. He does have good news, however. The children in the prison are going to be allowed to move into the home Czerniakow is preparing for them in the ghetto.

As Czerniakow drives back, he tries to feel reassured by this news, but his heart is beating too fast. His stomach knots with anxiety as the car drives in through the gates and the ghetto smells once again settle around him. All day asking questions, and still he has no answers.

The following morning he's in his office, trying to get the prison children released into a new home, when SS swarm over the building shouting orders, rounding up all the members of the Jewish Council. With no explanation the police bundle the council members into a van bound for Pawiak prison. His wife is also taken hostage, for what purpose it's unclear, but she's made to wait with Czerniakow in the office all day as he makes call after call to try and get the council members released.

Late in the afternoon, he and his wife are allowed to return to their apartment on Chlodna Street, but the Gestapo make it clear that his wife is still considered a hostage.

For what? What's coming? He's sure the Gestapo will keep the ghetto as a labour camp, but how many could they take away as unfit to work?

He lies awake as terrible visions pass through his pounding head.

And what about the children? Whatever happens, he will insist they are protected.

CHAPTER THIRTY-TWO

WARSAW,
21 JULY 1942

Across the ghetto, no one is sleeping; they are all terrified of some nameless thing that is coming. Few people have dared to go out that day, the soldiers shooting at random. In the little flat in Ogrodowa Street Sophia and Krystyna are also sleepless, nerves jangling from the confused panic in the ghetto.

The girls are drinking hot water flavoured with a few grounds of precious coffee dregs from Tatiana's café.

Misha has been and gone with a little bread. It's so rare and expensive now that everyone is dizzy with hunger. He's going to come tomorrow with more.

'But what do you think they are planning?' whispers Krystyna. 'A labour round-up? A pogrom? Those rumours about Lublin's people disappearing into thin air . . .'

'Rumours. Look at all the new German workshops that have opened. The Germans would never be insane enough to squander so much labour.'

'They can't go on for ever. They can't win, that much is clear now. If we can just hold out . . . Sophia, where do you think we will be this time next year?'

'That's only for God to know. I only pray that we will all still be together.'

Outside in the darkness, there's a volley of rifle shots and then complete silence.

Sitting up in bed, Korczak lifts his head, hearing several shots. He makes himself carry on writing, recording the strange things that have happened each day.

And what of the future? So many rumours and counter-rumours.

Talk about the ghetto being dissolved has now also reached the other side of the wall. Some while earlier, disguised as a water and sewage inspector, Newerly entered the ghetto to bring Korczak out. Newerly was a close friend who had worked in both the Polish and the Jewish orphanages with Korczak, later taking over the running of the children's newspaper for him. He had kept in contact with Korczak as much as was possible, but it had been some months since Newerly last visited the ghetto and he seemed deeply shaken by the state of the people on the streets. The children were very quiet and hardly moved about. Korczak saw in his face how he looked very ill and wasted, stooping over his cane, his uniform grown too large.

Newerly spoke urgently to the doctor. He must close the home, then he and some of the other workers could escape. Maryna had prepared a hidden room for Korczak at the Polish orphanage.

Korczak gazed at Newerly as if he was proposing some theft or fraud. 'You want me to abandon the children, run away and save myself? Thank you, my friend, but the Germans aren't unreasonable at heart. They will never let the orphanage be dissolved.'

Now Korczak puts down his pencil and rubs his eyes. Newerly was quite wrong to think he would ever run away and leave his children.

But he's so tired. It's an act of will each morning just to stand, put on his trousers, lace each boot, put one foot in front of the other.

In the meantime, the German machine rolls on implacably.

And what does he do in protest?

He clears the table.

No, no, people tell him, let me do it, Pan Doctor. And quite frankly, they're telling him he gets in the way. But he likes to clear the table. It soothes him, all the little clues to the children's character and disposition, a chair tipped over, a neatly stacked plate, a dented bowl. He refuses to put aside these human exchanges, these simple acts of care.

It's three a.m., time to catch some sleep. He checks on the children in the sickbay around him, turns out the carbide lamp and pulls his army blanket up round his shoulders.

Tomorrow will be his birthday. He'll be sixty-four.

CHAPTER THIRTY-THREE

WARSAW, 22 JULY 1942

Czerniakow wakes in his apartment on Chlodna Street. The scenes from yesterday and the Gestapo's arrests come flooding back. He dresses carefully, correctly, his uniform to do battle. Today he must get the men on the council released from prison. He drinks a watery coffee. He can hear a light rain falling. He goes to the window and his heart skips a ragged beat. Armed guards in black uniforms are stationed every hundred feet along the ghetto wall. Each one carries a rifle.

The small ghetto is surrounded. His heart racing, he hurries down to the chauffeured car that waits in front of his building.

'Who are they, sir?' the driver asks as he turns the car towards the Chlodna Gate.

'Ukrainians, I believe.'

The driver studies his face in the mirror.

By the time the car pulls up in front of the Jewish Council building, the rain has cleared, the air warm and damp. Across the road children are already in the playground, making the most of the quiet to enjoy the swings and the roundabout. He hurries in to begin making his first calls. As soon as he's in the sanctuary of his office, the stained glass of the artisan's window casting its soothing light – part of a scheme to pay starving artists – he wipes his neck with a handkerchief in the muggy warmth, picks up the phone to Gestapo headquarters. His secretary rushes in.

'Sir, the Polish doctor who had a pass to come in and operate last night, the SS turned up in the middle of the operation and shot everyone there.'

'They shot the patient? A sick man on the operating table.'

'The doctor, the staff, the family. And sir, there are lots more reports of people being murdered last night. And arrests, sir.' She places a list on his desk with an anguished and apologetic look.

Czerniakow's shoulders slump and he leans his arms heavily on the desk as he reads them. The news about the Polish doctor being murdered is shocking. Sickening images crowd before him as he picks up the phone and dials the Gestapo.

A voice at Gestapo headquarters informs Czerniakow in curt tones that he can no longer speak to Oberscharführer Mende in person. Kommissar Auerswald in the Bruhl Palace is also not available to speak to him.

He replaces the receiver, blanked by the German authorities. What can he do now if they refuse to negotiate with him?

He jumps, taut with nerves when the phone rings. It's a call from the Jewish police near the Leszno Gate. The man is almost shouting.

'Chairman Czerniakow, eight cars full of German soldiers have just driven into the ghetto. It says Pol. on the side of the cars. The streets are deserted here.' There is the sound of engines roaring in the background. 'Sir, there's more coming in, different now. They're in full battledress, sir, and there's SS with them.'

Czerniakow can hear the crack of gunfire. 'What's happening there? Hello?'

'Sir, they're shooting. My God, a woman on a balcony—' The phone cuts off. No reply when he rings back.

He rises from his desk fired with determination. He'll drive to the Bruhl Palace immediately and speak to Auerswald in person, but there's the sound of vehicles drawing up beneath the windows in a squeal of brakes and shouting, doors slamming. A rain of heavy boots comes up the stairs. The children's voices in the playground across the street carry through the open window, a scent of summer on the air.

Ten SS men burst into Czerniakow's office. He recognizes SS Sturmbannführer Hofle from the Lublin ghetto. Czerniakow met him briefly a few months ago when he and his officers paid a short visit to the ghetto.

It's clear that the Lublin men are now in charge. Mende and Brandt from the Warsaw Gestapo follow close behind.

Czerniakow stands, trying to show as much composure as he can.

'Disconnect that telephone,' Mende orders curtly. Hofle settles in the armchair opposite the desk, the leather of his long coat creaking. He does not remove his saddle-shaped hat. He sits down, crosses his legs in a relaxed, authoritative manner and taps a polished boot up and down in the air. Czerniakow watches how the stained-glass window casts patches of colour on the floor. Outside, one of the

Germans waiting in Mende's open-topped car has a record player, a Strauss waltz playing. From the playground opposite, the children's voices drift in like faraway bird calls.

All pretence at not knowing what is happening now gone, Mende barks out his orders. 'You will close the playground and send the children home. Listen carefully to the following instructions and make no mistake, they must all be complied with. Starting today, all Jews must be evacuated from the ghetto and moved east. By four o'clock today six thousand people must be waiting at the Umschlagplatz ready to be loaded onto trains.'

'But how can I? It isn't possible,' Czerniakow stammers.

Hofle stares at him from behind plain, round glasses. He has the face of an irritated bureaucrat, eager to finish the day correctly and go home. He gets up and places a written order for the deportations on the desk in front of Czerniakow.

'The trains are ready. There are to be no exceptions. Sign the order and give this information to all Order Police who will implement the instructions for deportation.'

'Where are you taking them?'

Hofle rises up in a fit of temper. 'I don't understand why you think you have permission to question me. You will comply with orders one hundred per cent or your colleagues in the prison will be shot. I think that's clear.'

Czerniakow listens to a faraway ringing in his ears as he reads through the report. He must not allow himself to react to Hofle's anger. He slows his breathing, remains studiously calm and begins to try to widen the categories exempt from deportation. 'It says workers and their families and the Jewish Police are exempt, sir? Could we also allow an exemption for the Craftsmen's Union and their wives, and for apprentices?'

Hofle shrugs. 'That is possible, yes, they may be exempted.'

'And I see, sir, you are exempting the sick in hospital. Might we broaden that to include children in orphanages who are also defenceless and in our care?'

Here Hofle's patience snaps and he takes the paper back abruptly.

'I will reconsider the matter of the children, provided that you agree to have six thousand people ready in the Umschlagplatz every day.'

'But if I can't find that many people willing to go?'

'Then your wife will be shot.'

The Gestapo leave, their boots thundering down the wooden stairs. Czerniakow sits alone in his office, their smell of leather and hair oil lingering in the room. He draws a sharp breath to counter the rising nausea now accompanying his blinding headache. He has to think. He has to act. He must focus on what he can do to stop the children getting on the trains. Surely the Gestapo must give an exemption for the children, please God.

He walks across to the open window. The swings are empty, nothing but a dusty wind blowing across the concrete under the morning sun.

All day, Czerniakow works to get the rest of the hostages released. At the same time he follows the reports on the number of people at the Umschlagplatz, knowing that if they fall short of the quota, the hostages will be shot. And he sends messages and makes phone call after phone call, trying to find out if permission has come through to get the orphans an exemption.

At their headquarters the Jewish police are given their orders and the number of people each one is required to bring to the yard next to the trains, the Umschlagplatz. There will be executions if the quota is not filled. They fan out into the ghetto and make up the required numbers by taking the homeless from the streets and the shelters, and the prisoners from Gesia.

To the rest of the ghetto, it looks like an exercise in clearing away the unproductive.

Sophia stands with the crowd in front of the poster that has appeared on the wall, trying to make sense of it, feeling the ground give way. So this is it. It's begun. Around her the ghetto seems to have been hit by an electric current, people hurrying off to try and arrange work permits, others wringing their hands.

Police are emptying the shelter of the well-dressed German Jews who arrived so recently. The people line up in orderly rows, four across, and march with dignity towards the freight yard where there are trains waiting to take them away to labour camps.

What if the Germans decide to divert Misha's labour unit there too, without him ever coming back to say goodbye? She spins round, not sure where she is, what to do.

Then she snaps to. She can't afford to panic. What she has to do is find work permits for her parents. She sets off at a run, not even sure where she should go.

By the time Misha and the boys return through the Krasinskich Gate late in the afternoon, the ghetto is in an uproar, people running to and fro, crowds gathered around notices posted up by the Gestapo, reading the announcement with cries of disbelief.

'They're sending us to work camps,' one woman tells him. 'But what does that mean?'

'If it says to take seven pounds of luggage, food for three days, then that must be a good sign,' another woman replies.

Is this the beginning of what Yitzhak warned them about? Misha steps closer to read the notice. Anyone with a work permit and their family will be exempt. So Sophia will be safe on his permit. And Krystyna's at the café. But the others?

He watches a cart rumble past, loaded with sick and elderly patients in hospital gowns, some crying or moaning with pain. Yelling to the boys to carry on, that he'll follow them to the home later, he runs to Sophia's flat to see what can be done about finding work permits for her parents.

The streets are in turmoil, people with anxious faces running to and fro to find work permits of any description. He passes long queues of people with drawn faces besieging the new factories.

Sophia meets him at the door. Marianek is clinging on to her in response to the tense atmosphere.

'Have you seen the notices?' she says. 'It's happening.'

'You'll be on my work permit as my wife, so you'll be safe. And Krystyna should have a certificate from Tatiana's café, but your parents . . .'

'My parents are queuing at the new boot works, but what can they do?' She goes to the window and stares out along the noisy street. 'It's such bedlam. Do you think they stand a chance there?'

'Let's hope they do. I'm going to run to the home now to see all's well but I'll be back later, or first thing in the morning before work.'

'Yes, you must go,' she says but her eyes fasten on him with panic. He picks up her hand and rubs her clenched fist against his lips. With a small noise she presses into his chest as his arms encircle her, Marianek looking on with a puzzled frown. He bursts into tears as Misha goes out of the door.

Mr Rozental returns shortly afterwards.

'Tomorrow. I'll definitely find something tomorrow. But I need to get my breath a while.' He sits by the table, one arm resting on it for support, stripped down to his vest, ashen white. He breathes raggedly for a while until the colour returns to his face.

Sophia gives him a glass of water and watches him closely while she cooks a pan of potatoes, the same meal they have eaten all week. No butter but at least they have salt.

A little while later Mrs Rozental returns. 'Nothing. They closed the queue as I got there, everyone shoving and shouting like madmen. And this in the twentieth century. Of course, if you have money to hand over it's a different story. Some people will be rich by the end of today.'

Krystyna bursts in, looking as if she's run all the way, her face moist with warmth, her hair blown from its clips, relieved and triumphant. 'Here, Mama, you are now a brush-maker at the factory on Swietojerska Street. I got a permit through someone in the café, not cheap, but it will cover you. And if Mother has one, then Father is exempt too.'

'Krystyna, you are such a clever girl.' Mrs Rozental examines it, looks alarmed. 'But what do I do with it?'

'You go to the factory every day,' says Krystyna, 'and if they have some materials you may even make some brushes.'

She turns to Sophia.

'But what's going to happen to Korczak and the children?'

Back at the home late that afternoon, Korczak assures Misha that the orphanage will be exempt.

'After all, what use would it be to the Germans to take children away to a labour camp? It would make no sense. No sense at all. And if we need it, I'll register us all as seamstresses and little tailors. After Stefa's lessons, even I can mend a sock.'

At five o'clock that evening the chief of police sends a message to Czerniakow in his office to say they have the required six thousand people waiting at the Umschlagplatz. Czerniakow hears the familiar sound of boots on the stairs. Hofle arrives to say that since the quota has been filled, Czerniakow's wife will not be shot.

But tomorrow is another matter. The quota will be higher: nine thousand people must report to the train sidings.

CHAPTER THIRTY-FOUR

WARSAW, 23 JULY 1942

The next day Czerniakow wakes with an inrush of anxiety to the terrible realities of another morning, wondering what he can do to protect as many of his people as he can from this vast labour round-up.

He hurries down to his chauffeured car – the only Jewish-owned car in the ghetto – but it's gone.

'Sir, the Gestapo took it,' says his driver. 'Can I get you a rickshaw?'

Czerniakow heaves his heavy bulk into the narrow bench at the front of the tricycle and directs the rickshaw driver to 103 Zelazna

Street, a modern apartment block commandeered by the Lublin Gestapo the day before as their headquarters.

Czerniakow hurries inside, hoping to get an interview with Hofle.

He is shown into a room and then left. Along the corridor he can hear Gestapo officers talking as they have a shave in the barber's room, the clink of a razor being rinsed in a metal bowl. Someone else is having their shoes shone, the brushes swishing rhythmically. A dog is barking in the yard behind.

At last, a German lieutenant enters, calm, polite. 'Sturmbannführer Hofle does not have time to see you,' he informs Czerniakow.

'But has there been a decision about the children? Has the exemption been agreed?'

'You must take that matter up with Sturmbannführer Hofle himself.'

'But if he won't see me . . .'

Czerniakow finds himself out on the street, a soldier with a rifle guarding the entrance.

'It's bedlam out there,' Lutek says, picking up his son and holding him close. 'No one knows where the next round-up will be. Half the Jewish police have deserted now that they understand what they are supposed to do, and the half that are left are going insane, beating people to force them to come down to the courtyards. And they're not just taking beggars and emptying the shelters now. They're cordoning off ordinary apartment blocks, emptying out families. Sophia, listen. Don't go out. Don't take Marianek out. Do you promise?'

'Yes, yes. I promise.'

'I have to get back to my workplace before I'm missed. I'll bring more food tomorrow. And Misha will come later?'

Sophia watches Lutek running along the road towards the houses that are now a German boot factory.

Groups of families are walking along the road with their bags, volunteering to go to the Umschlagplatz. Better to go and stay together than stay and be split up, people reason. And who knows if, after all, they are right?

In his office, Czerniakow is facing an avalanche of problems. Yesterday, the people cleared from shelters and from the streets had not resisted. Their conditions were so dire that they considered the deportations could be no worse and possibly an improvement. But today the ordinary families being evicted from their apartments are doing all they can to escape, screaming and hiding rather than let the guards split them up and deport any members without a work permit.

By three o'clock, Czerniakow is told that there are only three thousand people waiting to be loaded onto the trains in the Umschlagplatz. But the new quota is nine thousand and the deadline is only an hour away. His hand shaking, Czerniakow rings Hofle to ask for a reduction in the quota or for an extension in the deadline.

But before he can get through, the secretary rushes in, looking stricken. The Gestapo have sent in teams of Ukrainians and Lithuanians to carry out the deportations, men hardened to use any amount of brutality. They have opened fire with machine guns and herded the people, men, women and children, into the Umschlagplatz, everyone screaming and weeping. Work permits are torn up and thrown to the ground.

The news falls like a thunderclap. Czerniakow sinks into his chair, white as a sheet. He understands what this means. He's redundant now, a puppet head to catastrophic events.

He goes home at five o'clock, passing beneath the white cherubs above the portico of his apartment entrance. He climbs the steps to his door in a state of despair.

But he's still continuing to cling on to the hope that he'll hear from Hofle any time now about an exemption for the children. What kind of monster would deport the children?

Back in his apartment at last, Felicja has just put their meal on the table when the telephone rings. Czerniakow lays down his napkin and hurries to answer. It must be Hofle about the children.

The phone call is brief. He turns to Felicja, his face drained and grey.

'I have to go back to the Judenrat offices to meet with Gestapo officers.'

'But what are they doing, still in the ghetto at this time of night? What do they want?'

'I'm sure there's no need for concern. This may be news I have been waiting for. I'll eat this delicious supper as soon as I'm back home.' He kisses her cheek and returns to the rickshaw stand.

Felicja covers the plates of potato and herring and sits down to wait so they can finish the meal together when he returns.

Two SS officers are standing in his office, Hofle and his deputy. All pretence at civility gone, Hofle berates the chairman, shouting in fury. 'Because of your failure to carry out the deportations as instructed, there will be a new quota of ten thousand for tomorrow.'

'But how many days a week will these deportations take place?'

'Seven,' says the officer curtly.

'But the children. You haven't given me an answer about the children.'

Hofle is livid, screaming out his reply. 'There will be no exemptions for any children. Do I make myself clear?'

They leave before Czerniakow can raise an objection, their heels hammering down the stairs. A car engine starts up in the street and they drive away.

Breathing heavily, Czerniakow sits in the semi-dark in his office, staring at the order on his desk, the colours in the stained-glass window gone to night. What sort of work camp needs thousands of children? Only one where people die. These, he realizes, are trains to death.

He's always hoped to bring most of his people through these times, even though there would be deaths. But ten thousand people seven days a week. There's no hiding the Nazis' intentions now. Such numbers can only mean the death of the ghetto.

He is nothing now but an instrument to carry out the Nazis' death plan. He has nothing left but to comply with their orders.

It's been cold all day and now there's a wind getting up. Outside, the ghetto is in total blackness. No one he can turn to. The ghetto stands isolated and entirely without help.

He thinks of Felicja waiting for him to come home, waiting for news about the orphans she oversees in a shelter nearby.

In front of him is the deportation order that Hofle left for him to sign. He must sign it or be shot. No other choice.

But he can still protest. He can still refuse. In his desk drawer there's a small box with the cyanide capsule that he has always kept in case the Nazis forced him to act against his conscience.

He takes a pen from his desk and a clean sheet of paper and begins a letter to his wife, his darling Felicja.

I am powerless. My heart trembles in sorrow and compassion. I can no longer bear all this. They are demanding that I kill my people's children with my own hands.

He slides open the drawer in the large oak desk and looks at the rectangular zinc box inside. He clicks open the lid. A small innocuous-looking capsule. It's time. Not trusting his legs to go down the stairs, he rings for the night clerk.

'Would you bring up a glass of water when you have a moment?'

He can see she notices how much he trembles as he takes the glass and tries to smile as he thanks her. She closes the door and soon he hears the even tapping of her typing down below. He can see Felicja the day he met her. He can see the children in the playground.

A little while later, the cashier in a room nearby wonders why the phone in Czerniakow's office won't stop ringing. She thought the chairman was there, working late. She goes to the office, listens at the door, then goes in.

Czerniakow seems to be sleeping, his head on his desk. He's fallen asleep at his desk before, his nights given up to insomnia and worry. She puts her hand on his broad back to rouse him but there's not the slightest movement.

A moment later, she takes a step back with a small cry. Chairman Czerniakow is dead.

CHAPTER THIRTY-FIVE

WARSAW,
24 JULY 1942

Early the following morning, Korczak and a small group of people gather in Gesia cemetery under a cold, overcast sky. It feels more like autumn than summer. Czerniakow's family plot is among the lines of well-ordered stone slabs, but the wind blows a smell of caustic lime towards them from the communal pits where thousands of naked bodies lie buried in layers.

Korczak gives a short address commemorating all that Czerniakow did and all he tried to do for his people and then walks heavily back to the small ghetto. The day is already beset with problems. Some of the staff at the children's shelter are still determined to get him out so they can carry on stealing the children's provisions. They've reported Korczak to the Gestapo for failing to register a case of typhus – and the penalty for such an infringement is death.

He hurries to the Judenrat to get it sorted out. No matter how crafty those crooks are, he will outwit them.

No one has shown him Czerniakow's suicide note.

Throughout the ghetto, the news of Czerniakow's suicide has left everyone panicked. Does it mean the ghetto really is doomed? But surely only the unproductive should be afraid?

No one knows what to believe. Everyone concentrates their energies on getting hold of a work certificate in the hope that they and their family will be spared. Terrified, hungry and disorientated, people dash around the windy streets looking for someone to issue a piece of paper, queuing for hours outside factories and offices.

No one has time to look at the wider picture or to think about refusing en masse to comply with the Nazis' orders. Besides, such a move would mean certain death. No one in occupied Europe has ever staged a mass resistance in the face of Nazi power.

Just before four o'clock, Misha's unit returns to the ghetto. He hurries to Sophia's flat after work with some badly needed bread. The streets echo with the sound of trucks rumbling towards the Umschlagplatz, each one filled with people. He flattens himself against the wall as a lorry rattles by, the guard shooting into the crowd at random as they pass, then carries on as fast as he can. Has there been a raid in Sophia's street?

Since the arrival of the Gestapo officers and the Ukrainian and

Latvian soldiers from Lublin, a level of terror has entered the ghetto not seen before. Casual shootings and savage beatings have become commonplace. It's clear now that all the terrible stories from Lublin were true. These are men hardened by their experience of clearing the Lublin ghetto with great violence.

In the Ogrodowa apartment he finds the girls and their mother safe but beside themselves with worry.

With so little left to eat, their father has gone out to stand in line at the soup kitchen still operating from a window in a courtyard further along the street. But just being out on the street is a risk since no one knows which apartment block will be sealed off next with cordons of Jewish police and Ukrainian guards.

'Three hours ago,' says Sophia. 'Three hours and he's still not back. If there's been a round-up . . . I should . . .'

'No. Stay here.'

Misha hurries back out, down the stairs, and pounds along the street. A Jewish policeman stands at the entrance of the building where the soup kitchen operates from a ground floor window. The courtyard's empty, the courtyard scattered with broken furniture, burst suitcases and single shoes, the wind swirling dust and paper. There are dark patches on the ground, red streaks on one of the walls. Blood.

He shakes the Jewish policeman who is standing in the yard in a daze.

'Have you seen Mr Rozental – slight, dark hair greying? He was queueing for soup.'

The policeman looks at him – furtive, haunted, a wooden puppet in his made-up uniform. 'Everyone in the building has been sent to the Umschlagplatz. So if he was here at the soup queue . . . I didn't know what we had to do . . .'

Misha can't waste any time on words now. If he runs, perhaps he can stop Mr Rozental from getting on the train. Sophia's father is too frail to cope with a work camp in Russia or who knows where.

Misha runs through the streets towards the walls of the Umschlagplatz but German guards with rifles block the wooden gates strung with barbed wire that lead through into the freight yard. There's another gate beyond that and Misha can't see inside.

The guards make it clear that Misha must leave or they'll use their guns on him.

If Mr Rozental is in there, there's nothing more he can do.

Turning his back on the freight yard where cattle from the countryside used to be unloaded, turning his back on Mr Rozental, Misha walks away, the ground rising and falling beneath his feet as he returns to Ogrodowa Street with the load of his terrible news.

That same afternoon, Esterka, who ten days before organized the play for the children, sets out to fetch medicines from the hospital nearby.

As she nears the hospital building the street bursts into a chaos of running feet as cordons of police and guards in black uniforms begin herding people out of the archways of the nearby apartment blocks, lining them up four across in the middle of the road. Esterka is caught up in the panicked crowds, corralled into the middle of the street and made to crouch with the others in a cowed block while armed guards line the pavements. There are screams and shots from inside the apartment blocks and with each shot she flinches. The woman next to her is crying, holding her teenage daughter close. Everyone is terrified, with no idea of what will happen next.

They crouch there for almost an hour while the guards search the blocks with gunfire, screams and barking dogs. Suddenly they are made to stand, a column of hundreds of people, and told to march north.

'But where are they taking us?' says the woman, holding on to her daughter's hand. 'We've only got summer dresses on. Sandals. If they're sending us to a Russian work camp, how can we live through the winter with just summer dresses and sandals?'

As they near the Umschlagplatz, anyone on the pavements has been ordered to stand still as they pass. Behind a guard, Esterka sees a familiar face now stricken and open-mouthed with shock. It's Erwin. She manages to shout out to him to get a message to Korczak.

As soon as Erwin runs back to the home with the message, Korczak hurries to the Umschlagplatz, determined to get her released. He pushes his way through the crowd at the gate to where the guards bar the way into the main area. From here he can see hundreds of people sitting on the baked dirt of the old cattle-yard square, but he can't see Esterka. He pleads with the guard, cajoles, shouts at him to send someone to find Esterka.

Out of patience, the guard brings his rifle butt down on Korczak's shoulder and drives him through the gates into the freight yard.

Korczak looks around the crowds in a daze. An arm grabs him. A Jewish policeman marches him to the side, shouting and gesticulating at him.

As soon as they are out of earshot, he lets go of Korczak's arm. 'Pan Doctor, I'm sorry. I had to make it look like you were in trouble for something. Now leave. Go through that gate. Now.'

'But, Dr Winogron. She has glasses. She's here somewhere.'

The policeman looks behind him anxiously. 'Dr Korczak, you must go now or I can't help you any more.' He gives him a shove out of the side gate, closes it behind him.

Tears running down his lined cheeks, Korczak wanders home past empty houses and streets strewn with shoes and cases. A book, its pages fluttering back and forth in the heat. An empty baby pushchair.

In Ogrodowa Street, Sophia, Krystyna and her mother listen to Misha's news in stunned silence. Lutek sits with Marianek, cradling him on his lap.

'I'm sorry, but there's no hope of getting him out now.'

'Mother, stay home tomorrow with Sophia and Marianek,' says Krystyna. 'If there's a selection at the brushworks you might be picked out to go to the trains.'

Her mother is still as stone, her worn cardigan pulled tight around her shoulders. She speaks from a faraway place. 'The brushworks supplies the army. Why would they take the workers away? We need my permit.'

'Your mother is right,' says Misha. 'The factories are the safest place right now.'

Lutek gets up and reluctantly hands Marianek to Sophia, not wanting to part with him.

'I must get back before they close the factory gates. It's getting more and more like a prison, keeping people working through the night to supply the Germans.'

Misha too has to leave in order to get back to his registered residence before curfew.

'Be careful,' he murmurs to Sophia as they embrace for a long moment. 'I don't want to go.'

'I wish you could stay here.' They both know that the food that he and the boys bring in is more vital than ever. The only food entering the ghetto now comes from the labour gangs able to go outside.

*

When he's gone, Sophia sits by Marianek's side until he's asleep. Krystyna is helping her mother to bed, bowed and aged by years, it seems.

Sophia gets up and draws the blackout curtains.

Behind them night falls across the terrified and disorientated ghetto. How long will this cull go on before the Germans stop? Who will be taken? Where are they going?

'But we need Pani Esterka back. Can't you tell them, Pan Doctor?' says Sara when Korczak breaks the news to the children as they gather around him in the hall.

'The Germans won't listen,' Halinka tells her.

'But why did they take her?' Sara says, turning to Erwin who was last to see her.

'Perhaps they want her to be a doctor for them,' Halinka says.

Szymonek has a vital question. 'Will they take you, Pan Doctor?' he asks.

'No, Szymonek. I promise I won't be leaving you. We all stay here together and sooner or later the war will end. Sooner or later, the German people, the world, will understand what is happening in here.'

It's getting late. The children pull the beds out and unroll the duvets in near silence.

'Please don't leave the ghetto tonight, Erwin,' Halinka asks him.

He nods, wanting to stay and keep watch over the home tonight.

But as he goes up to sleep in the older boys' dormitory in the ballroom above, he knows that he'll have to go out again tomorrow night. They need bread.

*

Korczak takes down the blackout. A large pale moon, almost transparent, lingers on in the limpid morning sky. A chill wind comes through the gaps in the window frame, making bits of rubbish in the street swirl and drag along the pavement. What sinister happenings will today bring? Why can he do nothing to calm the madness all around?

Down in the main room Sara and Halinka are helping to lay the tables for breakfast up on the stage. Abrasha and Aronek hurry to finish their allotted chores, pushing the beds back, sweeping the floor, singing as they work, the alphabet song in Yiddish, 'Oyfn Pripetshik'.

Korczak looks round with pride. Even though they have had to move from place to place, each more inadequate than the last, the home has carried on with its same routines and values, not because he has insisted on it but because the children have carried them with them.

And the future?

Szymonek and Mendelek are carrying large jugs to the table. Is he doing the right thing in keeping all the children together? Could he really let them go to strangers to hide in dark corners, afraid and in terrible danger? He still feels sure that the Germans will never touch the home. Too many Germans know and respect the home for that to ever happen. But all the same, he's going to meet with a businessman called Gepner later and arrange to buy sewing machines, get the home registered as a workshop. A safeguard. And after Stefa's sewing classes over the years, even he is able to sew on a button or mend a sock.

*

In the crowded kitchen at the commune on 34 Dzielna Street where Korczak and Stefa gave lectures on education and child care to a room of hopeful students just a few weeks ago, Tosia, Yitzhak and his dark-haired wife Zivia are now holding a meeting with other youth-group leaders in the ghetto.

Yitzhak is speaking.

'It's no good waiting for the Jewish Council or anyone else to join us in resistance. They still insist it will only make matters worse.'

'And people tear down the posters we put up in the stairwells,' adds Zivia. 'They can't believe that our warnings are true. They shout at us for scaring people.'

'So it seems we're on our own,' Yitzhak carries on. 'But whatever happens, we won't let them take us. Whatever happens, we do not get on the trains. If you are taken in a round-up, you escape. If you are taken to the Umschlagplatz, get out of there. If you are pushed onto the trains, it's your duty to jump out before you get to the last stop. We do not let them take us. Resist, even if it means a fight to the death. And fight we will.'

There's a silence broken only by the cold rain.

'And if we die, at least we will have sent a declaration to the world,' adds Tosia, 'that the Jews will not go like sheep to the slaughter.'

Yitzhak has sent a message to Misha to let him know what they intend.

But Misha can't think like that. The youth movements are made up of young people without parents or children. Misha has too many depending on him to contemplate such a course of action.

Come what may, he must be there to make sure the children and Sophia survive these dark times, begin a new life after the war.

And at the end of the day, he too simply can't believe in the pessimism of Yitzhak's reports.

CHAPTER THIRTY-SIX

WARSAW,
3 AUGUST 1942

Sophia paces the room. Krystyna leans out of the window, watching along the street. The German guards have almost all left the ghetto and people have begun to appear on the streets, desperate to get out at last and begin to trade for food. Clothes, jewellery, shoes, everything's on sale, prices dropping fast. Food is what everyone wants, and prices are rocketing for the little that makes it in now. She's hoping to see Mother returning home from the brushworks on Swietojerska Street, threading through the crowds, but there's no sign of her.

'Perhaps they're making everyone sleep at the factory tonight,' says Krystyna. 'Don't you think that's it, Sophia? Or perhaps she's having to do a night shift. Or perhaps there was a disturbance on the street and it wasn't safe to leave.'

Sophia gives her a wan smile. It's not long till curfew when the street will rapidly empty. She's never been this late before.

Lutek has already been to see them and returned to his workplace barracks where he is now obliged to sleep. He has to hurry to bring food for Marianek and see him briefly each afternoon.

No one goes out in the morning. That's when the Germans from Lublin drive around the ghetto for the day's *Aktion*, selections and round-ups – new words that are now on everyone's lips.

Krystyna gives a whimper. 'Where can she be?'

There is no way they can find out. The room is filled with anxiety, with the absence of her mother. If only Misha were here, his warm arms around her. She knows that he will have gone straight from his work detail to the orphanage tonight, but she needs to see him, to know that he is safe. She has to stop her body from rising up and running through the streets to find him.

She stands by Krystyna at the window, resting her head against her shoulder in a numbed silence. 'She could still come,' Krystyna whispers.

And even though they know it's too late, long after curfew as night falls over the ghetto streets, they are still listening for her weary tread coming up the stairs, her little sigh as she sits down and pushes off her battered shoes.

Where is she?

*

In the morning Krystyna hurries to work at Tatiana's café early to get a message to Misha before he leaves for his work unit. The brush factory is opposite the gate he leaves by each morning.

He promises he'll find out what has happened.

But standing in rows waiting to go out of the ghetto gate, there's no chance for him to slip across and ask at the factory gate. He can see shoes scattered along the street, a heavy silence from behind the factory wall. His heart contracts with fear.

The guard gives a signal and they leave the ghetto in formation, shovels over their shoulders. The sun finally comes out and Misha works in the sudden July heat, next to the barracks wall, filled with foreboding.

He can hear the slow clack of trains going past. He stands and shades his eyes against the bright sky. Realizes he must be hearing trains that are coming from the ghetto.

As soon as Misha arrives back at the Krasinskich Gate that evening, he sees someone he knows waiting to go in to work at the brush factory and hurries over to ask if he's seen Mrs Rozental.

'Helena Rozental. Don't you know? There was a selection here yesterday. She was taken away to the trains with the others. She'll be long gone now, if she's still alive.'

Up in the apartment, he finds Sophia and Krystyna racked with worry.

His face announces the news before he can speak. The two girls hold on to each other.

'They had a selection at the brushworks.'

'Well, let's go to the Umschlagplatz,' says Krystyna, looking for her shoes. 'We must get her back, now.'

'Krystyna. It happened yesterday. You have to understand. She'll be gone now. I'm sorry. I'm so sorry.'

Marianek watches in alarm as his two aunts gasp with sobs.

A knock on the door. It's Lutek. He picks up Marianek and rocks him, hides the child's face in his shoulder as he listens to the news. Then he turns abruptly to the girls.

'You have to pack some things, quickly.'

Krystyna looks at him aghast, her face wet.

'Now? What are you talking about?'

'A friend in the Order Police says this building's slated to be cleared in the morning. A selection. There's an apartment in a block on Zamenhofa Street that's just been cleared. You'll be safer there. But we must go now, before curfew.'

'We can't leave here. Mother's things,' says Krystyna, looking around. 'We can't just leave them. And Father's books.'

'Lutek's right,' says Misha gently. 'We'd better hurry. I'll come with you as far as the flat, make sure you're in safely.'

Stifling sobs, the girls begin to pack a bag.

'Only what we can carry,' says Sophia flatly, eyes blurring with tears as she fills a bag with Marianek's clothes, what food they have left, bowls, spoons, a knife. The photograph of Misha and her on the steps of the house at Little Rose summer camp.

Glancing round the room at their few possessions, still redolent with so many memories of her parents, Sophia closes the door and taking Misha's hand follows Krystyna and Lutek with Marianek down the stairs.

The building on Zamenhofa Street has been ransacked by looters, windows left open, torn eiderdowns and bedding spilling out. Across the courtyard, bloodstains and odd shoes.

Lutek leads them up the stairwell to the top floor and unlocks an apartment. Inside it is stuffy with the day's heat, oppressive with silence. On the table, there's a pot of soup. Sophia puts her hand on the side. It's still warm. She takes her hand away as if burned.

Where are the people who were about to sit and eat it?

Misha puts down the girls' rucksack and checks out of the window along Zamenhofa Street. Once again people have come out in the late afternoon to try and buy food, but already the street is beginning to thin out and empty for curfew.

'Keep the door locked and don't let anyone in unless you know who it is. They're going to move police into this block soon so it won't undergo a selection again,' Lutek tells them. 'But you should find somewhere to hide, a wardrobe, the loft hatch, in case . . .'

He passes his hand over Marianek's dark hair, smooth as silk. 'I'm sorry,' he tells him. 'Papa has to be away again.'

Lutek leaves for the German boot factory where he's now registered, Misha for the home to join the boys ready for work next morning.

Misha lingers a moment longer, not wanting to give Sophia up as she rests in his arms. He kisses her once more, twice, then quietly leaves and closes the door.

After he's gone, Sophia shoots the top bolt shut. The apartment is weighed down with an ominous quiet. Even Marianek makes no sound. Krystyna curls up on a rumpled bed, eyes open and dry.

Sophia sits down by the lukewarm soup and ladles out a small bowl of it for the little boy, but she can't eat any.

She can't let herself think or feel until Marianek is asleep. Only then does she sit staring across the room, her limbs broken in pieces, longing for Sabina to walk through the door, to feel the comforting press of her father's hand on her shoulder, to hear her mother's voice once again.

The light is fading. Krystyna too is asleep. Sophia sinks into a stranger's sheets. She lays her cheek on a pillow, another's must lingering on the cotton. She tries to remember what it feels like to have Misha's shape next to her in the darkness. She stretches out her arm but touches only air and her hand drops back onto the thin blanket.

Around them, the rest of the ghetto huddles behind closed doors, hoping they can make it through another day, hoping that the Gestapo's labour round-ups will end soon.

CHAPTER THIRTY-SEVEN

WARSAW, 5 AUGUST 1942

Misha's determined to find a small cake, or something at least, for Sophia's birthday. As usual, he and Jakubek, Mounius and Dawidek leave early to report to Krasinskich Gate. Stefa waves them off as she sets out plates and mugs for breakfast on the stage and the children tidy away beds in the main area.

As is his custom, Korczak kisses each of the three boys and Misha on the forehead before they leave for work outside the ghetto.

'Bless you and may you have a good day as you work,' he says. 'Come back to us safely.'

As they cross the courtyard the air is still cool but soon the heat will begin to build and press down on the stone-bound streets like yesterday.

Misha turns to give one last wave, but Korczak has already gone inside.

Korczak finishes watering the pots of flowers at the back windows and moves to the front balcony. Hanna from the sickbay goes with him, holding tight to his hand. If he lets go, he thinks she will simply stand still, white and anaemic with hardly enough energy to smile. He lifts down one of the pots of red geraniums so she can carefully add a little water.

A small brown sparrow whirrs down onto the balcony ledge, and they look up entranced. So rare to see a bird inside the walls. He thinks of the sparrows that used to gather at his attic window at Krochmalna Street, almost invisible in their whirr of wings, the breadcrumbs in their beaks seeming to levitate away magically. He and Hanna hold their breath, willing the bird to stay, but it darts round the flower and is gone.

Korczak returns the geranium to the windowsill. Down by the wall he can see a guard standing legs apart, holding a rifle. He's one of the new ones, a black-and-yellow uniform. The young man looks up and eyes Korczak stonily. Korczak smiles back. Even now, he won't let himself hate, become like them.

In the hall they join the children at the tables, standing while Stefa gives thanks, then settle down to eat with a syncopation of chairs and chatter.

*

Halinka wonders when Erwin will appear. He's out of the ghetto almost every night now with a couple of the other boys, bringing in bread. She fills Szymonek's mug with milk that's almost all water. Szymonek drinks deeply, puts down his mug and leaves a thin moustache of transparent white on his top lip. The other children laugh and Szymonek wipes it away, happy with his joke.

Sara pushes back the ribbon in her hair. Halinka helped her tie it, but it keeps slipping down. Next to Sara's plate is a small doll made of hardened plasticine. Sara likes whispering secrets to it when she thinks no one is looking.

On the other side Aronek is explaining to a new boy how they all help with the chores here, not just the girls. Abrasha is humming a tune he's been making up. He says he's going to call it the wind in the trees. Halinka thinks it sounds nice and each time she hears it, she can see the poplar trees down by the river, silver and green running through the leaves like water in the sun.

The sound of a whistle. Halinka jumps and looks up to see a German officer in saddle-shaped hat and black riding boots, standing at the back of the hall. Another blast and he's shouting. 'All Jews out! *Alle Juden raus!*' The children have stopped talking. They're looking to Korczak and Stefa for an explanation. Outside, a dog is barking.

Korczak cannot understand what he sees now. He and Stefa exchange a long glance filled with grief and shock and a determination to protect the children as best they can now. The terrible moment they never believed could happen has arrived.

Then he's moving quickly towards the officer. All depends on calming the situation down. He's seen what happens if violence erupts among the guards, people thrown from windows . . . Up close, the officer smells of shaving soap overlaid by the sickly smell of the mothballs the Germans use for their uniforms.

'Please, shouting will only make the situation more difficult,' he tells the officer. 'If you would give me time to talk to the children, calm them down, and to get their things together then we will assemble outside quietly.'

'You may have fifteen minutes. But first you will provide the register with the names of all children and staff.'

In the hall Stefa claps her hands. 'We will be going on a trip today, outside the ghetto. So you must all go quickly and get ready. Put your shoes on. Your teachers will tell you what else you will need to carry in your knapsacks.'

'But Pani Stefa, we haven't finished breakfast,' says Szymonek.

'Go now, Szymonek.'

Startled by this urgent note in her voice, the children rise from the table, milk half drunk, bread uneaten.

Korczak comes back in. Her eyes fasten on his with hope but he shakes his head almost imperceptibly.

Korczak takes her hands. 'I'm sorry, Stefa.'

'Dear, dear friend,' she says.

One last squeeze of her hand on his and then they break apart, hurrying to ready the children as calmly as possible.

As fast as they can, the teachers fill metal flasks with water. But the German guards are waiting in the doorway and the first children are already hurrying out to the courtyard. Abrasha carries his violin, Halinka her soap from Erwin, Sara has her plasticine doll.

Aronek takes the postcard that Korczak gave him for waking up on time for a whole week.

Szymonek has a book.

They stream out of the door and line up under the morning sun, four across, the girls in their navy pinafores over summer dresses, hair in ribbons, the boys in shorts and summer shirts.

Guards in black uniforms are opening the back gate onto Sliska Street.

At the front of the column Korczak picks up five-year-old Romcia for her mother Rosa the cook, Szymonek on the other side, holding on to his hand. Korczak still wears no armband.

The guard gives the order to go out through the gate. Korczak glances back at Stefa and the other half of the children. He sees the thin young teenagers, helping the younger ones, Abrasha next to Aronek and Zygmus. Halinka next to Sara who holds up her doll to the sun.

The children walk out through the gate in a long column, four abreast. Gienia, Ewa, Jakub and Mietek; Leon, Abus, Meishe and Hanka; Sami, Hella, Mendelek and Jerzyk; Chaimek, Adek, Leon and little Hanna. Two hundred and thirty-nine children file out of the courtyard. With them are over a dozen teachers, many of whom have grown up in the orphanage.

In the buildings around, everyone has been forced out to stand on the pavement behind lines of armed guards while the action takes place, no one yet sure which buildings are to be cleared. When they see the children walking past, a cry goes up.

The children walk along Sliska Street and head through the warm streets towards the bridge over Chlodna Street.

'Are we going to play in the garden by the church?' Sara asks Halinka eagerly.

'I don't think so.' Halinka pictures the tiny garden through the arched porticoes next to the church on Grzybowski Square where they went to play once or twice before it became too unsafe to go out. She would like to lie down on the grass in the shade there now and watch the red roses on the wall as they tremble in the warm breeze.

Sara says she is hot. Halinka unscrews her flask lid and Sara takes a sip.

At Chlodna Street the children clatter up the steps of the wooden bridge into the blue sky, a lighter sound than the usual trudge of adult feet over the bridge. People in the Aryan cut-through walled in on each side look up at this stream of children passing over their heads into the blue sky. Behind them, group after group of children taken from other schools and orphanages follow in rows of four.

In the large ghetto, the Germans have given orders for people in certain streets to stay indoors. There are rumours of something approaching that's terrible even by the ghetto's standards but no one knows what.

When they see Korczak and the children coming, no one can believe it. The ghetto has seen nothing like this. People crowd at windows or stand stock-still on the streets, calling out to each other in horror, 'They've got the children. They're taking Korczak and the children.'

And behind, hundreds and then thousands more children follow.

Korczak walks on, in a mute protest of light against darkness.

*

Swallows shriek like fingers on glass, sewing up the sky with black darts. It's very hot now. The children walk slowly, straggling out into a long single file along Zamenhofa Street.

It's a procession of thousands of children walking the two miles to the Umschlagplatz. There are no voices or cries, only the soft footfall of still-growing feet, in sandals, in plimsolls, in wooden clogs, bare feet, as the children walk on exhausted by the heat. On and on they walk as the ghetto's heart breaks.

The march of the children pulls a dark cloud across the sky behind it. Finally, the ghetto understands what the Germans intend. If they can take the children, they will take everybody.

In Lutek's small apartment at the far end of Zamenhofa Street, Sophia is sitting with Marianek on her lap while he drinks a mug of water. The four-year-old is restless and clingy. He doesn't like this new little room and he wants to see Grandpa and Grandma. The window's open but the room still feels stuffy in the rising heat. In his short life, he has no memory of cool parks or paddling in the water on the white beaches of the river.

It's been quiet this morning, people told to stay indoors. A brooding feeling that something is going to happen. Only the sound of the swallows piping their tiny cries across the blue sky. Then she listens. There's a new noise, a distant sound of feet like a soft rain, light and immense. She looks towards the window, puzzled by this growing sound. If it were a selection, then there'd be screams and pistol shots and rumbling trucks.

She goes towards the window. Ukrainian guards are stationed along the street. There's a procession of children walking up Zamenhofa Street towards the Umschlagplatz. She sees Korczak at the front. The children. They are taking the children to the trains.

She can't breathe. Her heart races so fast that she thinks she might be dying. They are taking the children.

In an instant her eyes have registered that Misha's not there. He always towers above everybody else. But she can see Stefa. And she can see all the children. There are tears pouring down her face, she's covered in sweat. She grasps the windowsill and shouts, but they can't hear her above the clattering of so many feet passing over the cobbles, the sound magnified against the walls as they pass by under the hot sun.

She leans out to try and keep them in sight but moments later they have passed on and she can no longer see them. Through a blur of tears she watches the nightmare of more children following behind in a long procession. Hundreds. Thousands. She sinks to the floor, clinging on to Sabina's boy. The sight of the children leaving is burned into her soul.

All through the ghetto people stand stock-still and watch this crime unfolding. Everyone in the ghetto knows Korczak and all that he represents: justice, kindness, fairness and love. He is their candle held up against the darkness, the gleam of sunshine that makes the ghetto smile. Everyone knows how well he and Stefa care for their great family.

It's a mute march of protest, the Ukrainian soldiers along the pavement more like a guard of honour, for once not shouting or whipping their prisoners.

It's almost midday and very hot. Korczak stumbles from time to time, his shoulders bowed. The children straggle out, weary and thirsty.

*

At the top of Dzika Street, Halinka sees a barbed-wire gate. She grips Sara's hand tightly as they walk past German guards into a large dirt yard. The place has a very bad smell in the heat. There are red-brick walls with barbed wire on three sides, the tall square school building on the other.

It's now noon and the sun is at its height but the bare earth yard has no trees. The Ukrainian guards are standing immobile in the heat, holding their guns as if they are too heavy.

The guard sends the doctor and the children to wait by one of the walls near a gate. There's a strip of shade here where Stefa sends the youngest children to sit. She tells them to sip only a little from their flasks, to make their water last.

Halinka doesn't like this place, but Pan Doctor and Pani Stefa are here, walking around slowly to reassure the children. She watches as more children file through the gates and sit on the hard dirt. She's never seen so many in one place.

Nearby, Aronek and Abrasha are crouching on the ground. Aronek has a peaked cap pulled down over his eyes. Abrasha is tuning the strings on his violin. He tries a few bars of a tune but it's too hot to play.

Korczak squints up into the cloudless sky. 'Stefa, the boys have nothing but shirts. I didn't tell them to bring jackets. A clear sky like this, it will get cold tonight.'

'I gave the girls blankets to carry. Don't worry. I want you to sit down and drink some water.'

'I should have thought. If they take us east to Russia, we'll need warm clothes.'

She hands him the flask of water again and he sips.

'Pan Doctor, are we going to see the countryside today?' asks Szymonek.

'We may see trees, and fields. We may perhaps.'

A man in a white doctor's coat hurries over. Korczak recognizes him from the Jewish Council, Nachum Remba.

Korczak struggles to his feet. 'Remba, what are you doing here, and why are you dressed as a doctor?'

Remba's usually pleasant face is grave. 'I've set up a medical post just outside the gate as medical official and I've been telling the SS that certain people are too sick to travel. Once they're inside the tent, we make sure they look sick, add a few bandages and then send them back into the ghetto during the night. But Dr Korczak,' he says in a low voice, looking around for the guards. 'You shouldn't be here. Come with me now. You must go back to the Jewish Council offices immediately and get an exemption. I'll make sure you get out of here.'

Korczak looks around at his exhausted charges.

'But the children, can you get the children out?'

'I'm sorry, Dr Korczak, they'll never let you take them out of here.'

'I can't leave without my children.'

'But at least you could get an exemption for yourself. You must save yourself.'

Korczak studies Remba's face. Korczak has known that it would be a terrible journey for the children, that they would be sent somewhere with harsh conditions, a work camp for adults perhaps, but now he sees it is far worse than that. Remba knows there is no hope. As the realization sinks in, Korczak stands without words, the chasm in front of them reflected in Remba's hollow eyes. Too late now to do anything, the world flying apart.

Visibly aged, Korczak shakes his head slowly and firmly.

'Thank you, my friend, but you know I will stay with the children. No one knows what they're sending the children to. You do not leave a child alone to face the dark.'

The cattle yard is full. Guards are opening the gates through into a second yard. One of them approaches and tells Korczak and the children to stand and line up again. Remba is pushed back and watches aghast as the children begin to walk towards the gate through to the train sidings, the tears pouring down his cheeks.

On the far side of the cattle yard there's a loud noise of screaming and shouting from a crowd of desperate parents and relatives trying to get their children back. They press against the fence, weeping and yelling. The guards beat them back and fire shots into the air as the relatives push against the gates.

Erwin has managed to push and shove to the front of the crowd. As soon as he returned from his night's smuggling he heard the news and ran as fast as he could, his lungs bursting, to join the children at the Umschlagplatz. Through a mass of waving arms he can see Korczak across the yard, he can see Halinka and Abrasha and all the others.

'Let me through,' he shouts. 'I have to be with them. That man is my father, my father.'

But the guard won't let him through. No one is going in or out of the gate.

Then he sees Korczak and the children stand. They begin to move through into the next yard. Erwin screams out again, 'I have to go with them. He's my father.' Tears are streaming down his face but he can do nothing but watch them go through and disappear.

Waiting by the trains in the rail yard, the faces of the Jewish police turn to see Korczak and the children walking towards them.

Aronek and the boys look up with curiosity at the black engine encrusted with soot, massive wheels higher than a child's head. Behind it stretches a line of old wooden cattle trucks painted oxblood red. The doors gape open and narrow wooden ramps lead up from the dirt sidings.

Stefa goes in the first car, standing by the open door as children in ribbons and smocks climb the ramp, each holding a doll or a book or a toy. For once the Jewish police are not beating people with truncheons and shouting at them to hurry. They watch pale and open-mouthed, sometimes helping a child up the ramp.

When Stefa's car is filled, she looks out at Korczak with a long, sad glance. Then the German guard slams the wooden door across and solders the bolt shut.

Korczak walks up into the next truck with the children. An acrid smell of lime and chlorine assaults the back of his throat. No soil bucket. There is one small window, high up, criss-crossed with barbed wire.

When the rest of the children are in, the wooden door is slammed shut.

The train fills with truck after truck of children from the ghetto's homes and schools. The guard writes the number inside each truck on the door. When this train and the next and the next are filled, each pulls away.

A total of some four thousand children leave the ghetto that day.

*

In the acrid and hot train, it's hard to breathe. Korczak begins to tell a story to calm the children, knowing that if he is calm, they will be calm. The children, some of them crying, quieten and listen as the train clacks over the Vistula River. Passing behind the barracks where Misha and the boys are working.

There's no room to sit down, although the police have not crammed the children's trucks as full as they usually do, perhaps. Korczak's aware that they must have reached Malkinia station now, deep in the woods. He used to pass through here as a student with children on their way to summer camp. The train stops, no air coming in from the tiny window, the children drooping and half asleep in the heat. The chlorine air toxic. A military train thunders past, shaking the carriage. Shortly afterwards, the cattle trucks pull taut and they carry on again. Drifting in and out of consciousness, Korczak is aware that they are taking a track to the right, a spur that he doesn't remember existing.

The train clacks on and passes a sign, a village called Treblinka, a few tar-roofed huts with impoverished potato farmers who sent their womenfolk away to stay with relatives as soon as the Ukrainian soldiers arrived.

The villagers can't see what is inside the heavily screened camp within the forest, but they can smell a strange stench of rot and burning.

The train passes along a track where the trees are so close they brush the narrow window slat. After a while, the pine fronds disappear, the train stops and the doors open to a cacophony of shouting in German and Polish.

There are no work huts at Treblinka. It's a tiny place among the pine trees, sweet with a smell that makes the hairs rise on the scalp.

Thousands come here each day. None of them leave. Overheated and thirsty, the passengers who are still alive after the journey disembark. A narrow passage between barbed-wire fences leads to shower chambers where carbon monoxide is pumped out through the nozzles. Within two hours, everyone who disembarks at Treblinka is dead.

But in the Warsaw ghetto, no one knows this. No one has yet escaped to return and tell the people what Treblinka means.

CHAPTER THIRTY-EIGHT

WARSAW, 5 AUGUST 1942

Only in the sight of God is the apple blossom worth as much as the apple.

Janusz Korczak

L ater that afternoon Misha and the boys walk back to the ghetto with their shabby work unit. In the compartment under the tools in his bag, Misha has a small cinnamon bun for Sophia's birthday. He will take it to her at dusk.

But waiting at the gate while the guard inspects the men, Misha can see that the streets are deserted. The Jewish police are talking in low voices, faces aghast. Something's happened.

When he comes alongside one of them inside the gate, he asks what's the matter.

'My God. You don't know. They've taken Korczak and the children.'

'What do you mean? Taken them?'

'They've taken them to the trains. Gone.'

'You saw this?'

'I didn't see them, but everyone knows.'

The ghetto is always filled with rumours. Misha shakes his head. He knows the man is wrong. The boys have heard too now. They look to him for reassurance.

There's only one way to find out if the children are still there.

Misha pounds through the empty streets, the boys behind, the air clawing at his lungs. Hurrying over the wooden bridge, Grzybowski, Sienna Street. Tatiana's café is shuttered. The double door at Sienna Street is open. He runs up the stairs and into the main hall.

Silence. Everything is covered with feathers like unseasonal snow. Looters have been through and split the pillows. The chest with the children's keepsake drawers has been ransacked, buttons and pebbles scattered across the floorboards. Up on the stage the tables are still set for breakfast, half-full cups of milk, bread abandoned on plates.

No children. No Pani Stefa coming to see what they have managed to get.

The boys run up to the ballroom. Misha can hear them calling as he goes through into the side office that also serves as the sickbay. He's still hoping he'll find some clue to the children and Korczak being somewhere nearby, a temporary move or inspection.

Then he sees Pan Doctor's glasses on the floor, one lens cracked across like a star. He never goes anywhere without wearing his glasses, hates not to have them to see what's going on around him, scribbling notes in his notebook with a thoughtful look. Misha knows at that moment that they won't be coming back. He begins to weep silently and a look of pain enters his eyes that will always linger, there at the back of every thought.

He sees there's a sheet of thin paper in the typewriter, dated that morning.

I am watering the flowers. My bald head in the window. What a splendid target.

The soldier by the wall has a rifle. Why is he standing and looking on calmly? He has no order to shoot. Perhaps he was a teacher in civilian life, or a solicitor, or a street sweeper in Leipzig. A waiter in Cologne? What would he do if I nodded to him? If I waved my hand in a friendly gesture? Perhaps he doesn't even know that things are – as they are. He may only have arrived yesterday, from far away . . .

It is not in me to hate.

Tears coursing down his face, Misha gently pulls out the sheet and gathers up the rest of the sheets of paper scattered across the floor. Pan Doctor's diary. He puts them inside a small suitcase along with notebooks that the doctor filled with notes on the children. He places the cracked glasses on top and shuts the case.

The three boys come in, as frightened and lost as they were at eight years old, on their first day in the home.

'No one upstairs?'

'No one.'

They check through the rooms in the annexe at the back. The same disorder and signs of people leaving in a hurry, of looters turning things over.

The building is oppressive with disaster, like a landslide that will give again, a bridge about to topple.

'They'll be back to clear the area soon. We need to leave,' he tells the boys.

They make their way back to the bridge at Chlodna.

Misha is desperate to go to Sophia, but it would be too dangerous for her to turn up there so late, too risky for the boys too. And curfew is only minutes away. Too far to run the mile there and the mile back.

'Will she still be there? Is she safe?'

One thing is clear. They've been fooling themselves to think that anyone has a future in the ghetto. What sort of work camp in the east needs children to work there? Yitzhak was right. The ghetto is finished.

He has to get Sophia out, and fast.

First thing next morning Misha and the boys must report for work as usual at the Krasinskich Gate. All day he and the boys work at the barracks, listening to the trains clatter past slowly.

Yesterday, the cattle train with the children, Korczak, Stefa and all the staff, would have travelled along these very tracks near where he and the boys were working.

As soon as they get back that evening, Misha runs to Sophia's apartment on Zamenhofa Street.

If she's not there?

Sophia opens the door. They stand holding each other in silence, Krystyna in the shadows at the back of the room, rocking the little boy.

'I saw them. I saw them going by,' says Sophia. 'They passed by under the window. I didn't know if you were there too.'

Krystyna approaches. 'Have they really taken them?'

Misha nods, his face twisted with pain.

'Why? They're children.'

'It seems they mean to take all of us. Sophia, Krystyna, we have to leave,' Misha says.

Sophia nods. 'Yes, yes. But how? It's as dangerous outside the ghetto as inside, unless you have a lot of money, the blackmailers . . .'

'We have to find a way. But you're right, we'll need money, a lot. And we have to decide how we get you out.'

'There's a policeman at the courthouse who takes bribes,' says Krystyna. 'I can find out his name through people at Tatiana's.'

Misha nods. 'Yes, leaving through the courthouse is your best bet.'

For a large enough bribe, there's a way to walk out through the courthouse, the only building that still straddles the border, and out the other side into Warsaw.

Sophia stands in front of him. 'What do you mean, your best bet? But we'll go together?'

Misha takes Sophia's hand.

'It would be too risky. You and Krystyna are perfect Polish girls. Look at you.' He strokes her golden hair from her face. 'I think your husband was a Polish officer. He was killed fighting for Poland.'

Tears well up in Sophia's eyes.

'No, Misha.'

'Darling, it's safest this way.'

She begins to cry and shake her head.

'It will take all we have to get you both out quickly with Marianek. When I've got enough together to pay for my documents, I'll go back to Lvov, a workman from Belarus. I'll find work there, keep my head down. As soon as it is safe to, I'll come and find you.'

'No, Misha. I'm not going without you.'

'Darling, you have to. You know that if I come with you, it will put Marianek in danger. This is the best way.'

'Misha's right. We don't have a choice, Sophia. I'm sorry,' Krystyna adds.

'I promise. I'll come to you as soon as I can. But first we'll need documents. We need to get irrefutable documents.'

'Professor Kotarbinski,' offers Sophia dully. 'If we can get a message out to him. He's been sending in books so I can keep up with my studies. He may be able to help us find a Polish name so I can get documents, and perhaps even somewhere to stay.'

The next day as Misha hurries back from the gate towards Sophia's, he meets a friend with news that falls like a hammer blow. He tells Misha that the underground sent a blond boy called Zalmen Frydrych out of the ghetto to follow the trains to Malkinia Station and find out where they were going.

There, the villagers took Zalmen to two men they were hiding, escapees from Treblinka. They had appeared in the village square naked and bruised the day before with a harrowing story. When the trains arrive, the people are herded inside the gates with whips and told to undress for showers in readiness for transit to permanent camps, but once inside the shower blocks, they are suffocated with carbon monoxide – a slow death of over twenty minutes.

The bodies are added to the piles of corpses waiting to be buried in the vast pits. Mounds of cases and possessions can be seen above the fences in the sorting area.

'Everyone who gets on the trains, we won't see them again,' he tells Misha.

Misha walks back to Sophia, stumbling under the weight of what he knows. The evil news will have to go from his lips to her ear, burning the air, burning all who hear it. He hurries on, the street distorted by his tears. Now, more than ever, he must get Sophia out.

CHAPTER THIRTY-NINE

WARSAW, AUGUST 1942

What I'm experiencing did happen. It happened.

You drank and drank plenty, gentleman officers, you relished your drinking – here's to the blood you shed – and dancing you jingled your medals to cheer the infamy which you were too blind to see, or rather pretended not to see.

Janusz Korczak

Finally, the reply comes back from Kotarbinski through the policeman they bribed. Sophia opens the letter. Inside are the details of a birth certificate for a Catholic Pole, Zofia Dabrowa, born in 1920. They now have the name of one female Pole in the right age group. With it, Sophia can go to the church to ask for a replacement certificate, claiming that her Aryan papers have been lost in the bombing.

Taking all their courage, Sophia and Krystyna go back to the small ghetto to see Father Godlewski at All Saints Church. It's eerie to cross a deserted Grzybowski Square and enter the gloomy and bomb-damaged church, shadows filling its rows of vaulted arches. A candle burns at the far end. The priest in his vestry.

'My birth certificate was lost in the bombing,' she tells Father Godlewski. If you could possibly make me a copy from the register . . .'

He opens the parish register as if he fully believes her story. As he scans the lists of names for a Zofia Dabrowa, he pushes the register towards them so that the girls have a good view of the pages. He turns each one slowly, knowing full well that Krystyna is rapidly checking through the names for someone with a similar name and birth date, so that she too can ask for a copy of a supposedly lost Aryan birth certificate.

She spots one.

'And I'm Krystyna Kolvalska,' she says quickly. 'Can you possibly write out a replacement certificate for me too?'

The priest nods and continues to read names aloud as he scans the lists, like a man thinking to himself. He's giving them the gift of more names, to pass on to other girls so that they can also apply for Aryan birth certificates.

Sophia watches the priest write out her new certificate, queasy as the ground shifts and Sophia Rozental Wasserman born 1918 becomes Zofia Dabrowa, born 1920.

'So now I'm two years younger,' says Sophia as they come out of the church. 'I've just lost two whole years of my life.'

The small ghetto is empty, everyone ordered to be out by the tenth. They stand for a moment at the bombsite next to the church that was once their apartment block, their home. Longing to see something familiar, they decide to brave the deserted square and the unnerving silence, and go and visit the little white Nozyk Synagogue one last time, in memory of their beautiful sister on her wedding day.

Standing on the corner they can see that a wooden ramp has been placed over the white steps to the main doors. A German soldier is leading a horse in. The synagogue is being used as a stables. Sophia can feel Krystyna quivering with anger. Wishing she has not seen it, Sophia leads Krystyna quickly away.

Shortly afterwards, Professor Kotarbinski sends Sophia details of a Polish family willing to hide Jews, a middle-aged Catholic couple who live in Kopyczynce, a quiet rural backwater to the east, the sort of secluded place where a young Polish widow can live unremarked with her child and her sister.

It's agony for Lutek to part with Marianek, but he knows that his slim, dark looks would instantly put his son in danger. To rub salt into the wound, Krystyna's boyfriend in the ghetto, Bronek, with his blond hair and blue eyes, is going to travel with the girls most of the way. Then he'll leave them and try and get to England to join the Royal Air Force.

Above all however, Misha and Lutek are intensely grateful to the teenager. It will be a great relief to know that the girls have some protection on the journey.

'Thank you, Bronek,' says Sophia. 'It makes it a long route to get to England.'

'Of course, but it's only natural.'

Sophia looks blank.

'So you haven't told them yet, Krystyna?'

'Bronek asked me to marry him a few weeks ago and I said yes.'

Sophia bursts into tears. 'No, no,' she tells Krystyna when she begins apologizing. 'I'm not upset. I'm happy.'

For her new identity card, Sophia has her picture taken, a spare copy in case there's a problem. The developing is overexposed. She looks pale and shadowy, and so skinny. She gives Misha the spare copy. 'So that I'll go with you,' she tells him.

Biting his lip, he puts it away in his wallet. How many months, years, will pass when this little picture will be all he has of Sophia? He kisses her deeply, not wanting to ever let go of her slight and soft body.

The courthouse on the end of Leszno Street is a bravely modernist building, designed to express the spirit of a newly free Polish nation in 1920. Twenty years later it's under Nazi jurisdiction, a place in limbo, one side opening onto the ghetto, the other side leading to Aryan Warsaw.

It's not so difficult to bribe a guard to let you walk through to the other side. All you need is plenty of money, and then more money to pay off the greasy palms, the Polish blackmailers who wait along the street ready to pounce on anyone Jewish-looking who comes down the courthouse steps.

Dressed in the best clothes they can muster, a little lipstick rubbed into their cheeks, Sophia and Krystyna walk into the courthouse on the Jewish side, each holding the hand of Sabina's little boy. Krystyna's bag contains a brown envelope with all the money that Misha and Lutek have been able to raise.

Sophia feels a surge of panic as they walk into the dim, efficient air of the courthouse corridor but the child's hand in her own fills her with courage, deliberate and unstoppable. It seems miles to the waiting room on the far side of the building, bare walls and a high window letting in sounds of a summer morning from a Warsaw street. The guard does not look at them as they sit down. He waits until a man near the door leaves and then he walks over to stand next to the girls' bench.

'You have something for me?' he says almost under his breath, his eyes on the door.

Krystyna takes out the envelope from her handbag. The guard turns his back as he examines the contents. He slides it inside his jacket and begins to walk away towards the door. Sophia feels all hope drain away as he leaves with the money. Then he looks back and cocks his head at them to follow.

Suppressing an impulse to run down the court steps on the other side, they find themselves suddenly out on the street. Dazed, Sophia sees trees on the far corner, green branches above a garden wall. In the ghetto, every green thing has been eaten or burned for fuel long ago. Krystyna slips her hand into her sister's but Sophia pulls away discreetly. It's essential now that they look like two Polish women doing their errands as they cover the few miles between here and the station in Praga.

*

For the first few nights Sophia, Krystyna and Marianek hide with friends of Kotarbinski in a tiny village east of Warsaw, Krystyna becoming increasingly anxious as they wait for Bronek to join them. But he appears at the back door late one afternoon as arranged.

They board a train heading in the direction of Tarnopol in the Ukraine, dozing and playing cards or singing to Marianek. Sophia gazes out as they pass through misty fields of autumn corn. Further and further away from Misha.

At the last town before Kopyczynce they part with Bronek. He'll travel north towards Sweden, try and make his way to England from there. He searches inside his canvas rucksack and brings out a leather pouch. Inside is a small army knife.

'Have you carried that with you all the time?' asks Krystyna.

'I wish I could come with you and look after you, but at least you should take this.'

The train pulls away, leaving Bronek on the platform. Krystyna leans out to wave as long as she can.

'Do you think I'll see him again?'

'You must never stop believing that,' says Sophia.

There's a tight lump at the base of Sophia's throat. She closes her eyes and sees again Misha's kind eyes and his gentle smile as they parted, and something new, the knowledge of pain shadowing his gaze, his steely determination to get her out.

Now she must do all she can to survive, to take care of the others, and to make sure that she will see Misha again one day.

*

They have spent hours learning by heart the rough map of Kopyczynce they were sent. They walk out of the station trying to look as if they know where they are going. Kopyczynce is a small town buried deep in the Ukraine, with wooden houses and picket fences. The trees are beginning to turn, the green already burning away.

'Do you think they will still be happy to take us in, these people we've never met?' Krystyna murmurs in a low voice.

'If they are friends of Professor Kotarbinski then they will be good people,' Sophia answers, feeling sick with worry.

'What if they're no longer there? Then what will we do?'

At the end of a lane of low houses in small gardens, they come to an unremarkable house with washing in the back garden. A woman with hair in a grey bun, a retired schoolteacher perhaps, is taking in sheets.

When the woman sees them she drops her sheet into a basket and walks over to the gate, her head down.

'Sophia?'

She nods in reply.

'We've been waiting for you. You must be exhausted.'

They are not Jewish any more. The girls are Catholic Polish refugees, living with their distant relatives, Josefa and Michal Wojciechowski.

It's clear that no one believes Sophia's story that she's a war widow. They all think she's an unmarried mother, hiding away with her scandalously illegitimate son, and she's glad to let that be her story.

The days go by, the winter starts early, barely November but cold as ice. Krystyna's only news of Bronek comes through newspaper reports mentioning the RAF. For Sophia too, there's no means of contacting Misha. She knows he can't write to her and risk compromising her cover story.

At night she lies awake in the darkness and listens to the wind hissing through the pine trees in the vast forests that surround the town, and tries to sense some connection with Misha, some sign of hope that he is still alive.

But the truth is that she has no way of knowing if he's managed to leave the ghetto, no way of knowing if he's reached Lvov alive.

CHAPTER FORTY

WARSAW, NOVEMBER 1942

I cannot give you a Homeland, for you must find it in your own heart.

Janusz Korczak

Under a slate sky Misha walks in formation to his work at the barracks. Beneath the bridge, the river roils with yellow mud, a grey cast in the cold light. Here the numbing wind blasts in from the east, penetrating his thin coat. Each day since Sophia's departure, Misha has continued to go to his work detail at the gate near the Krasinskich Gardens, walking through the old town and across the bridge to the military barracks in Praga.

Before the deportations ceased at the end of September, three hundred thousand people were taken to Treblinka. Reports have come back about what's happening in the camp. No one left in the ghetto now doubts that Treblinka is the site of mass death.

The ghetto is a wilderness of empty buildings with islands of prison camp. Some thirty-five thousand remaining Jews live in workshops under German guards. Lutek is barracked in one of the factories. Conditions are harsh, with little food or heating.

And as many Jews again live 'wild', hiding in attics and cellars, only coming out at night to find food.

Misha turns to look at the broken skyline of old Warsaw one last time. He doesn't intend to return, not until he's a free man.

He's finally gathered together enough money for a train ticket and for false documents. The wind hits him with a vicious blast, dry leaves scudding round his feet. It's time to leave.

As the afternoon turns to frost, Misha pulls up his scarf around his chin, makes an excuse about needing to pee and walks to a quiet part of the barracks. He slips off his blue-and-white armband, walks on through a side gate, and heads along the street towards the train station. He concentrates on even steps, on breathing steadily, all the time waiting for someone to call him back. But no one does. He reaches the end of November Eleven Street with relief, and turns in the direction of the station, not far away.

A hand grabs his arm, tugs him towards a doorway.

A small Polish man with a half-ashamed, half-resentful, expression looks up at Misha.

'In a bit of a hurry? We look a bit dark for a Pole. How would you like to come with me to talk to a nice German policeman? See,

I've got a feeling you may not want to talk to him all that much, unless you've got something for me.'

Misha resists smacking the man in the face with his fist.

'What do you want?'

'Whatever you've got. And I'd hand it all over, if you know what's good for you.' He takes Misha's train fare, shoves it inside his jacket. Then he pulls Misha further into the doorway, making him turn out his pockets, checking his jacket hem and shoes.

'And the watch,' says the blackmailer.

Misha stares at him with hate.

'You really are scum, aren't you?' He takes out his father's fob watch. 'One day, you'll need help and then you'll remember what you did today.'

'I help myself, mate,' the blackmailer says with a whining tone.

Then he leans out of the doorway, looks along the street and hurries away, casting from side to side as he goes, to check he's not being followed.

The loss of his father's watch hurts bitterly, but the most dangerous thing is that Misha has nothing left to buy a ticket to Lvov. And by now the guard will have noticed he's gone. No chance left of slipping back into the ghetto and trying to get new funds together without being shot. And soon the streets will empty for curfew.

He's out on the street with nowhere to go and plenty of people who would hand in a Jew.

Near the barracks is the small shop run by the Polish couple. He's often slipped in there to buy bread during work detail and the woman has been kind, willing to quickly sell him a loaf of bread even though she can see from his ragged clothes that he's a Jewish prisoner from the ghetto.

He has no idea if she'll be prepared to risk what he's going to ask her, but he has no other choice. He walks back along the street to put his life in her hands.

The shop is closing, the old woman cleaning the shelves. She turns to say that they're shut, but when she sees Misha standing in the doorway her expression changes. She lets him in and closes the blinds.

He stands humbly by the counter with his cap twisted in his hands and tells her outright that he's escaped from the work crew. He was trying to get to the train when a blackmailer robbed him. He wishes he did not smell so bad, that he looked cleaner. She wears a peasant-style headscarf. Her face is stony, nobody's fool. He can't tell what she's thinking.

She nods to a door behind. 'Go in the back.'

They are good people. They feed him a large bowl of potato soup with bread and home-made cheese. He tries not to gulp it down as they watch, embarrassed by how fast it's disappearing. They go out into the back room and he hears them talking, a long discussion. They return and say they will lend him enough for a ticket.

That night he sleeps on the hard little sofa in the room at the front of the apartment over the shop, listening to the tramp of boots as a patrol goes past in the street.

Early in the morning, while it's barely light, the wife packs up bread and salami for the journey.

'I will repay you as soon as I can,' Misha tells her.

The old lady puts her hand on his stubbly face. 'Perhaps. Now go safely, and God bless you, boy.'

Hoping that Warsaw's blackmailers will still be asleep, he walks through the dark streets of Praga to the station and buys a ticket to Lvov.

Sitting on a wooden bench, with other workers in transit, Misha watches through the window as the industrial suburbs of Praga slip away. Sophia too would have taken this train. He closes his eyes, willing her to stay alive, to stay safe in Kopyczynce.

'I'll come to you again, my darling,' he whispers to the pale crimson sun, rising above the horizon across the fields. 'Stay well, my darling. Whatever it takes, I will see you again.'

In Lvov, Misha finds labouring work on a building site. A few weeks later, a German construction company requisition him to work on repairs at Kiev railway station. It's been badly damaged during the fighting, most of the buildings now a smashed collection of brick boxes wet with November rain.

All through the winter there's no news from Sophia. And though he knows her address, he can't write to her in case he endangers her cover.

CHAPTER FORTY-ONE

KIEV, JANUARY 1943

At the beginning of 1943, while the January snow blankets the ground, some extraordinary news reaches Kiev, whispered ear to mouth. The Gestapo have entered the ghetto to deport any Jews not in prison workshops, and a band of young people have fought back, killing dozens of Germans and forcing them to retreat. Inside the walls, a Jewish and a Polish flag have been hoisted above the roofs for everyone to see.

Misha knows Yitzhak, Tosia and all the others at the Dzielna Street commune will have been among the fighters. How many of them have fallen trying to repel the Germans?

His own hands ache to do something to make this war end. If only he could find a way to join up with the Red Army to push the Wehrmacht all the way back to Berlin.

Three months later SS Commander Jürgen Stroop enters the ghetto with a large detachment of soldiers and tanks to finally clear out the fighters. The world is electrified by the news that seven hundred teenagers are managing to continue to repulse the might of the Wehrmacht army with nothing but pistols, hand grenades and a couple of machine guns.

Misha and the other labourers manage to tune in to the messages on the Polish free radio, General Sikorski calling for all Poles to take courage from the ghetto fighters' example and do all they can to help them. The Jews in the ghetto are fighting not only for their freedom but also for the freedom of Poland, and of the rest of Europe.

The battle rages on for a month. But block by block, the ghetto is burned to the ground, its inhabitants forced out of their underground cellars with gas and smoke to be shot or taken away to camps

It's not enough to empty the Jewish ghetto of its people. Every building, except for the few in use by the Gestapo, must be dynamited and burned. The ruins are razed, every brick taken away. Finally, Jürgen Stroop sends a bound report to Hitler with extensive photographic illustrations. Its title: 'The Warsaw Ghetto is no more'.

But even so, the German soldiers refuse to patrol the ghetto ruins after dark. They fear Jewish ghosts.

*

In Kiev, Misha hears news from a Pole who has travelled from Warsaw, how the Poles watched the ghetto burning with cries of horror and compassion, nothing they could do to help.

'And yet,' he adds, 'it shames me to tell you, there were people riding the merry-go-round for the Easter fair, children in their best clothes rising up in the air in little bucket seats, laughing, as if they'd stopped seeing the clouds of smoke billowing up behind the walls.'

'But tell me, how many people do you think are left in the ghetto now?'

The man looks at him quizzically.

'There's no one left. It's gone. It's nothing but burned buildings and rubble.'

Misha takes himself away to the edge of the river and howls into the blackness.

CHAPTER FORTY-TWO

KIEV, NOVEMBER 1943

Perhaps this longing for truth and justice will lead you to Homeland, God and Love.
   Don't forget.

Janusz Korczak

M isha has been in Kiev for a year. He's living as a Ukrainian Pole and since he speaks both languages fully and has light brown eyes and hair, a tall Russian build, no one imagines he might be Jewish.

One bleak November morning, he huddles with the other labourers around a brazier in the sidings of Kiev station, a tiny fortress of warmth in the freezing cold fog. Over the past few weeks the constant thunder of Russian gunfire has sounded from the other side of the Dnieper River as the approaching Soviet army pushes the Wehrmacht west. In reply, the Wehrmacht has blown all bridges across the Dnieper as it retreats, leaving Stalin's army stalled on the far bank, unable to get their brand new tanks across. But now the Russians are building pontoons. Soon they will cross over the river into Kiev.

'At least when the Soviets get here we'll see the back of the Germans,' says Anton.

Kostya shakes his head. 'You're Ukrainian, you fool. What do you think is going to happen when the Russians come? Haven't you heard? The Soviets are enlisting every Ukrainian they come across, giving them half a brick and standing them in the front line to soak up a few German bullets.'

'They think we should have risen up and fought the Germans harder. They think we're all collaborators.'

'What difference does it make to us anyway – the Soviets crush us one way, the Germans flatten us another?'

'I'm just telling you, don't be a Ukrainian when the Soviets roll in.'

'At least the Jews are gone now. Hitler did that favour for us.'

Misha tips the grounds of his thin coffee into the flames and returns to the work site. He shows no outward reaction to the man's comments, barely registers any anger inside. His heart seems frozen by the deep winter cold.

Six months earlier, news of the ghetto's defeat reached him like a physical blow. He collapsed onto his bed that night, aching with grief, knowing that most of the young people from the Dzielna Street commune would now be dead.

And he aches for news of Sophia. He has not seen or heard from her for a year. His fingers numb with cold, he takes her photo from his wallet. Hunger has made her face fragile, a mere girl. But her direct look tells of her courage and determination. Her eyes are pale, almost luminous, the picture a little overexposed, pale washes of grey as if her physical matter is departing into light. He aches to see the precise shade of blue of her eyes again. And what would it feel like to hold her fragile weight in his arms? He recalls the emotion, the feeling of homecoming, but he can't recall the exact texture of her skin. Alone in grey and sullen Kiev, a cold city of strangers, he hopes and believes that she is still alive – just as he hopes against hope that his family in Pinsk have survived the German expansion east. He has heard nothing from his father or sister, only terrible rumours of mass shootings.

Some days, it seems as though he can no longer distinguish between the cold in his limbs and the cold in his heart. All it would take would be to stand still a while and let the icy wind penetrate him a little further. Then all would quieten and stop.

But he'll never give in to despair and depression, not while Sophia needs him. He has to keep on believing that she is breathing and waiting for him to come and find her.

The next morning, he mixes a batch of concrete, the spade scraping and slapping on the wet ground. He looks along the railway tracks heading west, towards where Sophia is hiding.

Everyone is muttering the same rumour. When the Soviets come they will enlist the Ukrainians like convicts, throw them under the wheel of the German army. The Soviets are also deeply suspicious of anyone who's arrived from Poland, and the risk of Misha being arrested and shot as a spy before he can explain himself is very real.

If he survives that long. The Red Army is rumoured to be the largest ever seen. To wait for the hail of rockets to rain down on Kiev is to wait for death.

He has to get out of Kiev before the Red Army arrives.

The following morning, Misha wakes to swirls of icy ferns on the windowpane, his breath clouding white as he washes. He dresses warmly, and packs a rucksack before he sets off to the station. The broken-off bust of Lenin is still there, askew on its stick. Beneath it are hand-daubed Nazi posters in black gothic lettering, mocking the great leader.

He walks on through the station, a white palace where light streams into the concourse through cathedral windows. Outside, he heads for the sidings, makes a small detour and hides his rucksack in the bushes behind the storage sheds.

At eleven the other workers break for a smoke. He walks to the outhouses, picks up the rucksack and walks on towards the far end of one of the platforms. At ten past eleven a train comes in, heading west. He's waiting, ready as it slows, finds an empty wagon with the door unlocked. He slides inside, hidden by a cloud of steam, and sits down in a corner of the boxy darkness.

He must have slept for a long time, exhausted and rocked by the train's momentum, his head on the rucksack. When he wakes, the sun is setting, a beam of red light passing through the slats, playing over his eyes. The train slows, stops. Cautiously he slides the door back a little way. He breathes in the deep green smell of orchards at twilight, a rising cold mist. It's a tiny station in the middle of nowhere, a halt to load on farmer's produce. He climbs out of the boxcar.

A thick frost is falling with the dark as he walks through winter orchards, the low trees seeming to float in the twilight, a few greying leaves still clinging on. Frost crackling on the grass, he finds a barn to pass the night in. He wakes cramped with cold and eats the bread from his rucksack and walks on through orchards of apple trees, bare of leaves, the frozen ground crunching under his feet.

At the edge of one of the orchards is a single-storey wooden cottage with a shingle roof, a picket fence and a garden of dark green cabbages. A woman in a headscarf is chopping a stump of wood into kindling. He watches her wearily raise the axe, the fall, the wood splitting. Her arms are too thin for the weight of it. When she finally notices him standing the other side of the fence, she holds the axe across her chest, frightened but fierce. She looks about thirty.

'I'm sorry to disturb you. I mean no harm. Do you have food to sell me? If it's no trouble, ma'am, I have some money.'

She still holds the axe across her body. After staring at him for a long time, she lays it down on the chopping block and goes inside.

She sells him soup and bread, at a very high price. She makes him stay the other side of the picket fence, asking him wary questions, scrutinising him through narrow eyes in a pale and yellow-tinged face.

She keeps a dog by her side. It looks close enough to a wolf.

After they have talked for a while, her demeanour changes, softens. She has decided to trust him.

'I'm sorry to be harsh,' she says in Ukrainian, her voice flat and weary. 'We don't see many men around here now. My husband was shot by the Germans. If you want to do some work for me around the farm, I can't pay you but I can give you food. You can sleep in the lean-to.'

Inside, she takes off her scarf. She has very pale blond hair like sun on water, in two girlish plaits, a shapeless skirt and jacket, a woollen sweater that may have been a man's.

A pretty face once, but now sunk into sadness.

He tells her about Sophia. She looks at the picture. 'So do you know if she is all right?'

'I haven't had any news for a long time, but she's with good people.'

The woman pulls a face and draws back. Not so interested. She has her own problems.

Winter deepens and the snow piles up against the walls of the house. The months pass and a bitter and wet March turns the ground to mud. Sometimes, she stands in front of the fire in her white nightgown and shawl, legs outlined in the light, brushing her pale hair for a long time, staring into the embers. She knows that Misha has a wife, but that does not stop her falling in love with him.

No news of Sophia. Almost a year and a half now. Misha leaves the heat of the tiny room, stands out under the acidic March sky and calls out Sophia's name.

Inside, the damp wood in the fire spits like miniature gunfire. She's still there, roping her long silvery plait back over her shoulder.

'Stay with me here, Misha. Don't think about her any more. I will take care of you so well. When the apples start to ripen here in Antonowka, it is the most beautiful time. You will see.'

She comes over and stands close, puts her head on his shoulder. 'So many people have died. You've heard nothing. Why do you hold back?'

He waits for a beat, then takes himself out and walks for miles until his lungs hurt from breathing the cold air.

*

A few days later, she comes back from market with the pony and trap and runs to find him in the orchard where he's digging in a new sapling. Her scarf flies from her hair but she doesn't stop to pick it up. 'There's Russian horsemen in the village. Misha, you have to hide. You know what they'll do if they find a Polish spy. They'll shoot first and they won't wait for you to explain yourself.'

His one thought is Sophia. He has to see Sophia again. But hide where?

In the end he lowers himself into the cesspit under the outhouse while the Soviet soldiers trample through the cottage, liberating her potatoes and apples. She keeps the dog next to her.

After they've gone, he washes under the cold pump.

The next day she makes him stay hidden in the attic space with the apples she saved from the Russians. He can't stand upright, his limbs cramped by the small space. He longs to be with soldiers, forcing the Wehrmacht troops back to Berlin, for Sophia, freeing her little town of Kopyczynce. In the cold, dusty air of the attic, the wind needling in, he can hardly breathe. He holds the tiny picture of Sophia in his hand and focuses on her clear, constant gaze.

That night he dreams of Szymonek and Abrasha, boys from the summer camp at Little Rose. He dreams that Sophia is shaking him to get up and join them at the midnight feast to roast apples and potatoes. He wakes in the attic, the air ripe with dust and old apples. He can't shake the feeling that she has just left the room, calling him to follow her.

When the woman comes back from the village she tells him that the Russians are behaving well, handing out bread. No one has been rounded up for forced conscription. There's an office in the village for men who want to enlist voluntarily, with papers.

'I've seen the commandant,' she says. 'He looks Jewish if you ask me, but then the Bolsheviks always were hand in glove with those Jews.'

She watches as Misha packs his rucksack. In the slanting sun with the dust of the room dancing, her pale gold hair and thin face, she's like a ghost of Sophia.

She blocks his way out of the door. 'Why join a war that isn't ours? You'll die. You think you'll see her again? Perhaps she's already dead. Stay.'

He stands with his head bowed until she moves aside.

Outside, the bleak trees and bushes are covered in green lights, buds of leaves opening. The Soviet soldiers in the village look rough, dirty brown padded jackets, sheepskin hats. They eye him with a blank-eyed lack of interest. He goes to see the enlisting officer with his three red stars on his cap band, his well-polished boots and leather gloves. Moments later, Misha is signed up to fight for the Soviet army and sent east to the Sumy barracks to train to join the Russian Polish regiment.

He signs with a firm hand. He signs for Sophia and for their future.

CHAPTER FORTY-THREE

KOPYCZYNCE, MARCH 1944

I can give you but one thing only – a longing for a better life; a life of truth and justice: even though it may not exist now, it may come tomorrow.

Janusz Korczak

Sophia picks up the old flat iron from on top of the stove. She holds it on the worn cotton tunic on the blanket spread over the kitchen table. She presses along the seams, listening for the crackle of a crushed louse. The boiling water has killed some, the heat of the iron finishes off the rest. So far they have not found any in the house, escaped from the partisans' washing.

She can hardly imagine the conditions for the men and women hiding in the forest in their muddy dugouts among the swaying trees. The bag arrives at the back door each week, smelling of leaf mould and woodsmoke. With the girls' help Josefa washes and dries the clothes and returns the bag to the back stoop a couple of days later, with food inside.

Sophia has seen the man coming to collect it at night, tall and with a sculpted nose and cheekbones, wiry black hair and a red scarf like a Gypsy. The typical Jewish looks you can't show in the street any more. He caught sight of her in the doorway, nodded his head, and said thank you, deferential to the good Polish girl helping the Jews. The clothes the partisans leave are stained with sweat and mould, running with lice. They go straight into the copper to be boiled, though she itches as she stirs them with the wooden tongs. So this is how it feels to meet a Jew. She thinks of the notices around Warsaw warning that Jews carry lice and disease.

She folds the ironed tunic, hangs it to air over the wooden rack in front of the fire, and picks up a pair of patched trousers. The iron has cooled. She places it on the stove top and takes up the second flat iron, hot from the black stove top, and presses it on the seam until she hears another crackle; a slight smell of singeing while she holds it in place for a moment, making sure the louse is dead.

Marianek is playing on the rag rug with a wooden train filled with bricks, a toy kept from Michal Wojciechowski's childhood.

'Mama,' he says, holding up his arms. It's important that he's learned to call her Mama. And each time he does, something grows in her heart. For Sabina, for her sister's beautiful dark eyes in the child's delicate face, she has let a mother's love grow for him. She hugs him, kisses his forehead and then settles the little boy with his wooden blocks, helping him build a tower before she carries on pressing the clothes.

The middle-aged Wojciechowskis are devout Catholics. On Sunday, Sophia, Krystyna and Sabina's little boy go to mass with them. It's important to take the communion with everyone else, Mr Wojciechowski has explained, or people will talk. God won't mind at all if their hearts are not entirely in it. Strange to look around those heads bowed in prayer each Sunday and think, you were there and you were there. You were there when it happened.

Six months earlier all the Jews in Kopyczynce were rounded up, shot in the woods or sent to camps where they were never heard from again.

She wonders what it is that makes a family turn in their Jewish neighbours for a reward.

And yet there are people like the Wojciechowskis, plain, serious – heroes now – taking a terrible risk to shelter three Jewish strangers. And they're not the only ones. Josefa has told them about a family living next to the Gestapo offices in the town hall who are hiding a Jewish woman in their loft. They play the piano to warn her to keep silent if the Germans come to the house.

The little boy is growing sleepy, leaning against the settle with his head nodding. She lays him down on the settle cushions by the stove. She strokes his head. Sabina's soft hair.

Sometimes they all ambush Sophia with their absence: Sabina, Mother and Father, and the gentle and wild children in Korczak's home. Korczak, Stefa. They ambush her with a sudden and violent grief that makes her gasp and empty out her heart, making her want to lie down and give up.

And Misha. She'd feel it, wouldn't she, if something had happened?

People still need clothes to wear. She returns to her task, picks up the half-ironed trousers.

Later, the sun setting, as she lights a lamp to finish the last of the ironing, she jumps at a loud knock on the door. She sweeps the ironing off the table into a basket, a cloth over the top, and answers the door.

There's a German soldier in the doorway. He looks her up and down approvingly, her pale hair.

Three other soldiers are getting out of the jeep.

'We're commandeering the house for billets for the night,' he tells her.

She hasn't got time to get Krystyna out of the house before the soldier spots her in the kitchen, cutting up cabbage. She stands close to Marianek as the soldiers come in. They smell of drink, jackets open, dishevelled and unwashed.

With a flash of hope, Sophia realizes that they must be on the retreat, heading west and helping themselves as they go. But the war's far from over yet. She sees reckless and bitterness in their faces. Defeat has made them more dangerous than ever.

She will have to tread carefully. One of the men kisses her hand, close and greedy and reeking of old sweat.

By the time the Wojciechowskis are back from work, the soldiers have made themselves at home. They've found the dried ham and are cutting off slices. They bring in bottles of vodka from the car and tell Krystyna to make sure there's enough stew there for all of them, seem not to notice when Mrs Wojciechowski serves most of it to their German guests.

Marianek is in bed. Grey-haired Mrs Wojciechowski excuses herself and goes up to keep watch over him, leaving her husband with the girls and three very drunk and very complimentary soldiers. The fat one next to Krystyna won't let her go up too when she says she's tired. He kisses her on the cheek, his arm around her neck, pulling her towards him while the other soldiers sing a maudlin song in German.

Sophia is flirting and filling glasses, watching as the soldiers' eyes grow red, perspiration on the fat one's forehead. The man next to her is young, callow. He pinches her leg and she smiles. Mr Wojciechowski, the awestruck old teacher, is carefully getting the soldiers to explain in great detail the rapid advance they made across Russia two years ago, their victories, making them concentrate on their explanations. He too fills glasses, this time from his own bottle of vodka – a very potent home-made moonshine.

The first soldier nods off, the other two take longer, sprawling drunkenly across the chairs, the sofa.

But Sophia knows that if they wake, they will come looking for her and for Krystyna.

She sees a spare leather holster in the jumble of bags the men have piled up by the door, all pretence at army discipline gone. With a skip of her heartbeat, sees there's a gun still inside it.

She knows how to shoot a gun.

Keeping her eye on the sleeping men, she slips it out and hides it under her arm, beneath her cardigan. She's just leaving when the fat one wakes, sees her and calls her over. He makes her sit by him and listen as he talks in German and cries. He leans his body towards her, heavy arms around her, his breath stale alcohol. He lays his head on her shoulder, whispering something, then he takes a deep, sighing breath. She realizes he's asleep again.

She stays rigid with him sleeping on her shoulder until the sun has almost come up over the dark line of forest trees behind the house. With the threat of dawn, the men have remembered the war at their heels and leave the house in a hurry, piling the bags in the jeep, shouting at each other to get a move on.

They roar away. She still has the gun.

A few weeks later, the Russians reach Kopyczynce. They are civilized and respectful towards these fellow countrymen they are liberating.

The gun Sophia stole from the Germans is now a danger in itself, with a death penalty if the girls are found possessing arms. Sophia's lessons in the ghetto mean that she can easily dismantle it. For the next few days the girls take a daily walk along the lake and every time they throw in a section of the gun, each splash in the water a sign of the war finally ending.

But still no news from Misha. If he were alive, wouldn't he have tried to contact her by now?

The wind bangs the door left ajar in the kitchen. She goes to close it. A wild March day, a black cloud low over the trees. The white blossom of a plum tree is blowing away like paper confetti, lit up from behind by the sun, flying bright across the ashy sky. She holds up her face to the feel of the light.

Coming along the path between the back gardens she sees the postman in his smock, his canvas cap pushed back on his head. She watches him turn in to their gate. He hands her a triangle of paper folded and glued at the edges, looking at it as if he's trying to see through the paper and read what's inside.

'From the Sumy barracks, then. From a soldier.'

She opens it as quickly as she can, trying not to tear the words, fingers trembling. She reads it, reads it again, leaning hard against the door frame, making out the words through a blur of salt water, swimming up to life again. It's from Misha. Misha's alive and he's written to her. He's alive.

She's surprised to see the postman's still there, mouth ajar, watching her with interest.

'From your husband, news at last?'

Sophia blinks.

'Yes.'

The postman looks impressed. Along with the rest of the village, he has not, up to this point, believed in the husband. She's been quietly accepted as a woman of shame, a Polish girl with a child, pretending to be married. He doffs his cap respectfully and she closes the door on him.

She doesn't care what they think of her. That's not the secret she's been hiding.

She reads the letter all morning, examining the writing, the ink, the smell of the paper, holding it against her face.

Misha is alive and well. He's written her a letter. He's training at Sumy in the Ukraine as part of the Polish First Army alongside the Russians. He thinks of her all the time, kisses her, longs to hold her again, his wife.

He's alive.

She finally bursts out of the back door, the room too small to contain her joy, and dances with the falling petals of the plum tree.

Misha has written again. The entire Russian army is on its way west and they're not going to stop until they reach Berlin. He's left the Sumy barracks and has been assigned to a reconnaissance unit.

The war will end soon, he tells her, and then he and Sophia will go home to Poland.

CHAPTER FORTY-FOUR

LITTLE ROSE SUMMER CAMP, JULY 1944

The Russian army's advance west is spectacular that summer and by July the Russians reach Poland.

After a long day's fighting, Misha finds himself standing in a grassy field next to a white bell tower pitted with shrapnel – the bell tower of the convent at Little Rose summer colony. Five years earlier he climbed it with the children to see Warsaw in the distance. A month after that, the nuns tell him, a plane landed in the field and Hitler climbed the tower to watch the siege of Warsaw, vast drifts of black smoke scarring the sky.

Now the Russians are on the verge of liberating Warsaw and as part of the Polish First Army under Russian command, Misha will be there to see it happen.

Across the field are the wooden huts where the children used to stay, empty now.

Soldiers run past wheeling a gun. Misha turns just as a large explosion sends him flying up into the air in a shower of dirt. He's unharmed, but there's loud ringing in his ear, a sharp pain. He'll never hear through that ear again, but today nothing can dampen his spirits as they press on under gunfire, heading towards Praga and the suburbs of Warsaw.

A feast that evening. The Russian soldiers have been liberating the German rucksacks left behind in the recently abandoned trenches, rifling their superior supplies, sardines, Belgian chocolate, Dutch cheese, even French champagne.

'Have to watch out for lice, though,' one of the Russians tells Misha. 'Germans don't know how to get rid of lice like Russians do.'

Misha's unit eat in the garden of an abandoned house. They sit along a bench in a small orchard, hard, new apples growing on the branches.

By the end of the following week they have taken Praga back. The Polish unit are welcomed home to Warsaw's working-class suburbs as heroes. The Russian army set up camp on the banks of the River Vistula, looking out across the water.

On the other side of the river in Warsaw the Polish underground army have risen up against the Germans in the expectation that the Russians will soon arrive across the bridge to join them.

The Polish First Army make one breakout attempt to help them, but the casualties as they cross the river are so high, they are forced back in bitter defeat – while the Russian army sit tight and watch.

Scant intelligence comes through but it seems the Poles are fighting with antiquated and home-made weapons against the most feared of German troops, the savage Dirlewanger Brigade. The reported losses are catastrophic, but the Poles fight on – and wait for relief. Impatiently, Misha and the Polish army stand ready for the order to move on Warsaw, desperate to go to the aid of their fellow Poles.

But the order to move does not come. The months go by and winter sets in. The Warsaw uprising is crushed.

Are the Russians happy to see a Warsaw broken and defeated, ready for a Russian occupation?

The sound of explosions does not stop. Hitler will never forgive the Poles' stubbornness in defying him not once but twice. It's not enough to march its entire remaining population away to camps. A furious Hitler has ordered a complete eradication of Warsaw's very bricks and stones. With an anguished heart, Misha watches the burning skyline across the river as a squad of Wehrmacht demolition engineers destroy Warsaw's medieval libraries and Baroque churches with dynamite. The city bursts into atoms of dust, crumbles to the ground. Flamethrowers follow and Warsaw blows away in mighty clouds of black smoke.

The Führer has fought the stones of Warsaw and won.

Months later, in January, Misha's unit is sent across the white waste of the river in the dead of night to find a silent Warsaw guarded by the corpses of frozen Germans. Dawn shows stumps of a broken city protruding from a blanket of snow. The ghetto is a ploughed field of salt and silence.

A few emaciated people in muddy rags appear from cellars to gaze wild-eyed at the blaring speakers on the Soviet jeeps proclaiming Warsaw's liberation.

Sitting in the icy jeep as the Russians move on to crush Berlin, Misha is silent: if you can lose an entire city, then how much easier to lose a slight, fair-haired girl with pale blue eyes. He understands now that there is scant hope of seeing his family in Pinsk again, Papa, Ryfka, Niura and all the many aunts and uncles. All he can do now is fight on, for Sophia, for all those he has lost.

CHAPTER FORTY-FIVE

WARSAW, MAY 1945

I cannot give you love of man, for there is no love without forgiveness.

Janusz Korczak

The room behind her is filled with flowers. Yesterday was Sophia's name day and the children at the Polish school where she now teaches came with so many bunches of lilac and mayblossom that she's had to use every jug and bottle she could find, stand them on shelves, on the table. It looks like an indoor garden – and it feels right on a momentous day like today. She's leaning on the windowsill, looking out for the first sight of an American Willys jeep. She's holding a letter from Misha in her hand, a small triangle of thin, army paper, light as a child's paper aeroplane. She's read it over and over. It says he's been stationed nearby and is due leave, so he's hoping he'll be able to drive out to see her today.

She and Krystyna have been living in Łowicz for the past few months. It's a small country town badly damaged by the war. But it's not just the buildings that are broken with whole sections of the town missing. She's seen no Jewish faces on the street, no Jewish businesses, no women with baskets of bagels in the market. She and Krystyna are two blonde girls living quietly. They don't often mention to people that they are Jewish. Officially, under the communists Jews have equal rights now, but Łowicz is a town of unexploded bombs, fenced-off buildings, an uncertain landscape.

Today, however, as she gazes from the first-floor rooms that she and Krystyna share, this humble street of low houses has become another place, illuminated by the morning sun, everything hyper-real and significant as she listens out for the sound of a jeep. In this street, among these buildings, she will see Misha again. The sky is a remarkable blue, small white clouds hurrying across in the warm breeze. Under this sky she'll meet Misha again.

She's not seen or touched or smelled Misha for nearly three years. Will he be the same? They will come to each other with three years of terrible experiences, piled up between them like a mound of unwanted luggage. She knows so little of what he's been through since they parted, the people he has met. He's said nothing in his letters about Berlin, the fighting.

His letters say how much he longs to see her, to be with her again, that he loves her as much as ever.

But she's not the same. What will he see? Her face looks a little haggard, she thinks. Small lines around her eyes when she looks in the mirror. She's done her hair three times with Krystyna's help, and then combed it all out again. And this dress. Isn't it a little dowdy? She's mustered lipstick, perfume, but she thinks it smells a little sour and faded.

She's made a good cabbage soup and set the table. There's bread, herrings, a humble meal for such a reunion, but what can you do when food, electricity, coal, supplies of everything are erratic and rationed?

In the distance she can hear the clacking of trains from the junction. And then, yes, the sound of a rough engine. When she sees it, unmistakably, a green-grey jeep with a canvas top approaching from the direction of the church, she can't breathe. She flies down the stairs out onto the street, waving. She's smiling like an idiot.

It must be him. Is it him?

The jeep stops and a tall man with a fine-boned brow and receding hair, thick black eyebrows and delicate eyes, a smile as broad as a summer sky, gets out and rises up to his full height. Different and just the same. She can't take it all in at once. He wears a uniform. He looks older.

And his arms are around her, the smell of woollen cloth, of cigarettes and Misha's own familiar scent.

'It's you. It's you.'

'You smell so good,' he says with a little moan. 'Like Sophia.'

His eyes wide, he stares at her face, checking some inventory as if he's not convinced it's really her. She kisses him shyly. How good to kiss his cheek, his lips, his eyes, slaking her thirst for him. A long, deep kiss as their lips meet. Passers-by turn their heads discreetly, smiling to see a happy reunion.

Franek the driver stands back on the pavement, grinning.

Misha doesn't want to break away and lose her as they go inside; his arm encircles her waist. She feels the pull when he bends down and picks up his kitbag. Franek follows with his arms loaded with packets from the jeep. For Misha's reunion with Sofia – all he has talked about since they left Berlin – the cook in the army's kitchens has loaded Misha with enough meat, cheeses, butter and bread for a week.

Misha stops when he sees the room filled with flowers.

'So many admirers. I'm not surprised,' he says with a grin.

'From the children, for my name day. From my class.'

'So you're teaching.'

'Yes. I'm a teacher.'

They eat surrounded by the scent of flowers. It's the kind of feast Sophia and Krystyna can only remember from before the war. And yet, behind the joyfulness, there's a current of sorrow.

'Have you heard nothing more from your family?' Sophia asks Misha quietly.

'No. It seems they may all have perished in Pinsk, murdered at the hands of the Einsatzgruppen. I still hope to hear from Niura. She said she was going to try and head back to Lvov, but I've had no news.'

'There's still hope.'

'And Lutek? Your uncles and aunts?'

Sophia shakes her head. 'We think they may have been taken to a camp. We've had no news. But Krystyna's heard from Bronek.'

'I had a letter from England. He's coming back soon.'

Marianek is clutching the toy car that Misha has brought for him, even though he's fallen fast asleep, his head on the table. Sophia carries him through to his bed and she and Misha stand and watch him for a while, hand in hand.

When they go back to the table, Krystyna has taken a packet of stubby candles from the parcels Franek and Misha brought. She sets them on plates and saucers around the table. Whispers a name each time she lights one. No one switches on the electric light. The sorrow always waits, like water behind a dam, seeping into the room, and pooling in the candlelight.

'Sometimes,' Sophia murmurs, 'I dream they are all alive again. Or I'm standing in the street and I'm back in the ghetto so clearly. And then I don't know why I'm still here.'

Misha pulls her closer. 'I know.'

'Do we deserve to live?' she whispers. 'Without them?'

'Yes. Because we will live for them. The world cannot be left as it is. We make it better.'

Korczak's words. They sit and watch the candles in silence.

Then Krystyna gets up, looks at Franek and nods to the door. She's going to take him to a nice little café she knows and buy him a beer for making sure Misha made it home safely.

They hear them talking as they go down the stairs. Krystyna laughs at something Franek has told her.

Sophia lays her head on Misha's shoulder. The candlelight keeps its vigil as they begin to talk. Giving the missing years to each other in small pieces. She holds him as he explains how he left the ghetto. She watches the shadows of pain that ghost across his face from time to time, even as he smiles. As he strokes her cheek, she knows he sees the same shadows in her own face.

She's been so afraid that they would feel like strangers, but as she holds him now, runs her hands along his spine, his neck, her lips across his lips, it feels so familiar – like walking home at last, the air beneath the trees cool with the scent of the forests. Familiar and tender. He pulls her gently towards him and she folds into his shape. Her husband. Her love.

In the morning, before he leaves in the white light, Sophia takes Korczak's book from the shelf, the same book Misha gave her on their wedding day, and writes in the front, 'For darling Misha, for our future. Never forget.' She places it inside his kitbag.

CHAPTER FORTY-SIX

In the long wooden cabins at Little Rose, the light is beginning to bring the room into focus as Korczak sits at his desk. The birds are stirring outside, whirring down onto the veranda to pick up the crumbs he has scattered for them. The curtains move with a breeze that brings a touch of damp coolness from fields still wet with dew. It should be a fine day. A good day to go swimming.

He hears a whisper behind him. Szymonek, a small boy again, is standing in his nightgown, their newest arrival, his head still shorn.

'Pan Doctor, is it time to get up yet?'

'It is if you are up. Do you want to be the first to hear some good news? Today we're going to the river.'

'Can I wake the others?'

'Gently. If they are ready.'

'I will sing.'

'That might work. Some people appreciate singing first thing in the morning.'

Szymonek begins a song he learned while he was living abandoned and hungry on the streets, with a full gamut of Yiddish swear words.

'Do you know another one, Szymonek, perhaps?'

He thinks.

'What about the one we sang yesterday?'

Szymonek nods and goes into the dormitory singing 'Oyfn Pripetshik', the Yiddish alphabet song that the children taught Korczak on his first summer camp.

Korczak watches the unforgettable sight of children waking in the dormitory: who yawns ready to jump out of bed, who is slow to rise and is perhaps not so well.

The sun will soon put that right. After breakfast, Zalewski will get the hay cart ready. The children will pile in and drive along the sandy tracks through the fenceless fields to a river that seems to run level with the land, the water clear above the stones shimmering with light while the day rings with the voices of children. Later, they will come home again, sunburned a little, the girls with headscarves, the boys with caps. No doubt they will all want to pick flowers and bring them home for Pani Stefa.

Rolls and herring for breakfast, and strong coffee and a cigarette, what better? The day is beautiful in its shimmering simplicity of hazy blue horizons and wide damp fields of new corn. In the cabin nearby, Stefa is calling to the girls.

He rises from the desk and leaves the paper he is writing. The child is not a person tomorrow; he is a person today. A child has the right to love and respect. He has the right to grow and develop. A child has the right to be who he is and to be taken seriously. A child has the right to ask questions and resist injustice.

Szymonek runs back in and takes his hand. 'Pan Doctor, may I sit next to you at breakfast?' he whispers.

'Of course, my son. Though I have terrible table manners. Perhaps you could give me some advice.'

After breakfast Korczak wanders along the tables collecting mugs and plates. The children are already out in the garden calling to him, the cart ready to go. Someone has put a straw hat on the horse and decked it with flowers. Someone else has taken the pennant from over the door and its green silk is now flying from the back of the cart.

Zalewski clicks to the horse and the cart moves off. The mist is burning away from the corn where poppies and butterflies dance in the breeze. Singing and chattering, the children set off along the sandy tracks to spend a day splashing and paddling in the calm pools along the river.

POSTSCRIPT

At the end of the Second World War, though Polish airmen had played a vital role in the decisive battle of Britain and though thousands of Polish soldiers had fought alongside the Allies, liberated Europe looked away from a Poland under Soviet occupation.

Slowly, with long lines of men, women and children passing salvaged bricks from hand to hand, the determined Varsovians began to rebuild their beloved old city centre by referring to photographs, architect's plans and memories.

This was the Warsaw that Misha and Sophia returned to, living in an apartment overlooking the vast levelled bombsites of Warsaw.

Sophia worked as a teacher in a building that had once served as offices for Nazi soldiers in charge of deportations from the Umschlagplatz site situated on the other side of the road. Misha was given a job in publishing and together they raised three boys.

Before the war a third of Warsaw had been Jewish. Now the vibrant Jewish community had disappeared. Misha and Sophia were among the one per cent to survive the Warsaw ghetto, out of an original population of four hundred thousand. The razed ghetto site was eventually built over with estates of Soviet housing blocks and a network of roads wide enough to take a Soviet tank.

Misha served as a father figure for the children who did not perish during the war, mostly made up of those children who had grown up and left the orphanage before the ghetto years, many emigrating to Israel, the US, Canada and France. Only a handful of boys from the ghetto home survived including the boys working outside the ghetto with Misha and Sammy Gogol and Erwin Baum.

Sammy and his remaining relatives were taken to Auschwitz. He was spared from the gas chambers because he was picked out to play his harmonica in the orchestra. He was forced to play to the crowds walking into the gas chambers each day. After he saw his family go by, he always played with his eyes shut. Still in striped pyjamas, Sammy travelled to Israel where he founded a children's harmonica orchestra and returned to play with them at Auschwitz on the very place where he had once stood as a prisoner – but now a free man. Erwin was also sent to Auschwitz but on arrival he managed to switch lines to avoid the gas chambers and was put on sorting prisoners' belongings. He was sent to Dachau and was later liberated by the US army in 1945. After the war Erwin went to the US and married with children and grandchildren.

To Misha and Sophia's great joy they heard that Niura was alive and living in France. She and her husband returned to Warsaw, but after her husband was imprisoned briefly by the Soviets, suspected as a spy, they escaped back to Paris where they remained for the rest of their lives.

Krystyna and Bronek married but later separated. A pilot for Polish airlines, Bronek defected from Communist Poland, remaining in Paris after piloting a Polish plane there. Krystyna later remarried and became a Polish member of parliament.

In 1946, following a Polish massacre of Jews in Kielce, Yitzhak was sent by the Polish government to investigate the situation and he persuaded the government to open Poland's southern border and allow Jewish emigration for a limited period.

Misha and Yitzhak were both sent to monitor the border crossing as some 20,000 Jews left through the Czech Republic. Misha and Sophia debated leaving Poland then, but as Sophia had a new baby they were unable to make the journey and the window of opportunity to leave Soviet Poland closed. Yitzhak and his wife Zivia managed to emigrate to Israel and founded the Ghetto Fighters' Museum in memory of those who died in the uprising, with a room dedicated to Korczak and the children.

In the late sixties, demonstrations and riots occurred in Poland's universities protesting against the Polish government, and Jewish lecturers and students were held accountable. Jews were pushed out of government jobs. Korczak's books were considered too Jewish by the authorities and fell into disfavour. Sophia and Misha feared for their future.

When, in 1967, their youngest son, seventeen-year-old Roman, was allowed to go to Stockholm to attend a technical summer school, Misha insisted on doing all Roman's packing. He fastened the case and ordered Roman not to open it until he got to Stockholm. When Roman arrived in Sweden and opened his case, he found not only summer shirts, but also thick sweaters, hats and gloves – enough for a Swedish winter. The message writ loud and clear was that Roman was not to come home but to remain in Sweden. He did not see his parents and brothers again until they were allowed to move to Sweden three years later.

Once settled in Stockholm, Sophia and Misha both worked in education, teaching Korczak's message of the child's right to love and respect.

The Nazis razed the Treblinka death camp to the ground in the war's closing days in an attempt to hide the evidence of their genocide. 900,000 people were gassed there during the war in the space of 14 months. After the war, the site of the death camp became a peaceful clearing in the middle of the woods, with a large monument erected over the site of the gas chambers and a trail of smaller stones laid to represent the people of the 1,700 Jewish towns and village communities killed in Treblinka. Before they left Poland, Misha and Sophia attended a memorial ceremony at Treblinka, their hearts full of pain for all those family and friends they had lost there. Only one boulder was inscribed with an individual's name. It read: Janusz Korczak and the children.

In Sweden in 1994, Roman raised funds and helped design a Holocaust monument commemorating the family and friends known to the community of Jews living in Sweden. Many of the people in this book have their names recorded on the granite wall. One of the granite walls carries just the same inscription to Korczak and the children as in Treblinka.

The real monument to Korczak, however, is his call to make the world a better place for children from all backgrounds. Korczak helped write the first International Declaration of the Rights of the Child in Geneva in 1924. Taken up by the League of Nations that same year, it was adopted in extended form by the United Nations in 1959 and remains in place to this day.

In Poland, Israel and all over the world, Korczak's teachings and his principles of respect and empathy are still followed and taught in schools, universities and at education conferences. His plea to treat all children with fairness, and to consider the welfare of the child as the most important basis for nationhood, irrespective of race, remains as vital and important today as it did when he first wrote *How to Love a Child* over a century ago, as a medical officer writing by candlelight in the hospital tents behind the battlefields of the Somme.

In 2016 the Polish government founded the Warsaw's POLIN Museum of Jewish History, with a children's room dedicated to Korczak's values of tolerance, justice, respect and empathy. There is also a museum dedicated to Korczak in part of Korczak's original orphanage on Krochmalna Street (now renamed Jaktorowska Street) where children once again play beneath the tree in the front yard, watched over by Korczak's statue.

Korczak's diary was smuggled out of the ghetto a few days after Korczak and the children were taken. One of the boys, probably Mounius with the red hair, delivered it to Igor Newerly, a teacher from Korczak's homes who ran the children's newspaper for Korczak for many years. Maryna Falska had the diary hidden behind a wall in the Polish children's home she once ran with Korczak, but she died during the war, and for several years no one knew where it was. The diary resurfaced in America during the sixties and was published, in English translation, by the Holocaust Library in 1978.

Poland remained under Soviet control until 1980. 59 years after the outbreak of the Second World War, Poland finally became a free and independent country.

AUTHOR'S NOTE

As a young mum and teacher, I had a lot of questions about the best way to care for children, and a lot of anxiety. I came across Korczak's words at a teaching seminar and they burst across the landscape like a ray of sunshine. He advocated not a prescribed best way to raise children but a relationship based on knowing who the child really was, respecting them as an individual and working out what they need from that understanding. In other words, how to love a child.

The tutor in charge of the seminar also told us about Korczak's life. I was surprised that I'd never heard about such a remarkable man and decided to attempt to write a book to bring his ideas and story to more people.

I had two problems however. I knew very little about his life, and I didn't know how to write a book. I attended writing classes, published three other books, and, ten years later, began to write about Korczak.

It was also a journey into some of the darkest history of the twentieth century. I read intensively, including the Warsaw Ghetto diaries and accounts of Janusz Korczak, Mary Berg, Adam Czerniakow,

Michael Zylberberg, Halina Birnbaum, Wladyslaw Szpilman, Janina David, Yitzhak Zuckerman and various first hand accounts from the Oneg Shabbat archives published in the book *Words to Outlive Us*. I visited the British Library, the Weiner Library and the Polish Library in London and the Bodleian in Oxford, searching for any books I could find on Korczak. I read biographies of Korczak by Betty Jean Lifton, Hanna Mortkowicz-Olczakowa, Igor Newerly, Shlomo Nadel and Adir Cohen. I also managed to source some of Korczak's works including *How to Love a Child, The Child's Right to Respect, When I am Little Again* and *Little King Matt*.

I contacted some of the various Korczak Associations worldwide for information, and found Misha Wroblewski listed as head of the Korczak Association in Sweden. His son, Roman Wroblewski-Wasserman, replied to say that Misha had recently passed away, but that he could help with any information. I travelled to Sweden to meet Roman, and over the following years he became a friend and trusted adviser on this story, providing a stream of information on Korczak and on the Warsaw ghetto years. This book would not have been possible without his hard work and his kindness in sharing his parents' story. Roman's parents, Misha and Sophia, worked with Korczak both before and during the war, living in the ghetto with him and the children. They were among the less than one percent who survived the Warsaw Ghetto, out of a population of over half a million. The book became their story also.

During my initial research, I also travelled to Warsaw to visit the Warsaw Korczak museum in Poland, the Korczakianum Centre for Documentation and Research, which is housed in a room of Korczak's original orphanage on Krochmalna Street, now Jaktorowska Street, where I was given a tour and talk by Agnieska Witkowska-Krych. I visited the new POLIN Museum of Jewish life in Poland, and read accounts of pre-war Jewish Warsaw by Isaac Bashevis Singer. Ewa Bratosiewicz, a guide to Jewish Warsaw, supplied answers to various queries through Roman. Roman was also in contact with Barbara Engelking, and I referred to her book, *The Warsaw Ghetto*, written in conjunction with Jacek Leociak, extensively to recreate the details of the ghetto.

Warsaw was all but razed to the ground in the war. The medieval centre is an almost perfect reconstruction that is in fact no more than 50 years old. The ghetto and many of the Jewish areas are now gone, covered by Soviet-era housing estates and modern office buildings. It is possible, however, to find parts of the wall and original buildings, and to reconstruct the area mentally by walking through from historical locations on a map. The Nozyk Synagogue and Grzybowski Square are still there, along with a few original buildings from the ghetto years.

My next big question after completing the first stages of research was, how do you write a book about the Holocaust?

I began by producing a manuscript so plainly factual that it was difficult to read, and so, following the advice of my agent Jenny Hewson and editors at Corvus, Sara O'Keefe and Susannah Hamilton, I re-wrote the book as a newly imagined novel, fully evoking the scenes and giving myself the same allowances as a filmmaker recreating a historical story. I was very grateful for all their advice and their willingness to stay with the project and put so much work into this book.

I decided to keep to the documented facts about Korczak and the war years and fill in the missing background details such as food and transport from research. I also used details from film reconstructions such as those in *The Pianist*, where Polanski went to great pains to provide accurate historical details based on his own memories of the Krakow ghetto. I watched Andrzej Wajda's

1990 film about Korczak for its wonderful poetic evocation. The Nazis were also avid film documenters of the Warsaw ghetto and this material is available online.

Janusz Korczak was a pen-name, acquired when he became a famous writer in Poland. Born Henry Goldszmit, in 1879, he was the son of a wealthy Jewish lawyer and his wife, who mixed freely with both Polish and Jewish friends in fin de siècle Warsaw. Korczak did not realise he was Jewish until his canary died when he was five, and, burying it in the courtyard, was told by a Polish boy that he couldn't put a cross on the grave because it was a Jewish bird. Poland in those days was divided between three superpowers; Germany, Russia and the Habsburg Empire. Korczak's first taste of school was at a Russian establishment where the beating reduced him to nervous terror and this memory led to his lifelong quest to give the child a voice and foster a better understanding between children and their carers. Korczak's beloved and brilliant father died in the Tworki Lunatic Asylum when Korczak was just 17, and Korczak's impoverished mother and sister relied on his income as a tutor, while hoping he would soon graduate as a doctor. Korczak later became a sought after paediatrician, also famous for his novels charting the lives of the street children he worked with in his spare time – when not dodging the Tsar's police for his involvement in the seditious 'Flying University', whose groundbreaking lectures on observational psychology had Korczak enthralled. Eventually, he decided to follow his heart and leave medicine to work full time with children at a neglected orphanage which was being run by a remarkable young woman called Stefa Wilczynska. He and Stefa formed a life long partnership dedicated to children. After WW1, Korczak also opened a home for Polish orphans in Warsaw with Maryna Falska as housemother.

Poland gained independence after WW1. The following decade was a golden time for Korczak's expansion of the kingdom of the child. He wrote and lectured expansively, on and for children, made child-centred broadcasts, founded a children's newspaper and served as a court advocate for teenage delinquents. But with the advent of the economic depression in the 1930s, a fascist spirit spread through Europe, and as a Jew in an increasingly nationalistic Poland, Korczak's work was curtailed.

Korczak was an early pioneer of child welfare and psychology. As a young man at the beginning of the twentieth century, Korczak had looked around and begun to ask why so many children were unhappy. There were vast numbers of slum children in Warsaw, neglected and unloved. Even the children of the rich seemed frustrated and resentful in spite of their material plenty. It was as if adults had forgotten what it was like to be a child. Adults had to learn to communicate with children and speak their language again. It was a lesson he understood from experience. As a young doctor in training, he wanted to heal not only children's physical ailments, but also their souls and lives. Determined to make children's lives happier on his first summer camp for slum children, he set out armed with a full knowledge of books on children, a bag full of games, good intentions and a carnation in his buttonhole. The week was chaotic. Korzcak found himself at odds with the boys, shouting at them to go to sleep and even resorting to threats. Ashamed and confused, he decided to ask the boys what they thought was going wrong. It soon became clear that his one-size-fits-all policy on childcare was missing the mark with such a wide variety of children who all had different needs for sleep, food, clothes sizes and interests. He realized that only by really listening to and knowing the children could he begin to devise creative ways to lead them towards who they were meant to be as people. Each child was a person to be respected in terms of their thoughts and feelings – that and a hefty dose of pre-planning for a group of 30 boys. The next summer, with lists, schedules and a lot of effort made in getting to know each boy, he and the children had a wonderful summer in the country. He realized that childrearing was about knowledge from failed attempts, an on-going quest to find out what works for an individual. 'I want everyone to know and love this state of "I do not know" when it comes to raising children – so full of life and dazzling surprises.'

For this reason, Korczak always put respecting and getting to know a child far higher than relying on books by child experts – although they were useful. 'No book, no doctor can replace your own careful observation of a child.' Mothers and fathers should trust their instinct about their own child, based on years of watching and getting to know who their child is.

And above all, he saw childrearing as a relationship, not an exercise in control. The adult was charged with the responsibility of the child's safety and happiness, but this meant accountability, not a free pass to lose one's temper or be unfair for one's own convenience. He loathed physical punishment, viewing it as wrong and completely ineffective. He understood that an adult has to be a grown up – 'before you start laying down the law to children and bossing them about, make sure that you have brought up and educated the child inside yourself.' And he saw no merit in treating childhood as if it were a mere preparation for the more important time of adulthood. 'Children are people today, not people tomorrow. They have the right to their cup of happiness.'

He taught children and adults to treat each other with empathy. He was quite happy to point out to a child that he was busy working or reading or simply tired, and that the child could perhaps amuse themselves for a while – while always remaining close at hand and in sight for help and comfort if needed.

He taught social responsibility through the court of peers where children brought their grievances against each other and debated the rights and wrongs of each case, considering the feelings of others and so developing a sense of justice and fairness. Punishments were mostly written warnings.

Korczak knew that children take comfort from the religion they were raised in and gave both Jewish and Christian children the chance to pray or go to services if they so wished. He wasn't a practising Jew but had been brought up in the tenets of the religion, and though he did not follow a specific creed, he believed in a loving God and read widely from wisdom literature. His religion, he said, was the sacred duty to protect children. He believed that a child belongs to itself and that it is the duty of not only parents but the whole community to care for the children in their midst. He had no children of his own yet he was father to hundreds of children. Korczak firmly believed that children held the world together and that the basis of nationhood was not an ethnic or cultural group, but the decision of a people irrespective of creed or race to come together to care for their children. He understood that where nations decide not to care for the child then civilisation is on the verge of flying apart, which is precisely what happened when the Nazi Reich decided to murder thousands of children in 1942, in Warsaw, in Poland, and across Europe. There can be no greater contrast than this terrible decision compared to Korczak's will to protect the rights and happiness of his children, even to the very end when he accompanied them to the death camp.

Korczak's message is as pertinent today as it ever was, both in how we define a nation, and in how we raise children who are independent, happy, loved and loving. Perhaps the best observation about Korczak comes from a child in care who was given some of Korczak's sayings to read: 'I wish all parents could read Janusz Korczak, because then children would be happier.'

This book is dedicated with thanks to my own children and my husband who lived with Korczak's story for so many years, and to Roman, and all the family and children of Misha and Sophia, with great thanks for sharing their story for the next generation, and also to Niura's daughter Tessa Valabregue and her family. Above all this book is for Korczak and for all children, everywhere.